PENGUINDRUM

PENGUINDRUM

NOVEL

WRITTEN BY

Kunihiko Ikuhara
Kei Takahashi

Seven Seas Entertainment

PENGUINDRUM VOLUME 1

MAWARU-PENGUINDRUM Vol. 1
by IKUHARA KUNIHIKO/TAKAHASHI KEI/HOSHINO LILY
© 2011 IKUHARA KUNIHIKO/TAKAHASHI KEI/
GENTOSHA COMICS INC.
© 2011 ikunichawder/pingroup
All rights reserved.

Original Japanese edition published in 2011 by
GENTOSHA COMICS Inc.
English translation rights arranged worldwide with
GENTOSHA COMICS Inc. through Digital Catapult Inc., Tokyo.

Seven Seas press and purchase enquiries can be sent to
Marketing Manager Lianne Sentar at press@gomanga.com.
Information requiring the distribution and purchase of
digital editions is available from Digital Manager CK Russell
at digital@gomanga.com.

Seven Seas and the Seven Seas logo are trademarks of
Seven Seas Entertainment. All rights reserved.

Follow Seven Seas Entertainment online at
sevenseasentertainment.com.

TRANSLATION: Diana Taylor
ADAPTATION: Nino Cipri
COVER DESIGN: Nicky Lim
INTERIOR LAYOUT & DESIGN: Clay Gardner
PROOFREADER: Kelly Lorraine Andrews, Stephanie Cohen
LIGHT NOVEL EDITOR: Nibedita Sen
PREPRESS TECHNICIAN: Rhiannon Rasmussen-Silverstein
PRODUCTION MANAGER: Lissa Pattillo
MANAGING EDITOR: Julie Davis
ASSOCIATE PUBLISHER: Adam Arnold
PUBLISHER: Jason DeAngelis

ISBN: 978-1-64505-537-2
Printed in Canada
First Printing: May 2020
10 9 8 7 6 5 4 3 2 1

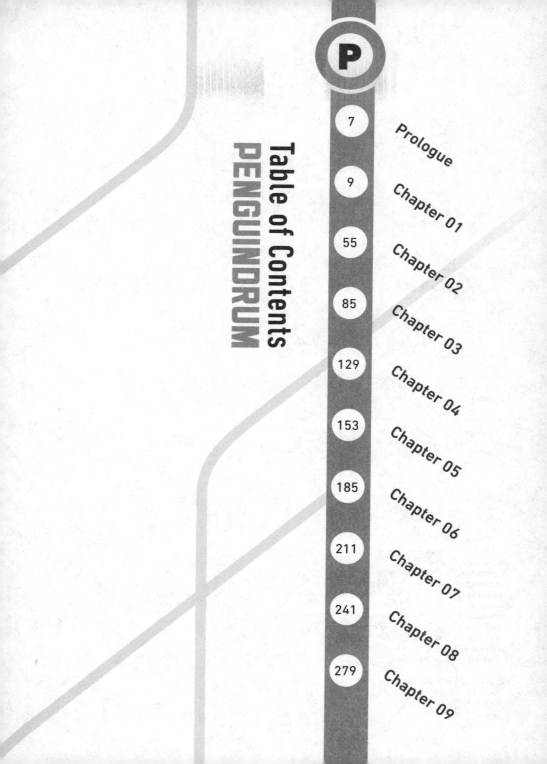

Table of Contents
PENGUINDRUM

PROLOGUE

•••→

AN IMPOSSIBLE COSMOS, swirling with all of creation. Clusters of stars, just like the beads scattered across that girl's desk.

Takamura Chieko once wrote, "There is no sky in Tokyo; I want to see a real sky." That isn't true, though the sky in Tokyo is a little shy. It's just intimidated by all the neon lights. If you focus hard and look, there in the distance just between the twinkling stars, you'll see a line of familiar creatures parading our way. Where have they come from, on those little flapping arms? Where are they headed? They fly onward soundlessly.

They are the penguins.

One penguin has sharp eyes, one penguin cradles a pot, one penguin is exceedingly cheerful, one penguin is licking honey. One penguin is singing on high. One penguin is crying. One is tying a pink ribbon around its head. One is eating taiyaki.

Through the black of the cosmos, neither cloudy nor clear, embroidered with twinkling stars, the penguins' silent procession spools out. They are captivated by something, these little birds in a row. Regardless, they cannot cease their movement. On and on they go. On and on, through the silent heavens, until they spot something. Or, maybe without seeing a thing. Until their consciousness is brought forcibly to an end. Until they know that it is over. They travel on together. So fate has decreed.

Their white markings stand out distinctly. Even within those silent skies, if you watch their motions carefully, you can hear their grand march. It is not a riddle or a foreshadowing or a memory. It is simply fact.

CHAPTER 01 •••→

I N A FAIRLY WELL-OFF part of the city, our house stood out. It was a little one-story building from a previous era, with a flat, unassuming red roof, and a bright red mailbox at the entrance beside the old wooden sliding door. The colorful sheet metal walls faced out on a narrow yard, which was still plenty for drying our scant laundry. Thankfully, the lot beside ours was long-vacant, with only a few pieces of playground equipment left behind.

On clear days like this, bright sunshine filled our parlor. Soaking up warm sunlight was surely good for the body. As I sliced up a green onion—rather efficiently, if I did say so myself—I thought of the dream I had that morning.

I dreamed about a set of train tracks hanging in the darkness, barely illuminated by small lights on the edges of the tunnel. Endless darkness and a comforting swaying: the view from the windows of the head car of the subway train. I felt stuck, unable to escape, my very consciousness adrift. I was filled with dread, convinced a monster would leap at me from the darkness, but I could not avert my eyes.

The train showed no signs of stopping at any station, and there were no announcements over the speakers, nor voices or any evidence of other passengers. Even straining my ears, I could hear no music leaking from anyone's headphones, nor clothes rustling. The only sound reverberating in my body was the *ka-chunk ka-chunk, ka-chunk ka-chunk* of the train running along the tracks.

I began to lose hope, praying the next station would arrive soon. This was a subway train, after all; it would be disastrous for it not to follow the timetable, to not stop at the station. It *had* to let me disembark.

I awoke with a voiceless scream—then realized that it was a dream.

It was hours before my alarm was set to go off, but I wasn't about to go back to sleep. Glancing at my brother sleeping soundly beside me put me a little at ease. I did a bit of cleaning, then killed some time flipping through the morning news. I prepared some miso soup, chock-full of tofu like Himari always wanted, then took the cucumbers from last night—Himari's favorite pickled vegetable—out of the nukadoko and piled them neatly in a little dish.

This particular nukadoko had been in our family for some time. It shocked me to learn that pickles were produced from such a smelly brown substance; I'd been stunned to see my mother casually plunge her hands into it. I wore rubber gloves when I mixed it, and tossed them in the trash afterward.

Honestly, for a high school boy to even be in possession of some nukadoko... I let out a self-effacing sigh.

I turned off the burner on the stove, took a taste right from the ladle, and gave a self-satisfied nod. Breakfast in the Takakura household was a standardized affair: white rice and a warm, hearty miso soup. Somehow, I inherited this routine without realizing it.

My brother awoke and put away the futons, and eventually our whole family was up and about.

Atop the low table in the tatami-floored parlor, three sets of bowls and chopsticks were laid out. Warm white vapor rose from the rice cooker. Fliers and coupons from the supermarket were pinned to the refrigerator with the cute magnets that Himari loved. All six of our shoes were lined up snugly by the front door. It was a perfect morning. A perfect, just-right morning.

As I carried over a tray lined with bowls full of miso soup, my eyes fell on our family photos. In one rectangular picture frame was a photograph of us three siblings and our parents, when we were young.

There was no Mother or Father on this perfect morning. Thus, it fell upon me, inheritor, to make our breakfast.

I despise the word "fate." If our births, encounters, partings, successes, failures—whether we achieve happiness or fall into the arms of despair—are all determined by "fate," then why on earth were we born into this world? What do we even live for?

Cured salmon and tamagoyaki, warm miso soup and pickles.

"Aniki, Himari, breakfast is ready," I called to them together.

Some are born into prosperous homes. Some are born into poverty. Some are born beautiful, to beautiful mothers. Some are not. And, some are born thrust into the middle of famine or war. If all of those things are set in motion by the hands of "fate," then God must be a horribly, outrageously cruel creature.

"Thanks for the food!" Himari said joyfully, pressing her hands together and smiling. Her hair was brushed out neatly, her lips glossy with lip balm. It always took her a while to get ready in the morning. I was relieved to see her looking bright-eyed and healthy today.

My brother and I shared our thanks for the meal in turn.

"Really pulled out the stops this morning, huh?" said my brother absently, rubbing the sleep from his eyes. We were both distracted, watching Himari pick up her bowl of miso soup, blowing a soft breath to cool it as she gently lifted it to her mouth. The sight set something aflame in us. Her face was beautiful in profile, her long eyelashes lowered. Her slender white throat moved ever so slightly as she swallowed.

"It's delicious," she said with a smile, enraptured.

"Is it good, then?" asked my brother, now wide awake.

"Yes. It's been so long since I've had hot miso soup."

"Of course. It was always cold at the hospital, wasn't it?" my brother said softly.

Himari's gaze lowered to her miso soup, smiling at the needless concern. "It was. But, more importantly, your soup tastes just like Mother's, Sho-chan."

"Himari." Indeed. We all knew there was something decisively lacking in this morning scene. And yet, as long as we could all sit around the table like this, our family would survive. We *were* family, after all. There was no reason besides that. Or rather, that alone was reason enough.

We were keeping the Takakura family alive.

"Right? This guy's already a perfect house husband, ain't he? He knows when all the grocery sales are on, sorts the trash, does the laundry and the ironing perfectly. He's even a master chef to boot," said my brother brightly.

Himari cackled in reply and said, "He'll make a wonderful groom someday."

"That so?" I asked. I had no clear memories of our mother's miso soup. But I was her child, so it's possible that our tastes aligned. And if that made Himari happy, then that was fine with me.

"Say, you notice anything special about the room?" Himari suddenly asked playfully.

"Hm? I mean, I did a bit of rolling this morning, but I didn't notice anything," I said dully. I'd used a roll of sticky tape to clean, rolling it along the floor and furnishings. Our old vacuum was incredibly noisy and blew up a lot of dust, so it wasn't suitable for prebreakfast cleaning.

"Did you make something again?" My brother whipped his head around quickly.

Himari was fond of crafting. She loved clothing, and her hands were small and skilled, so we often found her at her sewing machine or knitting. My brother and I didn't understand everything she made, but if Himari created them, then they were "cute things," and found a home as "new friends" in Himari's room or the parlor.

According to Himari, the world was mostly comprised of cute things. If you asked her what made up the rest, however, she would innocently reply, "Who knows?"

"The answer is: the curtains!" she announced.

We turned our gazes to the curtains. Now that I thought of it, I hadn't done any rolling on them that morning.

"Oh, there on the corner," I said as I noticed it. The words *I'm home* had been embroidered in English on the pink fabric in beautiful red cursive lettering. Next to them was a little flower design. "I didn't even notice this," I added.

"What is it?" my brother asked, peeking around me. "You're gettin' good at embroidery, Himari."

She smiled, clearly pleased.

Despite being shown the X-rays and receiving a thorough explanation, we never fully understood the situation. I'm not sure understanding it would have done us any good, anyway. All that mattered was whether Himari would get better.

"I'm very sorry, but unfortunately, there is nothing more that modern medicine can do," said Dr. Washizuka vaguely. "Himari-san has a few months at most. Perhaps."

"No way..."

I could feel the strength leaving my body. There was the familiar, characteristic smell of the hospital, Dr. Washizuka's disturbingly sterile white coat, the lightbox and its bright and hazy, translucent image of Himari's insides.

"Perhaps? Don't give me that crap, you're a friggin' *doctor*!"

My brother stood with such force he knocked his stool to the ground, reaching for Dr. Washizuka.

"Kanba!" I shouted, standing and trying to stop him, but he seized the doctor by the collar.

"If this is about money, we'll manage it! If she can't be treated here in Japan, then we can take her overseas! If you need a transplant or something, you can take whatever you need from me! Just don't tell me that there's nothing you can do! Please just don't say *that*!"

His grip suddenly loosened, and he collapsed on the spot, pressing his head to the floor.

"Please, you've gotta help her. Whatever the cost is, I'll pay it. I don't even care if that means my life for hers, just please save her!"

I was lost for words. Seeing my brother so upset tore my disbelief away, like the reality of our situation had been forcefully shoved down my throat. I stood there, unable to even wail like my brother, swallowed by a wave of memories and swirling emotions.

"Takakura-san, doctors are not gods," said Dr. Washizuka, his voice low and regretful, though still cut and dry. He placed a hand on Kanba's shoulder, urging him to raise his head.

"That's because God doesn't exist. He never has."

I could only watch in a daze as my brother's hands balled violently into fists, still trembling.

I hate the word "fate."

Himari was released from the hospital, so that she could live out her remaining days with us, never knowing when the tiny flame of her life might burn out. She muttered an awkward, "Welcome home," to us at the door, surrounded by her favorite dolls and stuffed animals.

Our little sister, braver and more precious than anyone else in this world. We could not fathom the idea of her no longer being with us. It was hard to truly imagine that this was reality, that our future might be snatched away from my brother and me, and most of all, from Himari.

A sluggish groan brought me back to my senses. Himari pulled away from the table and reclined on our little red sofa.

"Are you done, Himari?" I asked.

Looking at her dishes, I saw she'd left more than half of the food on her plate. She still couldn't eat very much.

"Yeah, I'm full now. I really gorged myself there!" she said, delighted, letting out a sigh and rubbing her gut. "That was tasty, thank you!"

Sipping his warm, post-meal hojicha, Kanba chided, "That's bad manners, Himari."

"But today's 'Himari Day,' so it's fine," she replied, puffing up her cheeks jokingly and blowing a raspberry.

"Himari Day? What is that?" he asked, glancing at me.

"Sho-chan said that I can do whatever I want today. That means today is Himari Day."

"Hm, I see," said Kanba, grinning at me. I averted my gaze, popping a pickle into my mouth and crunching on it.

"Kan-chan, Sho-chan, y'know something? I'm happy," said Himari, her eyes shut.

Her long hair fanned around her on the sofa. She wore her favorite nightgown, as she had even in the hospital, a warm peach color. Her slender white legs thrust out from under it.

Kanba stared at her, and then finally gave a warm smile, as though letting out a sigh. "That's true. You're here, Shoma is here, and we have a home. I guess that's what happiness is."

Happiness. That feeling didn't seem real to me, but I wasn't about to interrupt their joyful exchange with my gloom.

"Hey, hey!" Himari sat up suddenly, as though something wonderful had just sprung to mind. "Do you think they still have penguins over at that aquarium?"

Though there was no one else besides us, at some point we had begun saying, "Be back later!" to our empty house whenever we went out.

Himari Day was blessed with clear, lovely weather, and we boarded the train from Ogikubo, headed for the aquarium. Himari wanted to take a roundabout, nostalgic route to our destination, traveling on the line that our family most often used to take. This was Himari Day, after all, so my brother and I acquiesced, and the three of us set out on our first excursion together in ages.

Himari looked like a little doll. She wore a frilly blouse tied with a delicate ribbon at the front and long cowboy boots, her skirt billowing out from her waist like a flower. Her cheeks were pinked from the effort of her brisk pace. My brother sat lazily, even now still looking drowsy.

As I gripped the ceiling strap, watching the two of them, I was surprised all over again at the three of us being together. There Himari really was, right beside us, all dressed up and smiling.

"Hey, Kan-chan, do your otter impression," she said, tugging on his sleeve.

"Huh? Otter? Oh." His face reddened.

"That time we all went to the aquarium together, you kept doing the otter thing afterward. With an orange sitting on your stomach," she said, bursting into laughter.

"Hey, shut up! I was a stupid kid back then. I barely even remember that."

"Things were so fun back then," she said, gazing outside of the darkened windows.

Lost in my own thoughts, I did not see the gloomy expression she wore for just a moment. But as soon as Kanba, more sensitive, picked up on it, he called to me in a half-panicked voice, "Hey, Shoma. Wasn't your seahorse impression pretty great, too?"

"Hm? What?" I was still staring out at my own reflection in the window, and the darkness rolling beyond it.

"What's with you?" he asked. "You've been spacin' out this whole time."

"I was just thinking how long it's been since we've done something fun." Saying so made me a little afraid.

"It really has been a while," Himari said softly. "It's like a dream... Sorry for the big detour."

A heavy silence fell over Kanba and me. There was a difficult moment before we mustered up the strength to reply. "It's okay."

I looked back at the darkness rolling past the window. Floating in the darkness beyond the glass was the clear reflection of my own vacant face.

Because it was a weekend, the Sunshiny National Aquarium in Ikebukuro was packed. There were families and couples and groups of girls. And us. Even I grew a little excited as we bought our tickets and stepped inside, our first visit in so long.

The darkness in the aquarium was different from that of the train. The deep blue of the large, thick glass panes seemed like it might suck me right in. In that strange atmosphere, everyone walked along holding hands or chatting, walking along so as not to get separated, or else stood still, peering inside. There were tanks with large fish swimming quickly, and tanks with vividly colored warm-water fish, and tanks where strangely formed deep sea fish and kelp swayed.

"If you start feelin' bad, tell us right away," Kanba said in his usual reliable way.

"I'm fine," Himari replied, her gaze full of happiness mixed with nostalgia.

Kanba led us onward, diligently making sure that Himari did not bump into anyone. Popular guys really are their own breed, huh? We may have been brothers, but I didn't resemble him in the slightest when it came to how we treated women.

The penguins carefully climbed up an artificial rockface, standing still, tottering around. They formed into lines and dove into the water, gliding smoothly under the surface. They swam elegantly back and forth before our eyes, as swiftly and smoothly as if they were flying through the sky, a completely different creature from how they looked on land.

"Whoa. The penguins are such good swimmers!" Himari was impressed, watching with rapt attention from the front row. Honestly, I had long forgotten that penguins could move in such a way.

"Yeah, even though they look a little silly on land." Their wings looked both like fins and hands.

"I bet the penguins would be annoyed to hear that coming from you, Shoma."

"What's that supposed to mean?" I shot a glare at my brother. At roughly the same time, he pulled his cell phone from his back pocket.

He glanced at the LCD and said plainly, "Sorry, gotta go make a call."

"Another girl? If you don't cool it you're gonna get burned someday," I sighed wearily.

"It's fine, I'm playin' my cards right," he said, before leaving our row and disappearing into the crowd. Truthfully, I already knew this. Some days he received countless calls and texts from his rude ex-girlfriends, and even when he didn't, he was still ruthless in his dealings with the fairer sex. I once had the terrifying experience of seeing him thrust a girl's love letter back at her one morning at school, telling her, "No thanks, I'm good." He wore the same expression as when he was taking out the trash.

Girl after girl from various schools, wearing all sorts of uniforms, sought out my brother to confess their love to him. And then they went straight back home.

When I asked what he meant by, "No thanks, I'm good," he explained calmly, with a stony expression, "It means that I'm already fully satisfied right now."

"Playing his cards right?" I wondered aloud. "Ew. I wouldn't want to catch Kanba's filthy playboy germs."

Himari did not respond, or at least, she did not turn around. She seemed to be staring at something beyond the penguins in front of her.

"That penguin over there..." she said softly, pointing her finger.

"Huh? Which one?" I followed her gaze carefully, but only saw identical and indistinguishable penguins, shuffling on the rocks and darting through the water. I glanced back at her profile.

"Which one do you mean?"

"Honey, no running, you're going to hurt someone," came a voice, in the sweet but grave tone that mothers were so adept at. Even if you have no intention of listening, a voice like that always catches your attention.

A little boy wearing a hat with a penguin design came running up just beside us, stopping just before colliding with me. "Mama! There's a lot of penguins here!" he squealed.

"Goodness! Keep your voice down." The smile on the mother's face belied her stern words.

The boy's father caught up with them, watching over his wife and son. "You'll make all the penguins run away. Look," he said, gently lifting up the boy. He showed him the rockface in the enclosure from up on his shoulders. "Hello, Penguin-san."

The boy smiled, bursting with joy, clinging onto his father's sturdy arms.

"Someone's having fun." The mother's smile grew.

It was a perfect, just-right morning. The smell of hot miso soup wafting from the kitchen. A smiling family. A clear autumn sky. An outing, just like the old days. From the outside, nothing had changed. But really, everything had.

What expression was I wearing just then? Whatever it was, I knew I couldn't let Himari see it.

"Want to go pick out some souvenirs, Himari?" I asked cheerfully. "I'll buy you whatever you like today, my treat. How's that sound?"

"Really? Of course! This is Himari Day, after all," she said, beaming.

"And Kanba's taking a phone call over there anyway, so let's go."

I just wanted to get out of there. It wasn't that I hated the penguins, of course, nor did I hate the family standing next to us. Still, I had to get away. I was always felt wretched when I encountered children, useless and awkward even if I looked outwardly calm. Just seeing that thirty-second interaction made my heart twinge painfully. My sadness was so heavy it was painful to breathe, as if my lungs were being crushed. I know that Himari or Kanba would have been able to handle themselves. They would think nothing of standing there and smiling calmly. But I couldn't pretend that nothing was wrong.

Seeing Himari's slender back before me, I had no idea if I could protect her all alone. I was startled at how thin my own shadow was, stretching across the floor, so much smaller than life.

But I couldn't say such things, so I kept silent.

The walls and shelves of the aquarium gift shop were a uniform ocean blue. Himari looked around triumphantly at all of the toys and plushies of sea-dwelling critters.

"What's your favorite sea creature, Sho-chan?" she asked me as she carefully examined each of the stuffed animals, innocently stating her impressions of them. "This one's cute! The nose on this one looks too big, doesn't it? Didn't we see one of these today?"

"Hmm, let me think," I said, suddenly thinking of salmon and flounder—fish I liked to eat. "Uhm..." Scallops were going to be in season soon, and extra tasty. Squid and herring and urchin were expensive and hard to get, but I had seen them down in one of the tanks.

"Do you hate fish?"

Suddenly, I noticed Himari looking up at me, her dissatisfaction plain.

"No, that's not it. Look, I was just thinking, like, the penguins were really cute, but there were lots of other ones, too."

She smiled, with a "hmm," and headed for a different corner of the store. I felt more like a glutton now than a house husband.

"What's your favorite sea creature then, Himari?"

"Hmm, all of them," she said with a grin. I could only smile back at this unexpected reply. Of course, that was just like her.

"Wow, this one is awesome! It's just like the real thing!" she said, cuddling a large plush otter. "It's so soft." I could practically hear the heart emoji floating at the end of the words.

"Whoa, it really is." I let out a cry of surprise when I glimpsed the price tag. It was expensive. I hadn't expected that, either. But I already told her that I would buy her whatever she wanted.

"Oh, but..." she said, placing the expensive otter back on the shelf. Oh, good. "If I need an otter, I've already got Kan-chan, so never mind. I'll have him do his impression at home."

"I wonder if you can still get him to do that," I said, but I would graciously concede if she gave up the plush otter thanks to Kanba. There was no choice but for him to become a sacrificial lamb to save us the expense.

"He'll do it. Today is 'Himari Day,' isn't it? He's my otter, and you're my seahorse," she tacked on, triumphantly.

"Huh? I have to do it too?" I had no idea what a seahorse impression looked like. Apparently, it was something I had done in the past, but I had no memory of it. How was I supposed to impersonate a creature with no distinctive movements or expressions, like an otter had? I wished I could ask my past self, *A seahorse impression? Really?*

"Yep. Because today..." Himari grabbed a hat with a penguin design from a nearby shelf and placed it atop her head, puffing out her chest lightly. "...I'm the queen!"

At once my eyes began to sparkle. "Himari, that's perfect! That's disgustingly cute!"

"Right?" said our queen, giving a little spin. I was no match for her precious, cheerful face. My present to her would be that hat, and that was final.

This couldn't be bad at all, I thought, watching as the shop clerk carefully wrapped the hat up in bright gift wrapping paper. I was here and Kanba was here and Himari was here, the three of us together. This was a wonderful thing, wasn't it?

"What color ribbon would you like?" the clerk asked, showing me color samples for the ribbons. My gaze went immediately to the red and the pink ribbons, but I unhesitatingly replied, "The pink one, please."

"Yo, I was lookin' for you two." A hand clapped me on the shoulder, and I turned to see Kanba standing there, scowling.

"Yeah, we were looking for you, too. You got that call and vanished off to somewhere," I protested. I took the paper bag that the kind shop clerk handed me with a grateful nod.

"So, where's Himari?" Kanba asked.

"Hm? Right over there, isn't she?" I cast my eyes around the crowded gift shop, but there was no sign of her.

"Idiot, you were supposed to be keeping an eye on her." Kanba's face twisted.

"She was with me this whole time," I said.

Just then, a terrible voice rang in our ears.

"Hey, someone call an ambulance! Some girl just collapsed in the plaza!"

"No way." My blood ran cold. "It can't be."

Without a word, my brother broke into a sprint. I followed behind him, equally silent. We ran down the stairs to see a crowd of people near a stage, beneath a schedule for the sea lion show.

"Himari!" My brother shoved his way to the center of the crowd. I followed behind him, shouting, "Sorry, that's our sister! Please let us through!"

I tripped.

In the middle of the murmuring crowd, Himari was faceup on the ground.

"Himari! Himari!" Kanba held her up gently, shouting, but she was completely unresponsive, her eyes firmly shut, her pale pink lips open slightly.

"We've called an ambulance, *so let's get her to the medical office right away*," someone said. The voice was nearby, and probably belonged to an employee of the aquarium. But between the beating of my heart, and the sound of blood pounding in my ears, I could not tell who spoke.

"Please," Kanba murmured, as Himari was whisked away on a stretcher.

Once more, I felt the vivid sensation of being paralyzed and unable to act, the muscles in my face frozen.

Himari, who laughed and smiled not so long ago at all, was now as silent as a doll, unconscious in the ICU. An IV was taped to her arm, her face was covered by an oxygen mask, and numerous tubes that we could not make heads or tails of snaked around her. A small monitor indicated that her heart was still beating, though it was faint.

"Takakura-san! Takakura Himari-san!" the doctors called over and over again, but she did not reply.

We could only call out to her from the other side of a large glass pane. The doctors and nurses kept moving around frantically, the sight of which alone told us that her condition was critical.

"Her pulse is dropping!"

"Doctor!"

Just as Dr. Washizuka rushed to Himari's side, the small blips on the monitor ceased moving, the line going flat. All the numbers dropped to zero.

Both my brother and I understood what this meant, but neither of us could say a word. We knew what would happen next. Some nurse or doctor confirmed the time on the clock, and then looked sadly at us. And then, they stated it: the hour and minute at which Himari's life had run out. And then, their condolences.

"Takakura Kanba-kun, Shoma-kun, we are sorry to say that your dear sister has passed away," they said to us.

I felt the temperature in my body drop. My legs felt like they were floating. I'm certain that in that moment, my face was even paler than Himari's, who lay still in that bed, no longer breathing.

"Aniki," I managed to wring out.

Kanba stared at Himari like a statue, his face unchanging: not smiling nor crying, not showing anger, nor hatred.

"Takakura-san—or, no, Kanba-kun, Shoma-kun. Please allow me to offer my condolences."

Dr. Washizuka's speech ended before we realized it had even begun. Just what in the world did he mean by "condolences"? It seemed to suggest something like, "well, that's unfortunate, the poor thing."

If only this were a dream. I could open my eyes, slap my brother awake, and run to Himari's room. It might be three in the morning, or six. Kanba, always a grouch on waking, might kick me away, or complain loudly. It didn't matter—I would sit by the side of the large canopy bed where Himari slept, calming my frantic breathing, watching over her until the sun rose.

The surfaces within the high-ceilinged morgue became strangely translucent where the evening sun shone through. A strange and solemn atmosphere filled the room, like it was a church in some foreign land.

Atop the small bed, Himari was wrapped in unadorned white sheets, a white cloth over her face. Kanba slumped against the wall and stared blankly as I clutched the sheets, my face a mess of tears.

"Himari, why did you have to go so soon?" I whimpered. My throat was so tight, I could hardly speak.

"Guess that doctor wasn't such a quack after all..." said Kanba, his voice cold and blank. "He said that it was strange that she could even be walking around in her current condition. He said that we should be prepared for it to happen at any moment."

Even with the sun coming through, the morgue had a vague chill. The distinctive smell of dead people hung in the air, and Kanba's voice echoed.

"This was her fate," he said. "She got to go in a place from her favorite memories, without pain or suffering. At the very least, I think she was happy."

He took a deep breath and pulled away from the wall. As I held back my sobs, listening to his words, my face now twisted up for a different reason.

"Anyway, we should get in touch with Uncle Ikebe. There'll be a lot of arrangements and procedures to deal with."

"How..." My voice was quiet, still strained but steady. I shot up, turned, and grabbed my brother hard by the collar. "How could you, in front of Himari? How could you say something so cold in front of our little sister?!" I squeezed at his chest with a strength I didn't know I possessed.

"I'm just accepting the facts as they are," he coolly replied.

"What about this is *fact*?!" Still gripping his lapels, I shoved him against the wall. A *thud* echoed in the room, but neither his stance nor expression were shaken. "How is this *fate*?! Why Himari? Why would this happen to her?! She was a girl who would say that just eating breakfast with her family made her happy—why *her*?!"

I started to weep again, looking down so that he could not see my face. I'm sure that my eyes were already red and swollen.

Kanba rested his hand softly atop my head. I lifted my face and saw his eyes. His expression was lonesome, his eyes wide and wild and unexpectedly kind.

"Because this was probably the punishment that we earned."

I felt as though a nail had been driven through my heart. It was not as though I hadn't considered this. But I decided it was a coincidence, nothing more than a passing fancy of my wildly childish imagination. I locked the thought away inside a little black box that sat at the corners of my mind, and thrown away the key.

Punishment. Of course. We were children who could only expect to be punished. Children who were probably hurting others just by continuing to live as we were. And Himari had taken on that burden. Our little Himari, all on her own.

"Survival Tactiiiiic!!"

The two of us nearly leapt out of our skin at the sudden loud voice. Kanba looked toward Himari's body, and his eyes went wide. I slowly turned around as well, my shoulders tensed.

Somehow, Himari sat up, with the penguin hat that we just bought her at the aquarium gift shop atop her head. The white cloth that covered her face fluttered to the floor.

"H-Himari?" I said.

The loud voice sounded like an imitation of Himari's. It was certainly the same voice, but the strength, intonation, and force of delivery were all completely alien.

Perhaps because of the light of the setting sun, her eyes seemed to glow red, staring out from a hollow expression.

"We have come from the place where your fates reside. Rejoice! We have deigned to extend this girl's life. Kneel before us and show your gratitude, cretins!"

I was lost for words. I glanced at Kanba, but he was of course equally speechless.

A strange smile leapt to Himari's lovely face, and she continued, "If you wish for this girl to continue to live..." She spoke only that far, her words cut off with a haughty grin.

I leaned forward, continuing to listen.

Suddenly, her posture shifted, and she looked at each of us with cold eyes. Then she lowered her head slightly, and her hat slipped forward and plopped down on the sheets.

"Oh!" I reflexively reached forward to pick up the hat, then said, "H-Himari? Is that really you?"

I quickly forgot about the hat, peering at Himari's blank face.

"Where... am I?" she asked, looking nervously at the bed she had been lying in. "What was I doing?"

"Oh, um..." I didn't know what to say. I'd been certain that the Himari speaking now knew nothing about what was going on. Who had spoken before, then? And how was a girl who should have been dead sitting up and looking at me this way?

"You just passed out for a bit at the aquarium. Don't worry about it," Kanba assured her with a smile, coming up from behind me. He cast a glance at me and added, "Isn't that right?" He begged me with his eyes. *Don't say anything unnecessary.*

I nodded. "Right. That's right. I'm sure that being around all those people just wore you out. It was a pretty busy morning."

All that we needed right then was to confirm with our own eyes that Himari was alive. We had merely been mistaken in assuming Himari to be dead. Surely, it had all been a misunderstanding.

"Thank goodness you're alive, Himari!" I said without thinking, throwing my arms around her. As I spoke, tears welled up. These tears were different from the ones that came before. "I'm so glad."

"Come on, Sho-chan, you're making a scene," Himari said, placing her tiny hands on my shoulders. The faint warmth coming from her skin was more proof that she was alive.

"Right? He's such a weirdo," Kanba said with a chuckle, but his lips were twisted, and he kept having to wipe welling tears away with his sleeve. "Yeah?"

As he spoke, he made a surprisingly stern face, staring at the penguin-shaped hat that had fallen onto the sheets.

"Kan-chan?" Himari said softly, seeing his weirdly serious expression.

"Oh, never mind. I guess you really shouldn't try to push yourself just yet, Himari."

"Yeah, I guess so."

He was probably thinking of how Himari had been when she awoke, acting like a completely different person.

Seriously though, what had that been about? It was bizarre enough that Himari had come back from a declared death; it was even stranger that she put on some kind of performance when she did. Still, just like Kanba had yet to address it, I myself was of no mind to bring it up. I had no idea what I would even say.

Maybe this really was all just a dream. Just a fleeting nightmare. I had a peculiar dream just this morning, hadn't I?

"I'm gonna go get Dr. Washizuka," Kanba said quietly, patting Himari on the head as if to confirm she was really there. Then, he signaled to me with his eyes.

We *were* in a morgue, after all, and Himari had been dead for a time. I had no doubt that Kanba was off to tell Dr. Washizuka and ask him not to make a big scene in front of Himari.

"It's already evening, huh," Himari said mysteriously. "This is a weird room."

"I think this is, um, some kind of special examination room that Dr. Washizuka put you in just in case. They had to do some kind of emergency exam. They didn't find anything, though."

I couldn't find it in myself to continue, but Himari nodded. "I see," she said, as though this made perfect sense to her.

"Sorry," she added with a distant smile. "All I do is worry you two."

"Th-that's not true! Today's Himari Day, isn't it? You should be conducting yourself with even more regality, your Majesty!"

Sure enough, it was already dark outside. From here, we would head home, and I would rush to make us some dinner, which we would all eat together. Then I'd brew some nice warm tea, and we'd relax in front of the TV, then take baths in our usual order, say good night to each other, and head to bed. Himari Day would end without a hitch.

Seeing Himari's gentle smile soothed my troubled soul, and I felt like I was finally returning to a kind, uneventful reality.

A few days passed, and Himari's health showed no signs of deteriorating. On the contrary, she seemed exceedingly healthy.

The shock and bewilderment on Dr. Washizuka's face was clear when he saw this—he feverishly told my brother and I, "I can't believe it. To think that anyone could make such a recovery from that state... Right now, I would say her condition is completely stable. Honestly, I don't think it's a stretch to call this a miracle."

"I'd like to start taking on some of the responsibilities around the house from now on," said Himari. "It's gotta be hard for you to be doing it all on your own, Sho-chan."

Today she wore sarouel denim pants in saxe blue with large white polka dots, with black suspenders. With a tidy, round-necked t-shirt and her hair parted in two braids, she looked even livelier than usual.

"I can do it," Kanba interrupted in a mumble. This was followed by a large yawn.

"Can you actually handle anything more than cleaning out the bath?"

Kanba stuffed his face full of omelet, unconcerned with my protest.

"Look, that takes a lot of work," he muttered, his face emphatic.

"You're shameless," I said.

His chopsticks moved diligently as he looked up at the sky with bleary eyes, ignoring my snipe. When he was eating was the only time he seemed focused.

"Seconds!" Himari said forcefully, thrusting out her little bowl.

"Yo, you okay?" Kanba asked reflexively.

A smile leapt to my face. "Of course," I said, taking the bowl. "I'm making your portion a little on the small side, but you don't have to force yourself to eat it."

"I feel completely fine, though. Dr. Washizuka told me to start doing anything that I felt capable of, too." She then lowered her gaze, a little shyly, and muttered. "I wonder if I'll be able to go back to school soon."

I felt my heart squeeze as I looked at her. Out of the corner of my eye, I could see Kanba making a nervous face as well.

Honestly, I don't think it would be a stretch to call this a miracle.

I reflected on the doctor's words. If this was a real miracle, then I was sure that she would be able to return to school. But it was too early to say for certain.

We were still afraid. What if this miracle's power was limited and ran out?

"I'm sure you'll be able to go back to school soon," I said with a smile, thinking about how I would comfort her if the reality turned out otherwise. I'm sure that my brother thought the same thing.

He and I did not look that much alike, but we were identical when it came to treasuring our little sister.

"Here you go, seconds," I said, handing back Himari's dish. My eyes happened to fall on the penguin hat, which was sitting atop the globe in the corner of the room.

Just then, our ancient intercom crackled to life with a buzz.

"Coming," I said. I opened the door to see an out-of-breath deliveryman standing there.

"I have a refrigerated package for delivery. This is the Takakura residence, correct?"

I signed for the package and took the cold box from the man. There was no sender listed. If it was not from Uncle Ikebe, I could not think of a single person who would ship something in a cooler to our house. On the contents line of the slip, "Living Thing" was written in harsh letters.

I carried the surprisingly heavy box to the parlor, where I carefully opened the packaging.

Inside were three large black round things, thoroughly chilled.

"What are those?" Himari asked curiously, peeking inside.

"The label said they were alive, but..."

She prodded one of them with her finger, saying, "I wonder if these will all fit in the fridge." This seemed like an irrelevant concern to me.

"Are they edible? Some kind of giant eggplants? Are they seafood?" asked Kanba, watching on high alert as Himari continued to poke them.

"No idea. And who sent these, anyway?"

"Yo, Shoma, school time," he said, urging me on.

I looked frantically to the clock on the wall. It was already so late I'd probably be tardy no matter how hard I tried.

"Oh, crap!" I stood up, grabbing my school bag. "I'll trust Himari to you for today, then!" I ran to the entryway, shoving my feet into my loafers. Just as I slid the sliding door open, I heard a voice from behind.

"See you soon!"

I turned to see Himari, who stood there quietly, waving her hand with a smile.

"I'll see you later," I said. As a relaxed smile drifted to my face, I thought, *Ah, that's right. This, this is what they call happiness. Things will probably be fine. I probably don't need to worry anymore.*

I made my way cheerfully to school, gazing up at the pale, bright autumn sky.

Needless to say, I was late. Still, I felt good. Even being late couldn't put a dent in my good mood.

The class I was assigned to was year 2, class A, at Torigaienishi Senior High School. The classroom was infused with a lazy apathy after lunchtime. There was something suspicious to the drifting of the clouds outside the window, and I wondered if Kanba and Himari would notice and bring in the laundry before it rained.

Our homeroom teacher, Tabuki Keiju, delivered a tedious biology lecture, that combined with the postlunch fatigue nearly put the room to sleep. He was not particularly liked or disliked by the students of the all-boys school. Despite his relative youth, his main hobby was birdwatching. He wore glasses that were so unfashionable I'm not even sure where he could have bought them, and nearly always had a dopey, slightly uneasy smile. His lecture about the life cycle of a frog was about as lively as someone reciting a sutra.

"In other words, once the egg has been fertilized, through cleavage of the egg, the cells begin to multiply, growing into a morula from which the blastula is formed. Then, as we observed last time with the fertilization of the sea urchin, one part of the blastula moves to the interior. This is known as gastrulation, where the archenteron is formed."

Hm, I wanna eat some urchin, I thought. Had we talked about urchin fertilization in the previous class? With everything that had happened, I'd let my schoolwork fall by the wayside.

"When it reaches this point, the three germ layers—the ectoderm, the endoderm, and the mesoderm—join, differentiating into cells of different shape and function." Tabuki suddenly stopped speaking, looking at his wristwatch.

I breathed a sigh of relief. Any longer and I would've completely retreated into visions of urchins.

"That's all for today. Next time, we'll watch a video to get a more concrete look at those ontogenetic mechanisms." Tabuki closed his textbook. "Are there any questions?"

These were the only moments when the whole room was silent.

"Then we're adjourned. Frogs really are cute," said Tabuki, grinning to himself.

He really loved animals, there was no doubt about that. The bell rang, and Tabuki exited the classroom.

I was suddenly overtaken by a pure and earnest joy. God, who had always been a cruel, fickle being, decided to bestow a miracle upon my family. Perhaps even we still somehow deserved happiness.

There were doodles of penguins in the margins of my notebook. That hat. That was truly strange. I wondered if that was the voice of God speaking through my sister, though it had been pretty foul-mouthed for a deity. Maybe it was just Himari? Well, regardless of whether it was God, a penguin, or a frog, it didn't matter. Right now, I was happy.

After school was a busy time. There was shopping, laundry, and cleaning to do. Then, I had to prepare dinner, and after dinner I would have to peel some pears or something for us to eat together. I would cackle at some mindless television show and keep an eye on Himari to make sure she didn't eat too many sweets.

Now that she was home from the hospital, more and more of Himari's belongings had begun to appear around the house. There was facewash and lotion, a new toothbrush. The hairdryer, which my brother and I rarely used. New shampoo and conditioner. Treatment agents for long hair. Her clothes and underwear were mixed in with the laundry. The brilliant colors and scents of a young girl spread faintly throughout the house. Himari was definitely back home.

"Yo, little Takakura. How 'bout some tea on the way home? I found a place where this stupid cute part-timer works," my classmate Yamashita proposed, violently grabbing my shoulders and prattling on.

"Sorry, in a bit of a rush today." I gave him a wry smile, though deep down I was stunned that someone could be so loud and pushy.

"Whaaat? You're so cold, little brother." Yamashita pulled me closer unmaliciously and snuggled against my cheek. It was nice that he was so affectionate, but I never did well with this kind of clinginess. I was well aware that I didn't act like a typical high schooler. At the moment, I was more concerned that all of the special sale items at the supermarket would sell out before I got there.

"What's with you, though? Your bro would definitely have come. If you can't be like your brother, you should know that always turning people down is bad for you. At least if you wanna be a normal member of society like us."

Well, obviously. Kanba and I might have been twins, but we were separate people. Kanba was good-looking and had always been popular with girls. It wasn't that I didn't look like him, but I was kind of spacey and vacant. I would have made a great hard-working house husband, but I had no game when it came to girls. And I had no time for Yamashita's clowning.

"It's fine, get off me." I shoved myself free of Yamashita. Three girls passed nearby us.

"Oh sweet, those were girls from Oukagyoen!" he said, pulling my sleeve, his interest suddenly piqued. "You see that girl in the middle? Not bad."

The Oukagyoen uniform, with its refined black turtleneck t-shirt below a sailor suit, was well-known in this area. The girl in the middle that Yamashita had pointed out, her hair cut in a bob, glanced back toward us. More than likely, she overheard Yamashita. I quickly averted my eyes.

"Yo, you think that girl saw me? No, she definitely did. Wonder what year she is. Dang, I should've gotten her name or something. It's times like this I wish big Takakura was here..." Yamashita watched the girls from behind, his hands cupped around his eyes like binoculars.

I immediately took advantage of Yamashita's blessed distraction and made my exit.

Obviously, it wasn't that I didn't have *any* interest in girls. I always enjoyed it when idols or pretty actresses showed up on TV, and sometimes I even felt my heart race. But it was pointless. The number of responsibilities I had were like a large, open wound in my side. If I were to fall in love with a girl, I would have to show her that wound. I would have to ask her if she liked me, despite this gaping, unhealing laceration. I didn't possess that kind of courage.

I touched the back pocket of my pants as I went to pass through the subway ticket gate, only to find I was without my commuter pass. I searched in my bag to see if I had put it there, even though that was something I never did.

"Hm?" I checked my pants, jacket, and the breast pocket of my school uniform, but it didn't turn up.

It had to be here. I had it on the way to school, after all. Had I dropped it somewhere between arriving at school and now? I'd changed my clothes for gym earlier in the day, so maybe I'd left it behind in my locker. I decided to return to school and look for it there. If I did, though, then all of the sale items at the supermarket were definitely going to be gone. I couldn't even imagine sending Kanba to buy them in my place.

Just as I sighed quietly to myself, there was a strange, prickling sensation somewhere around my thigh. I turned around to see a rotund little penguin, its round eyes sparkling, holding out my pass to me.

I stared fixedly at the creature. Other people around just walked past us, not noticing anything.

"My pass." I took the pass from it. What else was I going to do? The penguin nodded firmly at me, just a faint motion.

"Crap, the sales!" I looked to the clock beside the gate in a panic, but when I looked back down, the penguin vanished.

"What?" I craned my neck while taking off in a jog through the gate and climbed onto the train.

If this was just a wild dream, then how could I explain the pass that I now held in my hand?

When I arrived at the supermarket in question, I found an empty cabbage stand beneath a sign proclaiming in bright red letters, "Advertised Item!"

"Too late, huh?"

My shoulders slumped in disappointment. As they did, I caught sight of the penguin from before, firmly gripping a sliced half of a cabbage and looking my way. It silently handed me the cabbage half, and then waddled off.

"Hey, wait a minute."

I glanced at the cabbage in my hands to see a tag with the words "Organic, Pesticide-free. 350 yen."

"That's expensive," I muttered unconsciously. Was the penguin trying to make friends with me? I hadn't done anything that would deserve this kind of gesture. Just then, the image of Himari's penguin-patterned hat flashed suddenly to mind. Nothing but penguins these days. All in ridiculous forms.

I returned the expensive cabbage to its place, but I hadn't been able to get my hands on the cheap ones either, so I bought a more mid-range cabbage. I stuffed other cheap ingredients and daily essentials into a fold-up nylon bag. I had a lot of points racked up at this supermarket. I grinned to myself.

By the time I left the market, it had already grown quite dim outside, and a light drizzle started to fall.

"So, it was supposed to rain, then? Wonder if they brought the laundry in..." I looked up at the sky and sighed. I could make out soft, faint trails of gray clouds in the pale sky. Just then, again I heard the pattering of little feet. I looked down, to find a round little penguin holding out an opened umbrella.

I really didn't think I was *that* exhausted.

I called out to a mother and child who were exiting the supermarket.

"Um, pardon me."

"Yes?" answered the woman.

"This is kind of an odd question, but this thing is a penguin, right? Or, what is it?" I asked, pointing to the penguin who loitered absently nearby.

"What?" A clear look of suspicion spread across the woman's face, and she pulled hurriedly away from me, as if to protect the small child.

"Mama, what's that man saying?"

"Shh, don't look at the man. Come on, let's go," she said, throwing in as a bonus the sort of line I had only ever heard on TV.

I looked down at the penguin, only to see its expressionless black eyes staring clearly back up at me. Declining to take the umbrella, I stepped away from the penguin at once, turned my back, and hurried away.

The smell of dampened clothes and vegetables and asphalt. The chilled air. Without even realizing it, I had begun running from the penguin. My wet bangs clung to my forehead.

"What the hell *was* that?!" Though the house was not far at all from the market, the rain grew stronger by the minute, and I was already soaked through. Along the way, I looked back timidly, to see the penguin waddling full tilt behind me, the still open umbrella wobbling back and forth. Now terrified, I ran as fast as I could to the front and opened the familiar sliding door.

"Yo, you finally home?" asked Kanba, poking his head out from the kitchen. "How'd you get so wet?"

"Hey. I'm beat. Something weird happened," I started to call inside, when I looked up into the doorframe and stopped. There stood another round little penguin, the spitting image of the one that followed me around, blinking at me with its little black eyes.

"What, did he not make it to you? We sent him out with the umbrella and everything," said Kanba, his expression blank.

"Did *who* not make it to me?" I asked, shuffling out of my loafers. As I stepped into the parlor, detouring around the penguin at my brother's feet, my eyes fell upon Himari, sitting on the sofa beside another identical penguin, doing some knitting. I felt dizzy.

"They're the 'living things' that came this morning," said Kanba in a way that suggested that was obvious information, pointing at the open cardboard box.

"'Living things'?" No way. Did he mean those cold, round things that had been inside the package?

I heard the front door open quietly behind me. A penguin folded its umbrella, and quietly shut the door, stepping right up into the house.

"What is going on here?"

"You should go dry off already, you'll catch a cold," Kanba said.

"I know that."

I headed first to the kitchen, putting the cold items I purchased today into the refrigerator.

"Welcome home, Sho-chan. Here's a towel," said Himari, draping a bath towel over my head.

"Hey there, Himari." A smile popped to my face at once.

"We took all the laundry in!"

"Thank you."

A penguin was following along restlessly at Himari's feet, but she did not appear especially surprised at all, merely patting it gently on the head.

Why was I the only one surprised here? Things were starting to grow absurd.

I changed into dry clothes and sipped some warm tea while toweling off my hair. Kanba sat cross-legged, quietly drinking his tea as well. My body was warm, and the sound of the rain was a comfort to my chaotic, confused mind. It finally seemed like things were calming down.

Himari was playing with one of the penguins. The penguin, who had now been decorated with a felt cap with a big ribbon on top, sat opposite her. She grinned, poking its cheeks and touching its tail, offering her stuffed animals to it. The penguin stared at her face, and then pecked at the stuffed animals in her hand with the tip of its beak.

"So, what is this? Why are these penguin-y things wandering around our house?" I asked.

"What do you mean? Can't you see? When we thawed out that delivery from this morning, these came out. They seem to understand what we're saying, so we can probably use 'em for gofers."

Hearing the word, "gofer," I thought of the train pass and the cabbage, and the umbrella. I glanced at the penguin sitting quietly at my side.

"I guess? But I mean, this is weird, isn't it? Having three penguins tumbling around the house. And besides, they..."

If I was not mistaken, we three were the only ones who could see them.

"You're gonna say that no other humans can see 'em, right?" Kanba said promptly, nodding toward the table. There sat a familiar bundle of traditional sweets from the Ikebe household.

"Uncle Ikebe was by, then?"

Our uncle's family ran an old sweets shop, and he worried about our family, not having any adults around, so now and then he stopped by to check on us. He always brought some sweets with him.

"Yeah, he came to see how Himari was doing. These guys were wandering around right in front of him, but he didn't seem to notice at all," said Kanba, casually opening up the bundle.

The sweets had a familiar taste, and though this variety was not especially delicious, they were comforting in their mediocrity, the kind of thing I craved now and then.

"Even if that's true, the two of you seem way too relaxed about this whole thing. How can you act like this is completely normal?"

"It's not like making a fuss would change anything. Plus, you seem just as chill with it, sitting there holding a cup and staring off into space."

The packaging rustled as he opened the box of sweets, unwrapped a manju, and began eating.

"I am *not* chill about this. I just have no idea what to do," I argued, but I could not deny that I sat there as calmly as my siblings, resigned.

I shut my mouth and breathed in deeply.

"Survival Tactiiiiic!!"

Kanba and I whirled around at the sudden scream.

Himari, who moments ago played with a penguin, was no longer there. Incidentally, neither was the living room we had just been standing in.

A blast of white winds disrupted my vision. I quickly tried to cover my eyes with my hands, but something warm brushed against my forehead and cheeks ceaselessly, and I forgot whatever I'd been about to say. I timidly opened my eyes to see that it was not the wind touching my face, but countless layers of fine lace.

I was in a place I had never been before, darkness stretching as far as the eye could see, with brilliantly twinkling stars scattered throughout like beads. It was like outer space, though of course I had never been there.

The three penguins stood in a line before the fluttering lace.

There was a rich, somehow nostalgic fragrance. A driving rhythm emanated from somewhere, steadily increasing in volume. Lights flashed in all the colors of the rainbow.

I momentarily met the eyes of my brother, who sat cross-legged a short distance from me, but both of us were struck completely speechless. There didn't seem to be anything to communicate, no facts or understanding.

Then came sharp footsteps. Himari suddenly appeared in the strange space from out of the ceaselessly fluttering soft, white waves, wearing the penguin hat. However, the penguin looked strangely mature, elegant, transfigured into something like a real crown. Bathed in white light, she spread both arms with the finesse of a ballerina, her long hair unfurling forcefully behind her like an angel's wings.

Her eyes were red, and a sharp light shone from them.

A peach-pink ribbon encircled the round collar beneath her face. Shining black gloves encircled her arms, ending just beneath her fingertips, leaving them bare. She was unmoving, a beautiful, doll-like form.

A black latex corset with white frills around the bottom highlighted her slender body, and from the bottom ballooned a skirt, so long it dragged across the ground. She wore high-heeled, knee-length boots, form-fitted to her dainty legs. These, too, were glossy and black. It was a penguin dress, through and through.

She walked forward with a cold expression, heels making a sharp *chk chk* on the floor. She looked down on us and smirked.

The driving rhythm shifted subtly, as though in tune with Himari's every movement, sucking in time itself.

Himari suddenly crouched down, and each time she glanced at our faces, the rhythm followed. It grew impossibly loud, so loud that I instinctively tried to cover my ears. But Himari's clear voice resounded.

"Surely, you worthless nothings shall be told!"

Himari straightened her back, waving her arms over our heads. A faint, mysterious light poured down above us from her fingertips.

"You must obtain the Penguindrum!"

This was the same voice that we heard in the morgue. It was Himari's voice, but somehow different. It had a forceful power, one that seemed to spring from the pit of her stomach.

"Himari, what are you saying?" I raised my voice in confusion.

"We are not your little sister. We come from the place where your fates reside."

Our sister, standing before us, said that she was not our sister. It was true that she was not her normal self, wearing that wild dress with those red eyes. But I could only see Himari as Himari.

"It's the hat," Kanba said with certainty. "That hat is controlling her!"

"But that's just a stupid toy we bought at the aquarium!"

Himari silenced me with a loud, purposeful clack of her heel.

"Currently, your sister's life has been granted a temporary reprieve by our power. However, nothing in this world comes without a price. We expect our payment for this boon!"

As she shouted this, another blast of wind blew in. Himari's hair danced around her.

Kanba glared at her inscrutable, glittering face.

"What's this about a payment?!" I started to say. "This is weird—whoa!"

As I spoke, there was a click, and a square-shaped hole opened up beneath my feet. I fell headlong into the darkness.

My consciousness grew hazy. The mysterious light and the grandiose rhythm that moved in time with this alien version of Himari drifted gradually farther away, and I lost consciousness.

Himari slowly approached Kanba, touching his chin with coquettish hands, lifting it ever so slightly.

Rather than reply to Shoma's question, she tilted her face close to Kanba's, so close that they nearly brushed cheeks, and whispered in his ear. Her voice was sultry, like the sweetest honey, just like the first words she spoke after a yawn when she was drowsy.

"Shall we initiate the Survival Tactic?"

She tore open the buttons of Kanba's shirt with her free hand, touching his now bare chest. Then, she plunged her hand deeply into it, as though there was no skin or bone.

"Guh!"

Her hand moved within his chest, as though searching for something.

"A-aah!" Even as he gasped in pain, a faint crimson spread across his cheeks.

Then, slowly, she extracted something that shone with a brilliant light from his chest, and held it up to the heavens. It spun, shining with a blinding light, and rose up into the sky, eventually disappearing into the far reaches of the alternate space.

Though it was now the middle of the night and the rain stopped, the disquieted atmosphere had not dissipated in the slightest. The intermittent sound of dripping water from the kitchen sink, which usually did not bother them at all, was strangely irritating. Shoma, already a light sleeper, seemed especially fitful.

Kanba sat up carefully, so as not to wake his brother, breathed in deeply, and walked to the kitchen to turn the faucet off more firmly. Then, after some hesitation, he decided to go and check in on his little sister.

Beside the living room, where Shoma and Kanba spread their futons out to sleep, was Himari's room. In the center of the room, totally at odds with the rest of the Takakura house, was a small bed with a luxurious red canopy. Both the canopy and the pillows piled up on the bed had been handmade by Himari, and the bed itself was surrounded by mountains of all her favorite things.

An angel blowing a trumpet, a candelabra, and a lamp shaped like a mushroom all glowed with faint light, and atop a vintage sewing table sat an old-fashioned sewing machine, fabric scraps, ribbons, lace, and bobbins. Embroidery thread and beads and buttons of every imaginable color and size were scattered around the room. Beside the closet were piles of books, above which were placed a number of Himari's so-called "cute things."

Beside a wooden rocking chair, which had been picked up from somewhere or other so that Himari could relax while crafting in her room, was a basket filled with yarn and knitting needles, along with a bunch of half-finished projects, doilies, and runners that could be draped over or used to decorate various things in the Takakura household.

In the middle of her bed, surrounded by curtains in her beloved peach pink that draped around her protectively, Himari herself lay like a princess beside one of the penguins, her eyes firmly shut.

Her long eyelashes. The buttons at the top of her nightgown were undone, her white skin bared.

The faint moonlight shone pale upon her slender throat.

Kanba stood at the side of her bed and brushed away the hairs that clung to her cheek with his fingertips.

Unwittingly bewitched by her face, he thought about the nature of humanity.

Why were people born? If humans drew breath only for the sake of being born, growing up, and slogging tediously through every single day until they grew old and died, then was this some grave sin? Or was this some cruel, humorless joke? If that was the case, wasn't the beast who stayed faithful to their survival strategies, living only for the sake of living, not the most lucid, the most beautiful?

If something like God existed in this world, then there was one question which Kanba would have liked to ask: Does such a thing as fate truly exist in the world of man?

For example, if a human were to ignore fate, his instincts, and even his genetics, and fall in love with someone—if he would accept even the destruction of his own self for that person's sake, could that person truly be called "human"?

"Or something like that," he muttered with a self-deprecating smile. He fixed the collar of her nightgown, and then quickly pressed his lips to her cheek. As he pulled away from Himari, once again he gazed down at her, aching all the more. His face was terribly sad, without a hint of insincerity in his damp eyes.

Anyway, Kanba hated the word "fate."

He stroked her hair once, unimaginably tender, then pressed his mouth to hers, her small lips parted in gentle sleeping breath. It was a kiss as reverent as that of a prince, awakening a slumbering princess.

Whether or not fate existed, Himari's lips were startlingly soft and sweet, and tasted of a deep, deep darkness.

PENGUINDRUM

CHAPTER 02

OGINOME RINGO *loved* the word "fate." Especially when it referred to "a fated meeting." A single encounter could alter the course of your entire life. Such special meetings could not be mere chance. Surely, such a thing was fate, she believed. Of course, life was not made up of fortuitous meetings alone. There were plenty of unpleasant, sad things as well. It was quite painful to consider that such misfortunes were also fated, entirely out of one's power to influence. And yet, she believed:

"Even sad and painful things must have some meaning to them. Nothing happens without reason in this world."

She stood at the corner of the subway station. She pulled a small mirror from her school bag and coated her lips in a pale pink lip balm. It had been advertised as making your lips, "as moist and glossy as a ripe apple," and caught her eye. Then, she combed her fingers through her hair, swiftly arranging it. Her heart ached with joy and nerves. But at the same time, it was a surprisingly blessed pain.

A girl from another school took up position beside her, chattering on her cellphone. Cradling her phone with her shoulder, she opened up a gaudily decorated folding compact, at least twice as large as Ringo's, and began applying additional mascara to her already overemphasized eyelashes.

"Yeah, I'm off to my date with Takashi. It'll be fine. I've got my triple lace strategy today."

Ringo glanced at the girl out of the corner of her eye. Her face was slathered with so much makeup, one might think she was about to step out on stage. Her hair was too bright to be called brown. She had visible cleavage, and the buttons of her blouse were open enough for her lacy bra to peek through. Her skirt was daringly short, and her thighs were bare. If anyone at Ringo's all-girls school were to dress like that, they would probably be stopped the moment they walked through the gates by the teachers who hung around for morning greetings.

"Huh? My triple lace strategy? Well, you know..." She cackled, and her boisterous voice permeated the space.

Ringo checked herself over again in her little mirror and nodded, a faint smile on her face. She was fine. Even if she wasn't wearing that much makeup, even if she didn't have mascara on top of false lashes, and even if her chest was rather modestly flat, she wasn't bad at all.

She put her mirror into her bag and walked to her usual place. She already felt painfully nervous, her diaphragm clenched so tense it was hard to breathe. It was coming so soon now that she couldn't contain herself, but she put her hand to her chest and steadied her breath. Every step of the way had been just as she intended.

Yes, Oginome Ringo was a believer in fate.

Roasted smelt, natto, and eggs. And some miso soup. Then the pickles. The three of us crowded around the table and said a proper blessing. Another fine morning, no better or worse than any other. Still, that penguin hat, sitting atop the cabinet, bothered me, and with the mysterious penguins sitting beside us, it probably could not be called a typical morning at all.

"Come to think of it, what should we be feeding these things?" I had unthinkingly only prepared enough breakfast for us three humans. "What'd you all give them yesterday?"

"We never fed them!" Himari gasped in realization, her brows pinched up in the middle of her forehead. "They must be starving!"

"They eat fish, right? They're penguins," said Kanba, not seeming especially concerned as he continued shoving food into his face. He looked fatigued.

"These guys aren't typical penguins, though." I looked at the penguin who stared at me. I had never heard of penguins who could be shipped in cold storage. Invisible penguins wandering around Tokyo in the middle of autumn seemed even rarer.

"The lady at the aquarium said they usually give them sardines and scad and mackerel," my sister said. Today, Himari's hair, usually worn in a loose ponytail, was pinned up with sparkling rhinestone pins, and she wore an autumnal violet dress. She preferred the kind with skirts that gave a gentle silhouette.

"Sardines, scad, and mackerel..." I repeated, carefully confirming that Himari was her usual self. I looked at each of the penguins. Sardines, scad, mackerel. Feeding them would cost a lot, wouldn't it? The price of blueback was pretty high lately. That aside, even butter and vegetables and other things would be nothing to sneeze at. Suddenly, my gaze stopped on the penguin next to Kanba, the biggest eater in our household. Somehow, I got the notion that this penguin would be the biggest eater as well.

Now that I thought about it the three penguins seemed to bear an unsettling resemblance to myself, Kanba, and Himari, in personality and mannerism.

"Here you go," said Kanba, suddenly picking up some smelt from my plate and offering it to the penguin. Without hesitation, the penguin chomped down the smelt, so readily it seemed it might eat Kanba's whole hand as well. "Oh, looks like they eat smelt too."

I was so wrapped up in thought that I forgot to be angry about Kanba stealing from my plate. At the very least, these were living creatures. Even if no one else could see them, and even if they looked nothing like typical penguins, as long as they were in our house, we needed to feed them. But we had no way of affording the extra cost.

"I wonder if we couldn't just give them some cheap dog food or something," I muttered, sighing.

"Survival Tactiiiiiiic!!!"

As I shot up in shock and turned to look at Himari, my vision was obstructed by a gust of white frills and lace. That sweet smell spread again through my nostrils. That familiar rhythm thumped so loudly that I was sure the whole house, maybe the entire world shook with it. I opened my eyes a crack to see Himari appear from out of the flood of dazzling light, the penguin hat atop her head, looking for all the world like a queen. Her black, enameled boots sounded wildly.

We were once again in that alternate space.

"Surely, you worthless nothings have been told!" Himari stuck her right foot out swiftly, her eyes shining red.

"So that... wasn't a dream," I said.

Unlike me, who looked around wildly, my brother calmly squared off against Himari.

"You must obtain the Penguindrum!" Himari shouted in a voice that seemed to rumble from the pit of her chest.

"Where is it, then? This Penguindrum," asked Kanba.

"Today, at 8:10 A.M., board the train headed to Ogikubo. Enter the third car and stand by the second door. At East Kouenji Station, Oginome Ringo will board," she said, her voice melodic and sonorous.

"*Oginomeringo?*" I repeated, like an incantation.

"Follow her and search her person. This girl possesses the Penguindrum. Probably."

The pseudo-Himari swiftly averted her eyes.

"Wait a minute, what's this *probably*?!"

"Hold up, are you seriously gonna tell us to do this when you don't even know for sure?" Kanba stepped in, coldly demanding the same information I'd asked for.

"What? Is that too much for you to stomach? Do you not care what happens to your sister?"

Shocked, I looked at Kanba. He wore a look of regret, but it did not seem that he had any more interest in talking back.

"W-We gladly accept your task, oh Lady of the Hat." I bowed my head seriously for the first time in my life.

"Lady of the Hat?" Himari, nay, the Lady of the Hat, furrowed her brows for a moment, but then continued. "Very well. You will be certain to locate the Penguindrum. Should that fail to happen, consider your sister's life forfeit!"

"Y-yes, ma'am!"

Kanba's face twisted, and he ground his teeth.

"But for you to expect us to take responsibility on such vague information, is..." I started to say, when out of the corner of my eye I saw a penguin pressing a mysterious button.

"...isn't very, aah! N-nooo!!"

A square-shaped hole opened up under my feet, and I fell at once into a space devoid of color or sound. A terrible void. Even a subway tunnel was not as dark and quiet as this.

"Shall we initiate the Survival Tactic?!" Far above, I heard the clear voice of the Lady of the Hat issuing a decree.

I fell straight down into the darkness. The Lady of the Hat, or rather, Himari. I wonder if she'd been angry because I suggested feeding the penguins cheap dog food?

There was no way that hat could be controlling her.

Kanba and I sat side by side near the door on the train we'd been instructed to find. Kanba nodded off, but I was on edge, throwing quick glances around the crowded train and checking the time on my phone.

Himari definitely died right in front of us, and then came back to life thanks to that thing. As if this was some malicious game that God cooked up, that thing instructed us to locate the "Penguindrum" in service of some "Survival Tactic."

"Hey Kanba, what kind of person do you think this 'Oginome Ringo' is?"

"Well if she's ridin' the train this time of day, she's either an office lady or a student," he replied, cracking his eyes open and rubbing them sleepily. "Either way, all that matters is we get the Penguindrum."

The announcement for East Kouenji Station came through the air, and we looked at each other and got to our feet, moving near the doorway. Just then, the train arrived at the station, and commuters on their way to work and school came flooding in, and soon the train was full. It took an enormous effort to make sure that my brother remained right beside me.

"Aniki, we're never gonna be able to tell who's who like this!" I said frantically.

"We're fine. We've got *them* here for that exact reason." He looked back at me, his face tense.

"I see."

Those little penguins might actually be useful here, I thought. However, when I finally spotted the penguins again amidst the crowd, they were pincered between the riders' legs, squished up and stuck aloft.

"This is impossible for them," I replied softly.

Kanba let out a deep sigh.

The penguins appeared to be attempting to return to us, making sorrowful faces. Their black eyes stared pleadingly as they were crushed between the legs of high school girls and women in pants suits. The way they were looking at us, it was like we really were their owners.

One of them pushed up tight against a high school girl's back, levering its body out through the gaps between the riders. It rolled out onto the floor and ran for me, looking at me with a desperate expression. When I instinctively held my hands out, it balled itself up, and embraced me, burying itself in my stomach.

"C'mon, what are you all doing? This is important," I said, quietly comforting it as I lifted it up.

"Just a minute!"

"Yes?" I looked up at the shrill voice to see a tall, long-haired girl glaring at me. Her lightly tanned skin and plump lips looked distressingly mature. Had she seen me talking to the penguin and been taken aback by how creepy it was?

"Don't *yes* me! You touched my butt just now, didn't you?!"

She stared directly at me. Perhaps because she was so loud, some of the passengers around us shot glances our way.

"That's not true!" I raised my hands in denial, dropping the penguin as I did.

"Stop lying! You were just groping all around back there, weren't you?!" She took a step forward and glared at me, unknowingly grinding her foot down on the penguin.

"Th-there's been a misunderstanding!" Obviously, I could not tell her, *It was that penguin-like thing that you're stomping on that did it, and I'm honestly not sure I would count as that thing's owner.* Of course, no one else could see the penguins in the first place, and I wasn't sure if they were even tangible.

"Then, what was it?" she demanded. "Come on now, spit it out!"

I shrank back, unable to even grimace. I knew that in cases like this, once you accepted the blame it was all over, but then again, I did feel somewhat responsible, as the penguin's caretaker.

Just as I was about to give up hope, I felt a presence at my back. A low voice spoke.

"That was probably my bad." Kanba had a listless way of speaking, one which barely concealed a bright and mischievous air.

"Huh?" asked the girl, looking beside me.

There stood my brother, attempting to hide something.

"My bag was caught. I was just trying to pull it free, so that might be what happened. I didn't mean anything by it. Still, if I made you feel uncomfortable, then I should apologize." Kanba gazed at the girl with anxious eyes and said sincerely, "I'm sorry."

It rung out as grandly as though they were the words of a lover, finally reunited after making his beloved wait for him for twenty years. My jaw dropped, forgetting myself as I looked at my brother, who acted like a completely different person.

"Well, in that case, I guess there's nothing to apologize for. With your bag getting stuck and all," the girl said haughtily, her cheeks flushing.

"I really am sorry." My brother, having repeated himself for assurance, glanced at me and gave a mischevious grin. It was, without a doubt, the face of a scoundrel.

"Shinjuku Gyouenmae, Shinjuku Gyouenmae," the train's speakers intoned. Once more the train came to a stop.

"Oh, this is our stop, then," said the girl, turning back to the friend who boarded with her and calling, "Let's go, Ringo."

Kanba and I looked at each other in shock. She definitely said "Ringo."

"You go," he said hurriedly, scooping up the penguin and handing it to me. "That uniform belongs to Oukagyoen Girls' School."

"What about you?"

"I need to make some arrangements."

My brother practically shoved me out into Shinjuku Gyouenmae Station, and, left with little choice, I began running after the two girls. The round, elastic penguin was oddly heavy, and carrying it was difficult, but I learned from our first encounter that it couldn't keep up with me while running.

As I hurriedly passed through the gate and exited above ground, I saw the long-haired girl again, and next to her, the girl I assumed was Oginome Ringo. They weren't far ahead. I could definitely catch up with them.

"Goood morniiing!"

Yamashita appeared in front of me, calling out in a carefree voice.

"Yamishita, stop it!" I stared at Ringo's back as she steadily moved away from me, trying to fend off Yamashita, who abruptly grabbed at me.

"What's with you? Lookin' all gloomy first thing in the morning. 'Sup, you havin' girl problems?"

Seriously, was there anything besides girls and romance in Yamashita's head?

"Sorry, just go on without me!" I said, running off and leaving him behind. I could not allow myself to lose sight of Oginome Ringo, the Penguindrum, or Himari's life.

"My, my! What's this? Has love finally found our little lord Shoma?" I heard Yamashita's voice from behind as I ran after the girls. How wonderful it would've been if this were truly something so frivolous.

As the name suggested, Oukagyoen Girl's High School was an all-girls' school. While it had been relatively easy to follow Oginome Ringo nearly to the school gates, now we were surrounded by throngs of girls wearing the identical uniforms. I hid in the shadow of a telephone pole, lost for what to do. I was very clearly a suspicious person—what was I doing here, and why? There was no way I could possibly find Oginome Ringo again without being a spy or a detective or something. But I could not afford to give up without doing anything.

I snuck up to the rooftop of a building near Oukagyoen. As I gazed at the buildings, which were far more beautiful than that of our school, I texted Kanba my location and waited, bored.

I leaned over the fence, taking in the autumn breeze. The penguin at my feet spaced out as well, as if mimicking me.

"An all girls' school, huh?" I said dazedly. "What do I do?

Do I need to dress in drag?" I asked the penguin, but it only looked back up at me, giving no response.

"Do you *want* to dress in drag?"

I flinched, turning around at the sudden voice. Kanba looked at me suspiciously, carrying a large paper bag.

"K-Kanba! Where have you been?!" I put my hand to my chest.

"Around. Anyway, take a look at this."

He pulled a laptop out of the paper bag, opened it smoothly, then took a USB stick from his pocket and loaded it up.

I held the penguin and gazed at the screen as a roster of individuals appeared: photos of the students of Oukagyoen. He flipped past several and stopped on what appeared to be Oginome Ringo's page.

"Is this a... roster? Where and how did you get something like this?"

"Hm? I've got an old girl who's good at this kind of thing."

"Good at *what*?" Was there a spy or detective amongst the number of my brother's ex-girlfriends? It was beyond imagining.

"Hacking," he said plainly.

"Isn't that illegal?" My face stiffened; that was distinctly more terrifying than what I imagined.

"Oi, lemme see yours for a sec," said Kanba, squeezing the penguin out of my arms. He pulled out a big, fat marker, and, perplexingly, wrote a "2" on its back.

"My penguin's number one, and this one's number two. The one back home with Himari is three. Better not to bother about it."

This made things less complicated, yes, but it wasn't very appealing. Wouldn't it be better to give them names? They didn't have to be complicated ones.

"Here we go," he said quietly.

He began pulling assorted electronics out of the bag and lining them up on the ground. He used duct tape to afix transceivers to the penguins' backs and small cameras to their heads.

"That should work."

Of course. It seemed his idea was to have the invisible penguins search inside of the school for us. He briskly gave the penguins a set of directions, and took a transceiver in one hand, switching the laptop screen to a feed of images captured by the two cameras.

"Will this really be okay?" The penguins were not especially quick-witted. My stomach started to ache from anxiety.

"Yep, that's good. Keep going straight ahead. Don't look around too much," Kanba said coolly into the walkie-talkie, not displaying a hint of worry.

The image swayed as the penguins tottered along, continuing down the tidy, spacious hall, just as they were told.

"Right there. Go up those stairs. Then, the third classroom on the left, that's class 1-C."

I scratched at my stomach in boredom—and also because the two camera images were swaying terribly, and staring at them was making me queasy.

"Head for the seat by the window," Kanba urged the penguin with certainty, flipping through the roster.

Suddenly, Penguin No. 1 looked up at the studious face of *Oginomeringo*, or rather, Oginome Ringo.

"Bingo," said Kanba.

She had thick bangs that hung just above strong-willed eyes. Maybe she *did* possess the Penguindrum.

"Now, look through her stuff. Check every nook and cranny and see if there's anything suspicious."

I looked up from the screen as he said this, startled.

"H-hey, are you sure it's okay to be doing this?" My voice fell softer as I spoke.

"What else are we supposed to do? We're investigating a total stranger."

I didn't have any other ideas, and it wasn't as if I had the means to get close to her on my own. Still, that was not the issue. As I fell silent, Kanba sighed softly.

"As long as we don't get caught, it's fine. It's not like we're hurting anyone."

"That's not the problem. I'm saying this is morally wrong. Just because no one else can see the penguins doesn't make it okay. Or legal."

Just as I wondered where exactly Penguin No. 1 positioned itself, given it was rather dim, suddenly her knees came into view from a strangely low angle. However, the next moment things went dark again, and I realized that it was rolling around on the floor. No. 2 appeared to have its eye on her commuter bag hanging from the side of the desk. It appeared to be trying to jump higher, so that it could peek inside, but it still could not reach. What on earth was it trying to do?

"So, what do we do?" Kanba asked flatly. "If we can't get the Penguindrum, Himari's gonna die. If this Oginome Ringo does have something so amazing, there's no way she'd just happily hand it over it us just because we asked. Do we really have a choice here?"

I knew he was right. We didn't have a plan, but morals were not going to be enough to protect Himari in these dire circumstances. Still, was this really alright?

As I fell silent again, Kanba said softly, "We have to do this." I glanced at his face. "It's for Himari."

Seeing his firm expression, his brows furrowed, I gave up. Now wasn't the time for any pointless arguments.

Somehow, No. 2 seemed to have managed to stick its head into her bag, but from there we could only see it squirming about, and the investigation could not continue.

The morning's lessons were long over. On the laptop screen, from a peculiar angle, we saw a scene of three girls, Oginome Ringo and her friends, eating lunch together. One of the three was the girl who had mistaken me for a pervert on the train this morning.

The benches were neatly arranged in the park-like courtyard. The penguins wandered around the girls' feet, as though trying to surround Oginome Ringo. At the moment, Oginome Ringo was eating a sandwich and playing on her phone.

"Ohmygod so like, he was *so cool*! He was all, 'If I made you feel uncomfortable, then I should apologize. *I'm sorry.*' Right, Ringo?"

The long-haired girl's impression of my brother was actually pretty good. I started feeling vaguely embarrassed, and noisily slurped milk from a carton. Kanba faced away, nibbling nonchalantly on some anpan, as if totally used to people saying things like that about him.

"Man, I wish I could've seen that!" replied a lively-looking girl with a short haircut. "That sounds like something else!" She shut her eyes, lightly touching her cheeks, sounding deeply moved.

"He really was cool."

"So, what about that first suspicious guy?" asked Short Hair.

"Mm, that kid who was with him? He was pretty much nothing," said Long Hair, instantly dismissive.

Kanba snorted laughter. Penguin No. 2, meanwhile, seemed wholly focused on the bento on the girl's lap.

"Ah, hang on, what is camera No. 1 capturing?!" I looked at the screen just in time to see a clear view up Oginome Ringo's skirt. I sputtered, "Pay attention to them, would you?! I swear, you're all terrible!"

I puffed out my cheeks, grousing at both my brother and the penguin. Just as I thought, Penguin No. 1 really did resemble Kanba.

"Which one?" Kanba looked to the screen, intrigued, focusing on the image from No. 1's camera with deep interest. "Oho."

"I think that guy's uniform was from Gaiennishi High," one of the girls said.

"No way, that's so close!"

"Seriously. Makes you wonder how we've let such a handsome guy escape out from under our noses all this time."

The whole time, Oginome Ringo only took quiet bites of her sandwich, staring at the screen of her phone, not participating in the conversation. Was she talking to someone? Looking something up? Reminiscing over photos?

"Ringo? What's up?" called Long Hair, suddenly noticing how silent Oginome Ringo had been.

"It's nothing," said Oginome Ringo, shaking her head, her face popping up from the screen.

"Now then, I was gonna eat that octopus sausage! Huh? Where is it? Did I eat it already?"

In reality, Penguin No. 2, standing at her feet, had eaten her octopus sausage, but there was nothing I could do about that.

"I'm going to head home a little early today," Oginome Ringo said suddenly, and both the cameras focused on her at once. She quickly cleaned up her sandwich wrapper, grabbed her bag, and stood up.

"Ringo?" The remaining two seemed dumbfounded.

Kanba and I hurriedly cleaned up the odds and ends we had spread around the rooftop like a picnic, so that we could follow her.

The penguins sluggishly followed Oginome Ringo, as per Kanba's instructions. The camera atop the more rambunctious No. 1 was now somewhat more lopsided than before, as though the tape had come slightly loose.

Oginome Ringo headed straight for Shinjuku Gyouenmae Station and boarded the train. We boarded the train as well, taking a seat a short distance away from her.

"Oginome Ringo's house was in East Kouenji, wasn't it?" Kanba asked quietly, holding a paper.

"She's going the opposite way from home, then."

I glanced at Oginome Ringo to see the penguins hanging around her. No. 1 seemed particularly interested in try to squeeze its head between her thighs again, but as though Oginome Ringo uncannily sensed this, she tilted her head and shifted in her seat.

"She's got something," said Kanba, making a strange face.

Obviously: we were only following her around like this because she had something. Though she did not appear to possess anything unusual.

"Kanba, what exactly is this Penguindrum, anyway?" I asked, as I watched No. 2 roll off of its seat.

"How should I know? Doesn't seem like 1 or 2 know either, and that Penguin Hat never said what it was. I couldn't even start to guess," he replied brusquely.

"I wonder if it's even something that we can actually take."

"Well, it's gotta have some kind of form, if we were told to find it and bring it back with us, right?"

"I guess all we can do is look for it, just like the hat said."

"It was for Himari." For once, as if we were both operating on the wavelength that twins supposedly always shared, my voice joined with Kanba's. However, unlike the unease that lingered somewhere within me, I saw determination stark on Kanba's face, reflected in the dark window beyond the benches.

In a teeny, tiny voice, Oginome Ringo muttered to herself. "A man's heart is through his stomach. Your underwear is your everyday weapon."

When we arrived in Ikebukuro, Oginome Ringo entered a book shop inside a large building, and flipped through the magazines with a serious expression.

"I mean, it seems like she's just standing around and browsing, pretty typical." My brother and I were standing by a shelf some distance from her, magazines flipped open for show as we pretended to read them, our eyes instead trained on her.

"Don't let your guard down. She might be giving some kind of secret code signal."

"Seriously? Just what kind of secret code..." Just as I spoke, the cheery ring of an incoming call came from my phone in my back pocket.

Noticing the sound, Oginome Ringo suddenly looked our way.

"Idiot! Put that thing on silent!" Kanba quietly raged.

"S-sorry, sorry!" I frantically hunched over, looking to see who was calling. It was from our house phone, which meant it was from Himari. "Sorry!" I said again, pitifully, and answered it.

"Onii-chan?" Sure enough, Himari sounded rather displeased. "Where are you right now, and what are you doing?"

"Where? Uhh, we're at a book store."

"Is that Himari?" Kanba asked from beside me. I nodded, moving a little way away.

"You two skipped school today, didn't you?"

"Huh?! How did you know that?" I asked, inadvertently letting the truth slip.

"Tabuki-sensei called because he was worried! You don't ever do anything like this!"

"Ah." I scratched my head, a warm smile on my face, as the image of my bespectacled homeroom teacher flashed before my eyes.

"Shoma!"

I turned around at my brother's voice, to see that Oginome Ringo finished her browsing, and was just about to leave.

"Sorry, Himari. I'll call you back later! I'm really sorry!" I hung up the phone and quickly followed after Oginome Ringo.

It was unforgivable to make Himari needlessly worried, but this was all for her sake. If we found the Penguindrum, we could return to our normal, peaceful lives.

"We're doing our best for you," I muttered to myself, catching up with the penguin that was following Oginome Ringo. From this distance, I probably wouldn't look quite as suspicious.

Just as she rounded the corner into a certain shop, the penguins' eyes flashed toward us. They each held up a paper with a drawing of a can of squid.

"A can of squid?" I muttered, slowing down. Where had they even gotten the drawings?

"I think they're saying we *can't* go in there?"

Just as Kanba suggested, the next papers the pair whipped out were a "No Entry" symbol. The shop front inside didn't have such a symbol though, so we kept following the penguins and rounded the corner.

"This is—!" I reflexively gasped, stopping in my tracks. Kanba made a complicated expression and stopped beside me.

The shop front was absurdly cute, drawn with pastel accents, looking for all the world like an amusement park. Wherever you looked, there was enough lace and frills to make your eyes sting. In the middle of the shop, a display of white mannequins, clad in bras and matching panties, spun leisurely around along with a small wooden rocking horse.

There was a poster of a smiling female model in her underwear, and women picking up that same underwear to look at it. Amongst them stood Oginome Ringo.

I gulped thickly. Even if it was my brother, if two men were to enter this shop together, we were sure to be questioned.

"Lingerie store, huh? Wish I had a girl here." I shuddered as my brother clicked his tongue. Was he saying that he could go into this shop if he had a girl with him?

"W-we absolutely can't go in there. We can't!" I paled, once more silently apologizing to Himari from the bottom of my heart.

We watched from a distance as Oginome Ringo wandered around the shop. She flitted between the displays, and then picked up a brassiere. I quickly averted my eyes.

"Don't tell me *that's* the Penguindrum," Kanba said seriously. "If it is though, then I've definitely seen one like that before." He sounded sincere, and I was too terrified to inquire where he'd seen such a thing.

"Would the Penguindrum be something mass-produced? Something store-bought? Either way, I cannot go in there and buy something like that!"

"I guess not."

I looked again at Oginome Ringo to see that she placed the brassiere back on the shelf. Then, she moved further into the shop.

"Hey now, going for somethin' a little more radical? Don't tell me she's gettin' somethin' with a hole down *there*." He furtively began to step into the store, breathing heavily through his nose.

"No way, seriously? Huh? Hole? A hole where?" These increasingly intolerable circumstances were making me dizzy. Even without any open holes, everything here was frilly and sheer.

"Obviously, a hole that connects to the cosmos, idiot." Kanba said strangely. Or, did he still have it in him to be telling jokes?

"Let's get out of here. I doubt the Penguindrum is here." Oginome Ringo really was just looking for underwear, and I was sure she would soon leave the shop again.

"Quit pulling my sleeve. Huh? Where'd she go?"

Suddenly I realized I'd lost sight of her. However, it did not appear that she had come out our way, near the entrance.

"This is because you were saying all that stupid stuff!"

"So this is *my* fault?! I'm going in! To the back!"

To the back, he said, but this was not a very large store. All that was in the furthest back, with its ornately painted walls, were piles of lingerie and an emergency exit.

Kanba shoved open the emergency door, and we went outside. The sun set, and I felt a slight chill on my skin from the wind.

"Damn it, which way did she go?!" We looked around the landing, but there was no sound of anyone climbing the emergency stairs, nor sight of anyone descending them.

"Oh, Aniki, there!"

Oginome Ringo walked along the edge of the building. Her skirt rippled in the wind, and some of the concrete that she was barely managing to balance on crumbled out from under her feet.

She dripped with a cold sweat, and her face was pale. But she continued sidling along.

"What is she doing over there?"

I couldn't imagine what she was thinking, creeping along practically on tiptoe. A strong wind blew her hair into her face, and she looked like she was about to misstep.

"What do we do, Aniki?" I leaned over the fence.

"Now's the time for these guys." His gaze fell to the penguins.

"I wonder." The anxiety in my heart was clear in my voice.

Now, just when had they ended up this way? No. 1 had a pair of panties on its head, or rather, its face, and No. 2 wore a brassiere on top of its head, the two cups just like two ears. Were these guys even stupider than we assumed?

The two penguins, now adorned with underwear along with their cameras and transceivers, began walking along the ledge.

"Oi, keep up the pace!" Kanba called. Though the penguins shivered at his scolding, they dripped with a cold sweat, and could not reach Oginome Ringo. All that we could see on the camera feed was the pocked and dirty wall of the building.

"I knew they couldn't do it," I said.

"Yeah, no hope here," Kanba agreed.

I watched as a gust sent the underwear adorning the penguins flying, and was filled with a deep sense of regret.

"Hm?"

Several meters from the penguins, Oginome Ringo stopped. She took out her phone from the pocket of her uniform.

"Found iiit!" she said cheerily, standing up as high on tiptoe as she could and holding the phone aloft.

"Was that a shutter sound?" I looked at Kanba.

"Is she taking a picture?" He looked back at me equally perplexed.

With her objective apparently having been accomplished, Oginome Ringo began to make her way back.

"Oi, hurry up and get back here." As soon as the penguins heard my brother's voice, they began to totter back. It seemed we would not be returning home yet.

We followed Oginome Ringo back to the train, and then to Ogikubo. She now sat by a flower box in front of the station and began flicking through her phone, looking up now and then as if waiting for someone. We blended in with a group of high school boys who were gathered in front of a nearby vending machine, trying not to draw attention to ourselves.

"Wonder if she's got a date with someone?" said Kanba. "The sun's already nearly set, though."

"Yeah, though given how weird she acted earlier, it might be with someone who has something to do with the Penguindrum."

"Seriously though, what's so important that she'd go to all that trouble to get a picture of it?" I still could not believe this Oginome Ringo was so important that she might hold Himari's life in her hands.

"Who knows? Could even be that picture itself is the Penguindrum. Oh, she's moving!" Kanba, who leaned on the vending machine, righted himself.

She stood up and waved as she caught sight of a man coming out of the station gate.

"Tabuki-san!" A smile leapt to her face, her cheeks pinking.

"Oh, Ringo-chan!" replied a familiar voice, smiling back at her as if it was completely normal.

He had slightly longish black hair, and totally unattractive thin-framed silver spectacles. A slightly crooked tie around his neck. And a plain-looking backpack. There was no doubt that this man was our homeroom teacher Tabuki Keiju in the flesh.

"Aniki, isn't that our homeroom teacher? That definitely is, right?" I asked. Somehow this felt anticlimactic.

"Yeah, that's Tabuki for sure." A grimace crept to his face as well.

"On your way home from cram school again today? We seem to be running into each other a lot lately. You're a hard worker," Tabuki said peacefully. He really was a carefree guy.

"Yes, well…" Oginome Ringo looked down bashfully, though she still shot glances back up at Tabuki.

"O-ohh! This is perfect! I've got something that you'll want to see!" she said, pulling out her phone at once, turning the screen so that they could both see. "It's amazing, isn't it? This was at that building in Ikebukuro you told me about the other day."

"The red-rumped swallow's nest?" He gazed into the phone screen, deeply interested. Oginome Ringo's face reddened happily as Tabuki stepped up right beside her.

"Yep! I just got a photo!"

"Wow, this is super rare! But, how did you get this photo?"

"A swallow's nest?" I thought of the luxury ingredient used in Chinese cuisine, but I knew this was something different.

Oginome Ringo tittered and said, "That's a secret." She was so endearing now; she seemed like a completely different person.

Kanba and I looked at one another. Just who exactly was Oginome Ringo? Kanba looked as though he realized something, but I still didn't have the faintest clue what was going on.

Their conversation seemed to be drying up. "Anyway. Give my regards to your mother. Take care getting home!" he said with a vacant smile, waving.

"I will, thank you very much!" She gave him a nod, then suddenly said, "Um!"

Tabuki, however, had already nearly vanished back into the crowd. "I'm really looking forward to going birdwatching," she added, very softly.

She remained there for a short while after, a bit wistfully, as if lingering in the echo of her words. Then she suddenly grinned, and began following Tabuki.

"Huh? Aren't they done, though?" I asked vapidly.

It was now thoroughly night time. The moon hung in the cold, clear sky. It would be dreadful for Himari if we weren't home soon. There was no doubt she would be angry with us.

Oginome Ringo followed Tabuki, who held a bag from a bento shop, and behind both of them were Kanba and I, along with the penguins. This was a thoroughly strange affair. It helped that it was dark out now, but following someone through a residential district was difficult. All the more so if that person knew your face. Oginome Ringo walked boldly on, however, never imagining that she herself was being tailed.

Finally, Tabuki arrived at an apartment building and entered a first floor flat. This was obviously where Tabuki lived.

Oginome Ringo peered at him from the shade of a nearby wall. We stood watching her from the shadow of a telephone pole, even farther away.

"Why do you think she's following after him?"

"That chick's in love with him," Kanba said at once.

"Huh? No way!" I tried to keep my voice down, but shouted louder than I meant to. Kanba quickly covered my mouth.

"You really are dense," he said, looking deeply and truly exasperated.

Suddenly self-conscious, I could only smile foolishly. Now that I thought about it, I supposed that did seem like an obvious conclusion, but frankly, had Kanba not said anything, it would have been a while before I realized.

"Hm?" Penguin No. 1 tugged on Kanba's shirt sleeve. I looked to see that the pair of them had taken it upon themselves to fix their cameras, lights, and duct tape, and were puffing out their chests.

Oginome Ringo was just about to enter the building's perimeter.

"Okay, time to redeem yourselves. Go," said Kanba, and the penguins started waddling across the dark asphalt, following after the girl.

We leaned back against the guard rail, once more furtively opening up the laptop, and peered at the screen.

The image was dark, of course, but it was enough to tell that Oginome Ringo was no longer by the front of the building, with its rows of old doors. The penguins swiftly rounded the building to the back.

"She's gone," I muttered. All we could see was the light flooding down from the balcony, along with a few weeds.

However, as No. 1 looked all around, we could see that below the balcony, the grate to the underground ventilation system had been removed. It had been placed to the side, and there were slight traces of something scraping against the dirt.

"Hm? What's that? Okay, get in there," Kanba directed.

It was even darker underground. We could see nothing on either of the penguin's feeds. Just as I thought this, however, a hazy shape of something moving appeared on No. 1's feed.

As I stared at it, I soon realized that it was the slender thighs of Oginome Ringo, who crawled ahead on all fours.

"Wah! Those again!" It goes without saying what lay beyond her thighs. I quickly covered my face with the bag I was holding.

"That's the second triple-laced pair of the day. Must be her fighting panties," said my brother nonchalantly.

"Don't say that so casually! And stop staring!"

"Yo." The tone of his voice shifted.

I slowly peeked out from behind the bag, looking at the screen again.

Oginome Ringo twisted her body, lying faceup in the vent. She seemed to be holding a small flashlight in her mouth. In a practiced movement, she shuffled something out of the commuter bag she dragged along.

"What's that?" Kanba focused on her hands.

"That looks kind of like the ones on the penguins, doesn't it?" My mouth opened dumbly.

"A microphone?" Once more, he said something dreadful without any hesitation.

I scowled, but stared at the girl on the screen, my mouth still hanging open. She twisted a knob on the side of the small black device, adjusting it. As she did, there was a faint noise, and then the sound of a television show drifted faintly through the penguin's microphones.

"No way, is she...?"

"Seems like she's doing the same thing to Tabuki that we're doing to her."

"In other words, that makes Oginome Ringo..."

Apparently, Oginome Ringo was Tabuki Keiju's stalker.

"Ah, gotta love a soda after work." Tabuki's nebbish voice felt even more ineffectual, filtered through the two microphones. You would think that he'd at least crack open a beer at home.

Oginome Ringo lay down in the dirt, a look of contentment on her face, as though she was listening to a lullaby, straining her ears for the sound of Tabuki going about his daily life. Seeing the dampness in her barely open eyes, I felt a shiver run down my spine.

"Don't you worry. Soon, you won't have to eat dinner alone anymore. After all, from now on, I'll *always* be with you. I'll never let you feel lonely. I believe in fate." There was a deep sincerity to her whisper. "In destiny."

CHAPTER 03 ••• →

A LITTLE GIRL ate curry. Behind her sat her beloved kappa and otter plushies, and on either side of her sat her loving parents, watching over her.

"It is good?"

"Yeah! I love your curry, Mama!"

"I see. You really do love curry, don't you Ringo?"

"Yeah, I love curry!"

"You're such a good girl, Ringo!"

"That tickles! If you squeeze me like that, I can't eat! Mama, what's wrong?"

"It's nothing. I'm just so happy."

"That's weird."

"Aw, no fair! Your Mama's hogging you all to herself! Time for Papa to get a squeeze in, too!"

"Papa!"

"Ringo, you are our dearest, dearest treasure. Let's stay together as a family like this forever!"

"Yeah! I love my Papa and my Mama! And curry!"

Even now, years later, the kappa plushie and the otter plushie were still by her side. No matter how old and dusty they got, no matter how frayed in places, their slightly vacant, gentle faces never changed, as constant as her love for them. She probably would never bring herself to throw them away. As if cursed, they were bound to one another, so close that they could be called family.

That morning, on the table in her empty living room, Ringo faced down her toast with a serious look on her face. She squeezed a bottle of chocolate syrup, carefully drawing a heart atop the toast. Inside this heart were two names: "Keiju," and "Ringo."

"There we go, all done. Time to eat!" Just as she lifted the toast and began to take a bite, her mother, clad in a suit, finally rushed into the living room.

"Oh goodness, it's so late already!" She looked at the clock on the wall, then back to Ringo. "I've got an important meeting today, so you can go ahead and eat without me tonight."

"Mama, today is the twentieth," Ringo said, casually folding the toast in half to hide the syrup letters.

"Yes, I know. Sorry, I'll have some curry while I'm out, so could you go eat out with your friends?" She readjusted her wristwatch and drank her milk coffee from a mug set on the table in one big swig. "See you later."

As her mother held up a hand, heading out, Ringo called to her, "Mama!"

"What is it *now*?" She turned around frantically. One large curler hung down from her bangs.

"You've still got a curler in," Ringo pointed out coolly.

Her mother held a hand up to her bangs, and gasped, "Oh my goodness!" She removed it and placed it down on the table, then headed back out while unraveling her coiled bangs.

Ringo let out a sigh. When she opened the toast again, the sweet-smelling heart was all a mess, the letters smudged beyond recognition.

The twentieth of every month was to be "Curry Day." This was a rule of the Oginome household. Furthermore, today was a special day. Today, for the first time, *he* would be eating Ringo's homemade curry.

Ringo had already perfected a special, love-filled curry. The carrots, which *he* hated, would be grated, and it was chock full of potatoes, which *he* loved. And it contained a secret ingredient: apple jam.

She slathered some apple jam atop the chocolate syrup.

Her dish might not look very appealing, but that didn't matter. *He* would adore a homemade curry. *He* and Ringo were bound by fate, after all.

She smiled in satisfaction, licking the syrup and jam from her fingertips.

Eating curry with someone you adored was the taste of happiness.

"Survival Tactiiic!!!"

A gust of white lace blew along with the shout.

I realized now that the sweet fragrance seemed to be emanating from the curiously sprawling lace. The air that filled this alternate space didn't quite smell like vanilla, or rose, or soap, or sunlight, or fresh grass, but it held us enrapt.

Today, the queen of our household, accompanied by the three penguins, once more wore the penguin hat atop her head. She had her feet planted haughtily atop the heads of Penguins No. 1 and No. 2.

Kanba and I stood, both looking back at Himari.

"Surely, you worthless nothings have been told! You must obtain the Penguindrum!"

I hesitated in the light of her cold and powerful red gaze. Then I took a breath and spoke.

"Himari. Quit messing with us with these elaborate illusions already!"

"Huh?" Kanba looked at me, a bit of surprise on his face.

"Oh?" Himari's eyebrows raised, and her bright red eyes opened wide.

"I mean, look, we already took your word on this Survival Tactic and Penguindrum thing once. It was right after that whole ordeal, after all. But, let's end this already," I said resolutely, looking up at Himari. "I know it was hard being hospitalized for so long, and

I understand how good it must feel to finally be released from that place. And I'd probably be lying if I said I understood what that's like. But I'd like to try to understand." I gave voice to the thoughts that churned in my head. "So let's work together. This isn't what you wanted to do once you were healthy and out of the hospital, was it?"

Himari looked at me, contempt in her eyes, playing with Penguin No. 3 as if it was a ball.

"Are you saying that you cretins still do not believe in our existence?"

"I..." Kanba averted his eyes from me.

"Aniki?" There was no way that he could have bought into this.

"Hmph. Are you still possessed of the base obstinance and suspicion so typical of you lower life-forms?" She cast a look to the penguins, grinning wickedly. "In that case, we haven't any choice. Shall we treat you cretins once more to that nightmare?"

Her eyes glowed as she looked at us.

"Wait! Before that, the Penguindrum!" Kanba quickly protested. "Please tell us more about the Penguindrum!"

"Aniki..."

So, he did believe in it. He truly believed that Himari was possessed by the penguin-shaped hat. And that the being that resided in that hat held Himari's life in its hands.

Unlike me, Kanba appeared desperate, fully convinced.

"It seems that you truly understand your place," said Himari, looking at Kanba, her lips twisted.

"Aniki, do you really believe this? Do you know something I don't?"

I got an uneasy feeling as I looked at Kanba, who seemed at a loss for words.

"Er, wait. I know how this goes." I looked down at the floor. Surely enough, a square shape snapped open and the floor receded. "No! Why?! Why are you only being mean to meeee?!"

As I fell, spiraling, into the darkness, I pictured my brother's anguished face in my mind. Was he able to comprehend, even accept these bizarre circumstances? To think that a single hat held control over our family's fate. The world went black before my eyes, literally.

"Shall we initiate the Survival Tactic?!"

All that was left was the booming voice of the Himari that was not Himari, ringing in my head. It was just like the dream I had of riding the subway. Where would this carry me to? And where would we be able to get off of this ride?

Later that day, we stood nervously before the automatic doors of the condo Oginome Ringo lived in, with their complicated art deco-style design. I wanted to bombard my brother with all the obvious questions floating through my head—were we really going to do this? *Should* we be doing this?—but when I saw the sullen, serious look on his face, I knew there was no way out of it.

We were going to break into Oginome Ringo's home.

We strode into the building's interior, attempting to look as casual as possible. As I tried not to act overly aware of the security cameras in the corners of the ceiling, I suddenly became unsure of where I should be directing my gaze. Furthermore, even though I knew no one else could see them, I could not fathom breaking into someone's home with two penguins in tow.

Unlike the automatic doors, the interior of the building had a simple design, and we quickly found the residence number indicated on the dossier that Kanba brought with him.

Earlier, we waited at East Kouenji station and watched as Oginome Ringo boarded the train. Her hair hung neatly around her chin. Her eyes peeked out from beneath thick bangs. This girl, dressed in the tidy uniform of Oukagyoen Girls' High School, looked nothing like someone who would crawl through an airduct underneath Tabuki's apartment and eavesdrop on him. Then again, the pair of us surely looked nothing like people who would break into the home of a high school girl we did not know.

Kanba pressed the button of the intercom with a surprising lack of hesitation. We waited, but there was no reply. Things might have been at least momentarily simpler for me if anyone, like the girl's mother, was at home, but I knew we could only postpone this for so long.

"Alright, looks like they're out."

Kanba took a pair of gloves out of his uniform jacket pocket and donned them, then pulled out a ring of what looked like metal earpicks.

"Uh, Aniki, those are..." I looked nervously up and down the hallway. Someone might emerge from the next apartment, or the next, or a different one and come this way at any moment. There might be hidden cameras in this passageway.

He slid some of the picks into the keyhole and began rattling them around.

"Unfortunately, for now, we need to do as that hat says. No matter how terrible it is, if it's for the sake of saving Himari's life, we have no choice but to accept it. The question is just how far we're prepared to go."

He switched to a different metal rod and tried again.

"Damn it, this really ain't easy for a novice."

Be prepared. That was one thing I did not need to be told. It should have been simple. I did not wish to do anything bad. But I couldn't bear the thought of Himari dying. Thus, I was troubled, at my wit's end.

There was a *ka-chk* in response. Kanba pulled, and the door quietly opened.

"It's for Himari," he said, pulling a second pair of gloves from his pocket and handing them to me.

I felt as if I was watching my own hands from a great distance as I accepted the gloves. My hands moved slowly, hesitantly. Gripping them was an act of final resolve that there would be no turning back.

"It's for Himari," I agreed.

I put on the gloves. When I looked at the penguins, they were staring idly, and I had no idea what they were thinking.

The Oginome home was a tidy little place, in line with the building's modern appearance.

The door to the living room was open as we entered from the spacious entryway and proceeded down the hall, so we quickly got a sense of its size.

"Whoa, this place is huge! Wonder how many tatami this is. This kitchen is super nice." The sink in the kitchen island was wide, much nicer than the narrow one we had at home, where Himari and I bumped elbows whenever we worked side by side. My eyes sparkled at the beautiful appliances, thinking how easy they looked to clean. Beside me, No. 1 and No. 2 were running around excitedly.

"C'mon, this ain't a home show on TV, let's get this over with," Kanba sighed deeply, sweeping his gaze across the room, obviously wondering where to start searching.

"This really does feel like burglary," I whispered.

There were two other doors, aside from the bathroom, before we reached the living room. That room seemed to continue on to another as well.

"If the Penguindrum is here, then I guess it will be."

"That's true."

We had come to take the Penguindrum from Oginome Ringo. No matter how you put it, we were stealing, weren't we? I set aside my desire to run away from this place. This was all a matter of resolve.

My eyes suddenly fell upon a calendar, where a red circle marked one particular date. It was today. Written in the same red ink were the words "Curry Day." Just what exactly did that mean?

"Yo, here's her room."

Kanba stood before a door.

"This is bad."

A plate in the shape of an apple hung on the door, decorated with small embellishments, and the words: "Ringo's Room."

"If the Penguindrum is something that belongs to that chick, then it's most likely to be in here." Kanba reached right out for the doorknob. Almost reflexively, I held his hand back.

"But it's cruel to intrude on a girl's room, isn't it?" It was an odd thing to say, but I couldn't help thinking of our sister. Just how would Himari react if two strange boys let themselves into her room?

"Cruel? Oi, Shoma. This chick's stalking our homeroom teacher."

It was true. There had been something strange about her that night.

"I mean, she's tunneling under Tabuki's floor and eavesdropping on him. She's a total pervert, just some stalker chick with her head screwed on the wrong way. She can screw off for all I care!"

"But..." But those were totally separate issues. The fact that she stalked Tabuki wasn't justification for us to be snooping through her room. But what about Himari? I resolved to do anything to save her.

I was truly between a rock and a hard place—caught between the weight of my conscience and the pressure of my resolve.

"If you can't do it, I will." Kanba ignored my hand and opened the door.

I reflexively averted my eyes. For a moment, I was overwhelmed by a wave of guilt. Was I not trying to maintain my integrity as a good person? Was I not trying to preserve, for myself at least, the love of a God that I was uncertain even existed? In doing so, had I just placed more of a burden on my brother, renewing my resolve again and again like some spell, complaining even though I expected this the moment I entered Oginome Ringo's home in search of the Penguindrum?

Who was I trying to save? And what did I hope to accomplish?

In a short time, I had fallen completely to pieces, but Kanba smiled warmly at me. He furrowed his brow, as if to say we had no other choice, and patted me gently on the head. "Well, that's okay. Hold onto that kind heart of yours, for Himari's sake. Yeah?"

Before I could tell him to wait, he urged Penguin No. 1 along and entered the room.

"Aniki..."

As I forced my body forward, the door shut in my face. I stood there, lost, unable to give any reply.

The courtyard of Oukagyoen Girl's High School was gorgeous, with well-tended quads decorated with white benches. It was a bright and lively place whenever the students were assembled.

The moment Oginome Ringo entered the courtyard, she saw a shrub trimmed into a neat, round sphere. It reminded Ringo of the ring of fate.

"Hey, hey, want an update on that hot guy we saw the other day?"

Yukina, who was the tallest among the three assembled on the bench, with full, mature lips, opened her mouth. The three girls each spread their bento out on their laps, and the school's midday break, lengthy enough to both let a lunch digest and allow the girls sufficient time to talk, began.

"Huh, what?! Tell us, tell us!" Mari—who had the same kind of cuteness as a small animal—leaned forward.

Ringo, once again, was elsewhere. Once she finished gazing at the circular shrub, her head filled with her plans for the day, which had warmed her heart since this morning. She did not even register the flavors of the sandwich she nibbled on.

"This is just between us," said Yukina, putting her hand to her mouth in an exaggerated gesture.

"Definitely! This stays here!" Mari grinned conspiratorially.

"I heard from a friend from cram school that that guy used to date Kuho Asami!" said Yukina, in a 'How do you like that!' tone.

"Kuho Asami?" Mari asked, tilting her head.

Ringo vaguely remembered the name, but she did not say so. For a moment, the image of Kuho Asami briefly interrupted the flow of her thoughts, but the shape of it soon vanished back into memory as more important matters returned to the forefront of her mind.

"No way, you don't know her? She was in *Sixteen* magazine!"

"You mean that model? What? That's *ridiculous*!" She placed extra emphasis on the last word.

Wow, neat, Ringo replied internally on cue without batting an eye, her thoughts still adrift.

"Yeah, but here's where it gets good! That guy flat out dumped her! 'Girls who're nothing more than their appearances bore me,' he said!"

"Whoa, that's kind of cool!"

Right? Isn't that cool? The pair nodded fervently at each other.

Ringo began muttering the words flowing through her head, counting on her fingers.

"Potatoes, carrots, celery, and pork. Kuho, no, apple jam." *And then*, she thought, lifting her head. White clouds in a white sky. As she thought of his gentle smile, a faint grin crept to her face without her notice.

This was by no means the first time that Kanba had been inside a woman's room. He had slept in the bed of such a room's owner, and he had taken her clothing in his hands, and had his taken in hers. He had sometimes shared kisses immediately after entering such a room, while other times it had abruptly turned to that after thirty seconds of light conversation.

Every woman's room smelled different. However, they were always sickly sweet, and spending too long surrounded by a woman's favorite things always started to give him a headache.

Oginome Ringo's room overflowed with assorted decorations and objects, all of them following a sea creature theme. Kelp and tropical fish hung amongst the glass beads of the curious, octopus-themed chandelier, and on the floor was a large pillow in the shape of a crab. Atop the bed sat old kappa and otter plushies, looking for all the world as if they owned the place. The suspended beaded curtain was primarily blue and translucent, with starfish mixed in here and there. Her jewelry holder, which seemed to have been crafted of coral wholesale, was hung with large-beaded accessories with the same sort of translucency as the curtain, and there was a cannister full of shells.

"She sure is thorough," Kanba muttered. He thought vaguely to himself that a girl who lived in a room of such single-minded taste must have a real one-track mind and it was not at all surprising that she would be a stalker.

He took a deep breath and pulled open her desk drawer, gesturing to Penguin No. 1 to start searching it while he investigated the closet. He did not find anything unusual. All of her clothes and underwear and socks and handkerchiefs looked incredibly normal. If he were to force an assessment, he might say that she had a bit of an excess of clothing with cutesy patterns along the hem. Still, that was all.

"Hey, you." Kanba turned around to see how the desk was coming along, and then immediately had regrets. "What the hell kind of investigating is that?"

The contents of the desk were poking out slightly from every drawer, and Penguin No. 1 itself pulled out the textbooks stacked atop the desk, attempting to open them.

Scratching his head, Kanba carefully shut the closet, and picked up a notebook that had fallen on the floor.

"Hm?"

Atop the windowsill was something that did not match the aesthetic of the rest of the room. It had nothing to do with the sea or sea creatures; it was not even blue. It was in the shape of a peach. It was a perfectly pink peach, like a peach manju, the sort of peach that would appear in a picture book adaptation of *Momotaro*.

Curious, he moved to the windowsill, picking up—was it an alarm clock?—but there was nothing strange about it. He put it back on the windowsill, assuming it had been a gift from a parent or some other relative, someone who would be offended if the girl didn't make use of it.

Kanba rolled his neck. His head hurt. He really did have a headache coming on.

Shoma was right. Shoma was always conscientious and bright. But always doing the right thing was not necessarily going to guarantee someone's happiness. But there was still a solitary softness in Kanba that would not allow him to blame Shoma for this, deep down. If Kanba were to lose this final softness, the balance of his humanity would probably be destroyed.

His headache worsened. He wondered what look was on Shoma's face right now, standing on the other side of that door. After checking that everything had been put back in its original place, all of the drawers and cabinets shut up tight, he grabbed Penguin No. 1 by the top of its head and once more put his hand on the doorknob.

The guilt and nerves of breaking into a stranger's home, of opening and shutting and rummaging through all of their things, had taken its toll on me, and I collapsed sloppily across the corner sofa in front of the large TV set. At first, I thought this to be a very clean house, but on further inspection, I started to get a different impression.

Oginome Ringo's home felt too sterile. Perhaps she had a tidy mother who loved cleanliness. But the overly straightened room was cold, with none of the personal touches to suggest that people actually lived there. Though, I was uncertain if this was a good or a bad thing.

"Hey, Aniki," I called from the sofa, hanging my head.

"What?" he asked suspiciously, scrutinizing whether the potted ornamental plant he investigated had been placed correctly back into its previous location.

"Just what the heck *is* the Penguindrum?"

"Who knows." He stared at me, the furrow of his brow deepening.

"We keep searching around aimlessly, but we have no idea what color, what *shape* the thing is. Even today, we haven't found a single unusual thing."

Kanba ignored my questions and opened the drawer on the TV stand, pawing through the DVDs and other detritus inside. "If you've got time to gripe about this you could at least help a little. It's too early to say that there's *nothing* to find in here."

A movie that I thought I might have once seen started playing in fast-forward on the TV screen.

"That's true, but, even if you did find the Penguindrum, you wouldn't even know if it *was* the Penguindrum, would you? What I'm saying is, what are we even looking for?"

"Well, the Penguindrum, obviously. Stop complaining and make yourself useful. We still haven't searched the whole kitchen. Get up already."

I sat up, pressing him, interrupting his gloomy, exasperated words.

"Listen, I know we're looking for the Penguindrum, but we have no idea what the Penguindrum is, so that means we have no idea what we're searching for, right?"

"Yeah, I know. But the real issue here is that you don't want to be doing this dirty job anymore, right? This one's no good either, eh?" he said cynically, and stopped the DVD.

Just like I feared, I foisted the whole task of entering Oginome Ringo's room and searching her stuff off onto my brother. But he was the one who let me off the hook. Furthermore, that *wasn't* what I was saying. It wasn't remotely the same thing.

"If you hate this so much then you don't have to help anymore. I'll look for the Penguindrum on my own, and I'll save Himari on my own. *Just me*," he emphasized, taking another DVD from its case.

"What are you saying?" I asked. "We decided the moment we set through that door. We're ready. We're going to do this together, for Himari."

Kanba shrugged.

I continued, "I know that! We still gotta try, right?! It's not that I'm not willing to do this. It's just, I have some questions." Deciding that I was finally on board with his plans, I stood from the sofa. Just then...

"I'm home!"

We looked at each other, and practically dove behind the sofa, curling ourselves up out of sight. Not giving us a moment to think, Oginome Ringo entered the living room. We held our breaths, bodies numb. There was nothing more we could do. This was no longer just a simple trespass.

With a little tune, Ringo sung and danced down the hallway into the living room.

"Hooray, it's Curry Day!"

She put her bulging grocery bag of curry ingredients into the kitchen and went straight to her bedroom to change from her uniform into her normal clothes. Her eyes fell upon the clock on her windowsill. If she started now, she was certain she would have a hot curry ready just in time for dinner.

She went back to the kitchen, clad in a blue apron that fit with the rest of her favored color scheme. She washed her hands neatly, heart already bursting with the anticipated happiness that she knew was just a few hours away.

"Wonderful, tasty Curry Day! The taste of happiness, Curry Day!" she sang.

She took the ingredients from the bag and lined them up on the counter to the beat of her song. Carrots, potatoes, onions, pork, apple jam, and big round apples. A new type of curry roux, cumin, cinnamon, and ginger.

Once the pot and ladle and cooking chopsticks were all perfectly prepared, she set vigorously to work.

As she worked, Ringo's thoughts wandered frivolously, wondering if curry might have been the first dish ever cooked in human history. Naturally, it would not have been a curry like the one she made now, but some curry-*like* dish. Surely, it had been a young woman who made this dish, making all of her cooking implements from scratch, using fruits and leaves from trees in the forest as her seasonings, exhaustively fanning the flames, drawing the water and pouring her heart into it, all for the sake of feeding someone she loved, so that they would smile and tell her how wonderful it was. Curry truly was the taste of joy.

She packed some grated apples in with the pork, so that it would not get tough once stewed. This was the secret technique of the Oginome family.

She toasted the spices well, then cut the carrots up finely, the potatoes into large chunks. She wondered briefly if she ought to prepare the roux as written on the box, or if she should alter the amount slightly, but given that it was her first time making this kind, she decided to follow the instructions.

The apple jam was the very last thing to go in. Just a little spoonful, the secret ingredient.

Ringo loved the sound of the ingredients stewing in the pan. It was as if the ingredients were whispering to each other, bursting with innocent mutual encouragement, *Let's be delicious, let's make whoever eats us happy.* In the lulls of the warm lullaby, gentle white steam rose like the sweet tones of a mother speaking to her babe. Curry had to be eaten with someone special, someone you hoped to spend the rest of your days with. These were the rules of Curry Day.

Stirring the pot, Ringo peered quietly inside.

Her mother, wearing a black apron and dishing out curry. This was a recollection from March 20th, five years prior.

At the table were little Ringo and Tabuki Keiju, who, though he looked quite grown up, was still a boy at the time. Ringo, age eleven, donned her black velvet dress, just as her mother told her to. Looking back now, she didn't think it was a material suited to mourning clothes, but that was the only black garment Ringo owned at the time.

"No need to hold back, you can eat as much as you like," her mother said with a smile.

"Of course, thank you very much," Tabuki replied in a soft voice, though his posture did not at all relax.

"So, you're in university now then, Keiju-kun. My how the time flies. Is your mother still doing well?"

"She is, thank you." As the refined, well-mannered Tabuki finished speaking, he politely brought a bite of curry to his mouth.

"Your curry is always so delicious."

The smile on his face was a kind that Ringo had never seen before now. It seemed to have a ludicrous sparkle. Seeing him in his black suit, which his wry smile suggested he was unaccustomed to wearing, Ringo thought him a mature, handsome young man.

"Why, thank you. To be honest, we have a secret family recipe. Isn't that right, Ringo?"

Ringo continued watching Tabuki, her mouth slightly agape, barely hearing her mother's words. She was caught up in trying to determine just what feeling had overtaken her, but she hadn't the faintest idea.

Even now, she still remembered that it had taken Tabuki looking her way to finally reclaim her senses. He was superb. Thus, curry was something to be eaten with the one you cherished.

The smell of well-stewed curry wafted from the kitchen into the living room.

"All done!" she said proudly, shutting off the flame, scooping a little bit up in the ladle to taste it.

"Mm, perfect."

She ducked into her room to retrieve her diary from her bed, and then flopped heavily down on the sofa, stifling a laugh.

"Step one is complete. No need for me to worry. Everything is proceeding according to fate," she said to herself, flipping through the diary. She could not hold back the smile that bubbled up naturally from her heart.

Up next was the main event of Curry Day.

Oginome Ringo wrapped the whole pot of curry up in a furoshiki, then packed all her things into a small tote bag, which she slung over her shoulder. Our empty bellies rumbled at the smell, and my stomach let out a loud growl at least once while she stood in the kitchen. "Control your guts, would ya?" Kanba absurdly demanded, his face frightful.

The penguins kept peeking into the kitchen and drooling, but I had to wonder if they could even eat curry.

We managed to follow her back to the train without being spotted. We boarded at East Kouenji in pursuit, and then disembarked at Ogikubo.

Oginome Ringo cradled the pot carefully in her arms as she passed through the shopping district.

"What a weirdo," said Kanba, almost entirely to himself.

"That aside, where does she intend to take the curry she made?" We were beginning to grow accustomed to following Oginome Ringo from a fixed distance. She seemed to spend most of her time lost inside her head, or focused on whatever task she was currently set on.

She had spent the entire time on the train looping back and forth between grinning and hanging her head and tensing up her face. She seemed to be in a happy mood. Even now, watching her from behind, we could tell that she was in high spirits.

"It might not be just any old curry," Kanba muttered, a seriously twisted smile on his face. "Maybe there's some secret code in the combination of the spices. We can't rule out the possibility that maybe that curry itself is the Penguindrum."

"I guess not," I said doubtfully. No matter how you looked at it, it really was just a normal curry, in a normal pot.

Oginome Ringo walked steadily on, proceeding into a familiar residential district.

"Hey, Aniki. Isn't this the same road as yesterday?"

"Yeah. That chick's headin' to Tabuki's place."

Would that really be making her behave so erratically? That energetically? Did she intend for Tabuki to eat that curry?

I then recalled the words I had seen marked on the calendar: Curry Day. Was it really a day so joyful it was worth singing about? Was eating curry with Tabuki what she meant by Curry Day?

Tabuki sat across the table from Ringo.

"Um, so, today is Curry Day, and I was thinking we could eat this together," said Ringo, opening the pot lid. A gentle steam and the pleasant smell of spices wafted out. "Still, maybe I should have cut the carrots a little bit smaller, so if you like I'll try to serve it so that you don't get any! I don't mind at all if you eat around all the carrots. In fact, I even think that's cute!"

As Ringo spoke, she spooned the curry over glossy, shining, freshly made rice. Tabuki was moved by her care.

"Ah, I thought it would still be warm," Ringo fretted, "but maybe I should've reheated it once. I can microwave it if you like."

Tabuki halted Ringo with a smile as she spoke.

"Looks plenty warm to me," he said. "Plus, you've gone to so much trouble. I want to eat it as it is."

The messy length of Tabuki's hair. His eyes, behind his glasses, took Ringo in deeply. She suddenly could not speak another word. And then, Tabuki smiled back.

It was simple, but it was a Curry Day for just the two of them, with a homey, practically candlelit warmth. Before the two plates of curry, the pair said their graces.

"Mm, this is delicious. You're a great cook, Ringo-chan. I'm sure you'll make a wonderful wife someday," Tabuki said, grinning again as he took another bite.

"No way, it's just curry!" came the fervent reply.

Tabuki happily ate, and then ate some more. Seeing this gave Ringo courage, and she opened her mouth bashfully.

"Oh, that reminds me, I'll make us some bento for the bird-watching trip!"

Tabuki's eyes widened in pleasant surprise.

"Really? I can't wait. Are you sure, though? You have cram school, won't that be difficult?"

"No, not at all! I, well, I'll do anything if it's for you. I can make a little bento anytime you like."

As Ringo spoke softly, eyes downturned and her face growing red, a wide palm reached out to her, gently stroking her hair. Ringo's gaze drifted further and further downward in shyness.

"Tabuki-san," she called to him, in a voice both joyful and troubled.

"Ringo-chan," he said sweetly.

For the first time, Ringo truly understood what it meant to feel as though your heart was ready to leap right out of your throat.

Ogikubo, in the dim evening light. Ringo returned to her senses before the door of Tabuki's home, still shivering from the powerful reverie she'd been caught in. If things went as she imagined, then the plan might end up proceeding even further along than expected.

Shoving all her expectations and fantasies down into the heavy, curry-filled pot, Ringo cleared her mind, and knocked twice on the old-fashioned apartment door.

"Welcome home, Tabuki-kun."

A beautiful woman opened the door, her wavy, mid-length, brightly colored hair arranged in a casual style, her smile like a freshly-bloomed flower. Loose hairs hung around her cheeks.

Ringo stood stock still, staring at the woman suspiciously, unable to move a single muscle.

"Oh?" said the woman with a smile, and then, "Come in," inviting Ringo in as though this were her own home.

The woman wore a soft-looking knit dress with a thin, gentle silhouette, and matching black leggings. She led Ringo to the living room, her seemingly well-worn slippers pattering across the floor, and took some barley tea from the small refrigerator in the adjacent kitchen, pouring it into a cup.

This sucks, Ringo muttered to herself, but the words reached no further than the walls of her own heart.

"Here you go. Not too cold out yet, is it?"

The woman placed the cup in front of Ringo, then sat across from her, placing both elbows on the table and resting her chin. Her fingers were long, pale, and slender. Her nails were trimmed in an oval shape and painted neatly in a pale pink, each nail decorated with a thin strip and a single rhinestone. On the pinky finger of her left hand sparkled a delicate gold ring.

Ringo sat up straight, not reaching for the tea.

"Are you one of Tabuki-kun's students from school? My apologies. He isn't home yet."

The woman's eyes narrowed gently. Her eyelashes were long and delicately arranged, and her eyelids, painted with a pale beige eyeshadow, shone. Her lips were glossy and coral-colored.

She spoke nothing further. She did not ask who Ringo was, nor show any unpleasant expression. Ringo internally bit her lip and stamped her feet in frustration.

"Who are you?" Ringo asked, fully aware that she was asking something absurd. Presently, no matter how you looked at it, Ringo was the interloper here. "Who might you be?"

"Me? I'm Yuri. Pleased to meet you." There was a composure to her gently smiling face.

Ringo squeezed the cloth-wrapped pot of curry tighter. She averted her eyes, unable to look at this woman named Yuri, and saw in the kitchen a pot of the same type that she had brought atop the stove.

Yuri followed her gaze. "Ah, I was making tonight's dinner. It's just a curry, but if you like, why don't you stay and eat with us?"

"Curry." Ringo was at a loss for words.

"Yes. 'Today is Curry Day,' he told me. What a weirdo, he's such a little kid sometimes," Yuri said with a smile, affection clear in her tone.

Ringo thought fiercely that there was no way that this woman could understand. There was no way this cheap floozy—with her blatant, sweet smell, glittering every which way—could understand Curry Day. The strings of fate that joined Ringo and Tabuki could not be so easily severed.

However, that did not change the fact that there was quite the unanticipated problem here. *Someone else had already cooked curry.* This was quite a wrench in her plans. Her eyes fell to the curry cradled in her arms.

The curry that Tabuki ate tonight would be the one that Ringo made. She would not permit it to be the one made by this witch of a woman before her.

There was a knock on the door.

"Oh! Now *that* must be Tabuki-kun."

Yuri stood with a smile as sweet as honey.

"Welcome home. There's an acquaintance of yours here right now," she told him quietly, putting on airs.

"Huh? Who could that be?"

Ringo could never have imagined the voice of her beloved sounding so distant. It had come from just a few feet away, but it was as if a wall had been erected between them.

"A very cute girl. You're quite the smooth operator, Tabuki-kun."

"No way, I would never."

His bashful voice reached her ears. From the other side of the wall, she could hear their muffled conversation.

"Oh, here's the yogurt you wanted. Hope this brand's alright."

There was the rustling of a bag.

"Thank you."

This was her only chance. It was unforgiveable, but this sole moment, while Tabuki and Yuri were enrapt in yogurt and conversation in the narrow entryway of Tabuki's apartment, was her only opportunity.

Practically crawling, she slipped as quick as she could into the darkened kitchen, and easily arrived at the stove. She would have to stand in order to lift the pot, and Tabuki aside, the woman was already so near that there was no way that she wouldn't be spotted. But there was no other way. Ringo stood, seized the pot, and crouched right back down, returning to the living room. She swiftly unwrapped the furoshiki from her curry and placed the pot atop the counter. Then, she picked up the pot with Yuri's curry, and, still in her socks, walked to the window, opened it, and jumped out.

She sprinted through the Ogikubo evening streets.

At least, thought Ringo, things were proceeding according to fate. Her curry would be the one to pass Tabuki's lips tonight. The pots were very similar, so surely, they wouldn't notice. That woman was nothing in light of the bonds of fate they shared.

She ran through the still bright shopping district, toward the train station.

"Yes, this is all perfect, all according to plan. Nothing's gone wrong," she muttered, assuring herself.

Suddenly, she was halted by a cat crossing her path. The cat carried a fish in its mouth, just like in a manga, and wore an aloof look upon its face. It threw a glance at Ringo, and then walked calmly on.

"You little thief!" she screamed, unthinking, conflating the cat with the image of Yuri in her mind, sending the cat running, scurrying around the corner.

She had done well. Her project was still underway. She would not be crushed by a setback as simple as this.

She steeled the muscles in her cheeks so as not to let any emotions show on her face, and once more took off running.

Eating meals when you're home alone had to be done according to schedule. The meals did not have to be especially fancy, or particularly delicious. As long as she ate properly at lunch time, if she filled her empty stomach and satisfied her minimal nutrition needs, that was sufficient as far as Himari was concerned.

Someone else was there with her, though, and at least at first the meal had simply appeared before her. But with no other witnesses there, such details as whether she had been the one to eat the omurice grew hazy and faded away.

Himari flipped through a fashion magazine, stroking Penguin No. 3, who was always by her side.

"We asked musumeyaku actress Tokikago Yuri, of the East Ikebukuro Sunshiny Opera Company: What is 'elegance' for the modern-day maiden?" she read aloud, then muttered, "This actress is so pretty." The words weren't meant for anyone's ears, and she meant nothing more than precisely what she had spoken.

"I'm bored... I wish they'd come home already," she said to No. 3. Today, a number of hairpins in various motifs were affixed to No. 3's head. On its back was the numeral "3," which Kanba had written.

She breathed in the smell of the aged tatami in the parlor.

"Y'know, I'd like to grow some little tomatoes or something outside. I wanna grow strawberries. I wanna eat strawberries." She set down the magazine and lay back, arms and legs spread out wide, and grinned. "Do you think that tomatoes and strawberries grow vines?"

It was a meaningless question. Himari just thought that plants that grew trailing vines were wonderful. Thinking of them encircling a building, like a castle in a fairy tale or a haunted mansion, made her very excited.

Mimicking Himari, No. 3 rolled around the tatami.

"Oh, it's Asami-chan," Himari muttered, turning the page.

What's inside a popular model's bag? read the spread. Himari read the page with deep interest. Seeing what other people carried was always interesting. This model is really into the color red, while that model isn't that fond of brand names. Some walked around with tons of makeup brushes, while the studious types carried around electronic dictionaries or a library's worth of novels.

"This bag has gotten the most miles with Asami in recent days!" Himari read aloud. "She adores its vivid colors, and that it has plenty of pockets to hold things. Besides her lipstick, she stores a compact, eyelash curler, mascara, and blush in a pouch. Her signature sunglasses are a superior brand, and effective for those with smaller faces."

For many years now, in Himari's bag there had been a wallet, lip balm, a handkerchief, and the keys to their home. She often brought her knitting supplies with her as well on trips to the hospital and such, in order to pass the time. But the contents of her bag didn't show much of what her life was like.

She set down the magazine and headed to her room, lifting her basket of knitting supplies up onto her bed. She plopped down No. 3 onto the bed before climbing up as well.

She first started knitting while she was in the hospital. One year, around Christmas, one of the hospital tutors taught it to any of the children who wished to learn. The first thing that she knit had been a too-short, wonky scarf. Still, she'd been happy. Soon, winter would be here again. She decided to knit something epic this year—though she still was not entirely sure what.

"What do I do if my brothers turn delinquent? Lately they've been skipping school, getting angry, and not listening to me at all. Right, San-chan?" Himari had affectionately begun referring to Penguin No. 3 as 'San-chan.'

No. 3 nodded, seeming to echo her exasperation. It sidled up to Himari, pressing its round body against hers.

"Wait a minute! If you're with me, San-chan, then it doesn't count as going out alone!" Himari smiled widely.

No. 3 forced its nonexistent neck into a cramped tilt.

Himari had been forbidden to leave the house by her brothers, who still worried for her physical health. She felt like Rapunzel, locked away atop a tower. Dr. Washizuka told her she could do whatever she liked, and honestly, she'd been feeling pretty fine. She was eating plenty, sleeping plenty, and finally, finding more time during the day than she knew what to do with, napping plenty. She spent her days knitting, stealthily elaborating on the embroidery on the curtains, reading books, doing household chores, and sometimes just staring dazedly into the sunlight.

She adored her room. It was filled with all the things she loved, and her bed was constructed comfortably. Himari herself selected or made the light pink canopy, the sheets, and the many pillows stacked upon it. But she'd crafted all of it in an effort to distract herself from the fact that her body itself was not free.

She was the sickly Princess Himari, passing the days in her own beloved castle.

"Let's go shopping." She stood, clearing her thoughts. No. 3 tried to stand up in turn, but its feet caught in the sheets, and it tumbled back onto the bed.

Today, as always, Himari's little bag held her wallet and lip balm and handkerchief, along with the keys to her precious castle.

Himari and Penguin No. 3 headed to a nearby supermarket and bought ingredients for curry. She couldn't think of any other recipes whose ingredients she could easily remember and assemble by memory.

"I wonder if making dinner for my brothers will make them happy." She smiled at No. 3, who nodded back earnestly. "I'm gonna need to get better at cooking!" Her eyebrows pricked up, and she rolled up her sleeves, forcibly flexing her pale, thin arms. No. 3 bounced as if to say, "How splendid!"

Just then, a cat with a fish in its mouth ran out in front of them.

"Whoa!" It was so close Himari staggered back in surprise.

The cat slowly dropped the fish from its mouth. Seeing this, No. 3 ran up to the fish and snapped it down whole.

"C'mon, San-chan! You can't eat things off the ground!"

Just as Himari scolded the penguin, the cat seemed to pick up on its strange presence. It stood up, let out a fearsome yowl, and flew claws-first at Penguin No. 3.

"Oh, Mr. Cat, stop that! Be nice!"

Himari ran flustered after the cat and Penguin No. 3, who had fused into a scuffling, yowling ball, and were presently rolling away. Apparently, the penguins were visible to any creature who *wasn't* human.

Up ahead of the two animals was a T-junction in the road. Himari looked up, wondering what she would do if a car or something came running through, and saw a girl with a clean bob cut, clutching a pot and a furoshiki. It was Oginome Ringo.

"Watch out!"

It had been a long time since she had done any running. It felt good, but Himari was dreadful at it, and incredibly slow. By the time she screamed for the other girl to watch out, it was already too late.

The cat and the balled-up penguin collided with the girl, and she and the pot she carried went flying. Himari went slack-jawed in surprise, her eyes wide.

The pot tumbled through the air, and the curry inside splashed out across the pavement. The cat ran away, and No. 3 collapsed on the spot, not moving.

Himari finally caught up with No. 3. It stood abruptly up, and leapt up, clinging to Himari. She squeezed it tight, stroking its head.

"U-Um, I'm sorry," said Himari. She had not been the one to cause the accident, but No. 3 had already become a dear friend to her. Naturally, she assumed responsibility for anything that No. 3 did. Plus, the girl was on the ground and dumbfounded, covered in curry from head to toe.

This was already a huge disaster.

"It's fine." The girl's voice was low and hoarse.

"My name is Takakura Himari. My house is nearby, so you can come by and wash your clothes, if you like!"

Ringo looked up at Himari dazedly as she spoke. Her skin was pure white, and her hair long. What a delicate girl, she thought. She did nothing but running into strange women today. Beautiful ones, at that. As for Ringo, however, her socks were thoroughly dirty from running, and she was covered all over in the curry that woman had made. She was thoroughly miserable.

Unable to hold it back any longer, her face twisted, the tears welling up.

"Are you alright? Are you hurt?" Himari quickly knelt, looking the girl in the face.

Hiccupping, Ringo shook her head, saying softly, "I'm fine." Indeed, such a thing as this was not enough to alter fate. "I'm really okay, my butt is just a little sore. I'm Ringo. Oginome Ringo," she replied tearfully. She let her guard down a bit; Himari's voice was guileless and kind.

"You want to come to my house? You aren't even wearing shoes."

Penguin No. 3 pulled itself away from Himari's arms and approached Ringo, stroking her head even though the other girl could not see it.

"Um, maybe," said Ringo, quickly checking the contents of the tote bag she dropped nearby.

This girl's eyes were strong-willed and beautiful, Himari thought. Her thick bangs only emphasized her eyes all the more. Moreover, she seemed very much like Cinderella, running without any shoes on like that.

"Um, sorry about your curry. We're having curry tonight, too. So, well..."

Himari wanted Ringo to come back home with her. She wanted to talk with another girl.

"I'm actually not that good at cooking, though."

For a short while, the pair both looked downward in silence.

"I could teach you? Curry's my specialty," said Ringo, as if dusting herself off.

"Really? Then you should definitely eat dinner at our house tonight!" Himari smiled like a blooming flower.

"Are you sure?" asked Ringo.

"Yeah, I mean, when you make curry you always end up with a lot, right? It's only me and my two brothers at home. It's bothersome to have leftovers." No. 3 nodded in agreement—though of course, Ringo could not see this.

"In that case..." *That's not true,* Ringo thought. There were only two people in her house, but they still made curry, and had no

119

qualms about eating the leftovers the next day. Himari was being too fussy. "In that case, I guess I'll take you up on that."

Ringo's home that day, as always, was sure to be spotless and deserted. More importantly, this might be fun. Visiting the home of a new friend, made by chance.

Himari held her hand out to Ringo, helping her up. The two smiled bashfully, picked up the pot, and headed towards the Takakura home, introducing themselves properly as they walked.

It was already fully dark when we made it home from Tabuki's place, exhausted. When Oginome Ringo stopped by Tabuki's place and encountered someone who looked to be his girlfriend, I was worried that she would do something terrible, but I was relieved to see the situation resolve without incident. And yet, our trials continued.

"Himari's gonna be mad at us."

The day that Tabuki contacted our home, Himari hounded us when we returned. Obviously, we could not tell her that we followed some girl around, so instead we lied that Yamashita had been bummed out after a girl rejected him, and so we had spent the day cheering him up. Once again, we had spent today doing something that we could not divulge.

"Probably." Kanba tried to sound unaffected, but his lips were twitching, his eyes were lowered, and a rather dark expression was on his face. He was weak when it came to our sister.

"Ugh, we lost Oginome Ringo's trail, *and* we didn't get the

Penguindrum." And we'd have to apologize to Himari, who was probably angry or sad. I felt the urge to cross myself.

"I know that that chick went into Tabuki's place, so how'd she slip out of there?" The perplexed look returned to my brother's face.

"Aniki," I said, holding out a loosely balled fist.

"Hm? Ah yeah," he replied sincerely.

"Throw or else you're gonna lose! Jan Ken Pon!" we chanted.

I didn't want to think anymore that night. I was worn out, and starving, and feeling weak.

"We're home!" Finally, I opened the door. I was always bad at janken.

"You're late!"

Himari waited for us, arms crossed and feet planted out firmly. Penguin No. 3 stood beside her, mimicking her pose.

"Sorry, Himari!" I bowed my head and rounded my back, eyes shut and hands clasped as I supplicated myself, just like some salaryman who had gone out drinking after work and come home late.

"I won't forgive you again today!" she said. After a moment, she added, "...Is what I wanted to say, but I'll make a special exception. We have a guest today. Hey, Ringo-chan! My brothers are home!" she called inside.

I shot up in a reasonable shock. I wondered before what we would do if Oginome Ringo realized that we were following her. What if she started staking out our house? She was already stalking Tabuki, after all. She seemed a bit reckless, but maybe she was far more alert than we realized.

If Himari ended up telling her something, it would be all over.

Oginome Ringo appeared from within, a slightly nervous look upon her face.

Kanba finally entered from the entryway behind me, muttering a soft, "No way."

"This is Oginome Ringo-chan. We just became friends today!" Himari smiled brightly, deeply pleased.

As far as I could tell, Oginome Ringo did not react particularly to seeing our faces. On the contrary, she gave a reserved nod, saying, "Sorry for the intrusion. I'm Oginome Ringo."

For some reason, she was wearing my clothing.

We were both too shocked to respond for several seconds.

"I-I'm Himari's older brother, Shoma. This is Kanba," I managed, with some difficulty.

I hoped that I would finally get a break today, but at this rate, inevitably, the mission continued.

It was a strained, uncomfortable dinner. There was someone in our parlor who was not Uncle Ikebe, and the fact that it was Oginome Ringo made it difficult to breathe.

Presently, the girl in question was in the kitchen cooking with Himari, smiling and chatting.

"How the heck did this happen?" I asked Kanba in a low voice, widening my eyes.

"Don't ask me," he said, casually flipping down a picture frame atop the cupboard. It was a photo of our whole family.

I pretended that I hadn't seen him do it.

"Sorry for the wait!" Himari entered the room with a grin upon her face, carrying a pot. "I bet you're hungry. Today we're having a specialty apple honey curry!"

There it was, the long-awaited curry. Himari must have been some kind of genius, to have such timing in choosing a curry for tonight's menu. Both our stomachs growled on cue, and our faces went red.

Himari chuckled at us, and swiftly served up the curry with Oginome Ringo's help.

"Oh, maybe I should've made a salad, too?" Himari said absently.

"This is plenty, Himari," I warmly replied.

And so the Takakura Curry Evening began.

"Mm, the meat is so tender and tasty. You're really good at cooking, Ringo-chan." Himari seemed to be in high spirits.

"Not really, all I can make is curry. My mother taught me how, a long time ago," Oginome Ringo replied solemnly.

"Hmm. It must be nice, having your mom teach you things," Himari said with a smile, though her expression was clearly clouded.

"This curry really is good. Himari, how'd you know I'd been craving curry all day?" I asked, as brightly as I could muster.

"That's because we're family," she said with a grin. "Right, Ringo-chan?" She tilted her head, her spirits renewed.

"Yeah." Oginome Ringo's voice was soft in reply. She gently placed her spoon down upon the table. "You live a happy life, Himari-chan."

"Happy?"

"You get to eat curry with people you love. That's what eating curry is all about."

"Is that so?" Himari tilted her head further.

Oginome Ringo nodded once, a lonesome look upon her face.

"Ringo-chan... Y'know, Ringo-chan, I'm happy that I get to eat curry with you. You're my special friend, after all," Himari said bashfully.

I was moved at what a kind and gentle person our little sister was.

"It really has been a long time since we've had a guest over. Right, Sho-chan?" Her wide eyes peered straight at me.

"Ah, yeah, a really long time."

"So, you're always welcome. Any time you have to eat alone, just come over here, we'll eat together!" said Himari, innocent as a little child.

"Yes, thank you," Oginome Ringo replied, with a slightly bewildered smile.

Himari seemed thrilled. Having female friends probably was a necessity for a girl. I wasn't sure how to feel about the fact that this particular friend happened to be Oginome Ringo, but I supposed it was fine for now. Even Oginome Ringo probably didn't do weird things *all* the time, and as long as she didn't have a bad influence on Himari, this would probably be good for her.

"By the way, how did it go?" Kanba asked abruptly, having finished all his curry and now plucking off the grains of rice stuck to his mouth to eat.

I looked at him in shock. What was he doing? Oginome Ringo seemed to have no idea what we had been doing, and her finding out would be a problem. Plus, if we were discovered, Himari would lose a friend.

"You had some important errand today. You had a plan, didn't you?"

For a moment, Oginome Ringo stared at my brother in silence. My face twisted up nervously. Himari looked confused.

Was Kanba trying to feel her out? Even so, this was as good as asking her straight to her face, wasn't it? He stepped out onto the stage.

Sometimes, I had no idea what Kanba was thinking, and not just when it came to dealing with girls. This was only natural, as we were not the same person, but sometimes he felt so different from me, it was like he was a completely different species. Not that this made it any easier to shrug off.

"It was fine," Oginome Ringo replied straight away.

I was shocked. She answered him as though this was a completely normal question.

"Things went a little off course, but it's fine for today. Everything is still going just as written."

Just as written? What did she mean by that? I looked to Kanba, the interrogator, but he did not appear to have any idea, either.

Oginome Ringo nodded, self-assured, and continued, "Yes, that's what's most important. Bringing about the words engraved by fate is the reason I was born, and my most important mission. I am going to see this through."

Oginome Ringo was fired up now, and Himari watched her, intrigued. To both Kanba and I, this girl—now fully confident, the opposite from before—was an even more inscrutable creature than the penguins. We looked to each other, finding that both of our mouths were hanging open dumbly.

Ringo swayed on the train, wearing her own clothes, now warm and dry, and a pair of too-big sneakers borrowed from Himari's brother. As she dangled her feet, the shoes flopped around amusingly.

She slowly pulled her phone from her bag and drafted a text to her mother.

"Mama: I ate curry with a friend tonight. It's been a long time since I've eaten curry with someone. But really, it's family—" was as far as she got, before stopping, and erasing the word, "family."

"But really, it's at home that eating curry tastes best."

She took out her diary and opened it carefully.

She stared at the line that read *Tabuki-kun eats my home-made curry,* and then muttered, "It's destiny," before generously reapplying her red-tinted lip balm. She hadn't been able to let Tabuki see her lips tonight.

The train continued intently along its dark, lengthy road, toward the station where Ringo's home was. Even this dark rail, seeming to stretch on for eternity, had to end somewhere. Perhaps that was its fate, decided sometime in the distant past. Or perhaps it was something that everyone had all unconsciously decided.

Yuri. Even that woman's lips had been vibrant. They were soft-looking, and glittered in a pale and delicate way, in a way that tinted lip balm could not compete with. She smelled sweet.

Ringo let her head loll back onto the headrest and gently shut her eyes, while the darkness passed outside her window.

PENGUINDRUM

CHAPTER 04

As soon as my eyes cracked open, I wondered why my alarm clock had not rung yet this morning. Moments after, I realized that in my own fatigue, I had half-consciusly shut off the clock, which had done its duty properly. Still, it was a day off, so I was in no big rush. Plus, for the past several days, Himari diligently helped me out all day.

Still thoroughly groggy, I changed my clothes with some difficulty, and headed to the kitchen, yawning. Penguin No. 3 came running up before me as I did. I patted it on its head, which today was decorated with a blonde wig and three cheap-looking flower barrettes.

"Oh, morning, Sho-chan!" Himari called happily.

"Morning. Sorry, looks like I over...slept?" I looked up to see a cheerful Himari standing in the kitchen, along with Oginome Ringo.

"Why is... she here?"

"You've got a case of the bedhead, Sho-chan," Himari tittered, trotting over and poking my hair.

"Sorry to barge in," said Oginome Ringo, with a lighthearted nod.

"Welcome," I returned the greeting, running my hand over my head.

"Hey, hurry up and wash your face, and then show me how to make tamagoyaki," said Himari, grabbing my arm.

Today, Himari's loose ponytail was arranged briskly with a hair clip with a flower decoration, maybe just to keep her hair out of her face while preparing the food. She wore denim jeans, with a beige cardigan over a lightly embroidered white dress. Her rumpled socks were a light pink, matching the color of the flower ornaments. A tender pink really did suit our little sister.

"Sure, I can do that, but..." But what was Oginome Ringo doing in our home first thing in the morning? I was suspicious, but instead I wedged myself between the pair, showing off my skills.

I preferred to make rolled omelets that weren't too sweet. Don't overbeat it, don't use too much heat. Don't pour too much of the egg mixture into the pan at once. Make it fluffy by adding just a little more milk.

"You're amazing, Sho-chan! It looks so good already, I wanna eat it!" Himari jumped up, No. 3 bouncing around as well.

Oginome Ringo watched my hands eagerly, mumbling the steps in repetition.

Feeling like I had suddenly aged many years, I sipped some warm hojicha, watching as Oginome Ringo and Himari battled it out with the omelets, mimicking my preparations and chattering to each other. "That's right." "This looks good." "Like this? Like this?" "It's gonna burn!"

How was it that girls could still shine while doing something so childish, conducting themselves as if a music box played? We were all humans, but they seemed like a totally disparate life-form.

"Ta-da! A special deluxe field trip bento!" said Himari, placing an exaggerated, multitiered bento atop the low table. Penguins No. 2 and No. 3 applauded joyfully.

The way that Himari intoned her words was murderously adorable.

"We did it, Ringo-chan!" Himari and the penguins circled around Oginome Ringo, like Snow White and her dwarves.

"Yeah," Oginome Ringo said happily, her cheeks pinking ever so slightly.

"Are you taking these out somewhere?" I asked with my eyes narrowed, like a sweet old grandfather, holding my teacup.

Himari grinned wide, as though she had been waiting for me to ask, and announced, "Ringo-chan's got a date!"

"Huh?" The kindly look upon my face suddenly turned serious. Oginome Ringo looked bashful, while Himari muttered, "Sounds nice."

"She asked me to show her how to make a tasty tamagoyaki, but I'm no good at it, either. Your help really saved us, Sho-chan!"

"Oh, well, that's good."

I did not want to dampen the smile blooming over Himari's face, but the other party involved in said date was likely Tabuki

Keiju, and there was a high probability that it was not a date, but another exercise in stalking. None of that sounded *good* at all.

Kanba, having finally finished his carefree morning routine, appeared from out of the washroom.

"Oho, looks like you did good. That's our house husband for you," he said, swiping a piece of the cut-up omelet on my plate and popping it into his mouth.

"Who are you calling a house husband?" I shot a glare at my ill-behaved brother. Kanba, who was terrible at mornings, seemed strangely alert for it being relatively early.

"By the way, Oginome-san, where are you going birdwatching today?" Kanba asked her, without hesitation.

Birdwatching. I could not readily remember where I had heard a discussion of that.

"In Wadazuka Park," Oginome Ringo replied, without a hint of suspicion.

"Whoa, what a coincidence! Shoma had something to do over there today too. Right, Shoma?" said Kanba, flashing me his best smile.

"Huh? N-no. I do not!" I started to say, when I was suddenly gripped in a headlock and dragged to the corner of the room.

"Hang on, what is going on?!" I asked, my voice naturally growing softer.

"Listen. This is our chance to search that chick's bag." I followed his glance to see Oginome Ringo's tote bag. "We gotta find the You-Know-What."

"By the You-Know-What, you mean the Penguindrum?"

Kanba pressed a finger to his lips with a "*Shh!*"

Looking around to ensure we hadn't been heard, he said, "This chick said that things were going, 'just as written.'"

"So, you're saying that it's something written on paper, like a book or a journal?" She mentioned something about things being written, or engraved. We flipped through plenty of books, journals, and other written items in Oginome Ringo's home, but we wouldn't have found it if she carried it around with her.

"Yeah, that's a good assumption. It must have some connection to this Penguindrum we're after. It's probably the key to unlocking this mystery."

"Yeah." I nodded, glancing at Himari and Oginome Ringo, who were now quietly sipping some freshly brewed hojicha. What a cruel irony in this scene, if the girl sitting next to Himari was the one who held her life in her hands.

"The reason that it hasn't turned up yet is probably because she keeps it hidden on her at all times. Maybe even somewhere even closer than in that bag."

"Huh? Somewhere closer than her bag?" I momentarily imagined something improper, and felt my cheeks flush with embarrassment.

"I'm kidding, stupid. Though, we can't entirely rule that out, either." As usual, no color appeared on Kanba's face.

"In that case, why don't you go? You're way better at getting close to girls, aren't you?"

"Hm? I've got some stuff to take care of. I'm leaving today's mission to you. Break a leg out there!" He slapped me on the back heartily.

"Another girl? Aniki, you're definitely gonna face some divine punishment one of these days." I pouted, deeply exasperated with him.

"Whatever." My words had fallen on deaf ears.

Things went rough after that. Oginome Ringo made a dreadful face when I tagged along on her date. The effect of Kanba's killer smile was lost on Oginome Ringo, who was smitten with Tabuki, and even Himari chided me, but in the end, I followed her along to Wadazuka Park.

The train ride was awkward. I sat beside an unhappy Oginome Ringo, my head slightly hung, occasionally looking up at our reflection in the window opposite us. Oginome Ringo, her tote bag on her shoulder, wore a hat down over her eyes and a vest with many pockets, with a pair of binoculars hanging from her neck. She seethed in quiet anger. I was in casual clothes, my back rounded, carrying the heavy, three-tiered bento, a sullen look on my face, looking utterly forlorn.

"Um, so. You're going to the park to do some birdwatching today?"

"That's right," she said, quite curtly. Girls were scary when they were angry.

"Is this also, um, how did you put it, part of your, 'fate'?"

"*Huh?*" She did not even spare me a glance.

It was a single word, and yet I felt as though I had been thoroughly redressed.

"Ah, well uh, the other day, you were saying something like that."

"That's right," said Oginome Ringo, though she didn't seem to be speaking to me. "Everything that happens from now on today is a matter of fate. I'm on a very important mission. There is no room for failure," she elaborated, as though to herself.

"I... see."

Her reflection in the dark window seemed like a completely different person from the girl who smiled with Himari this morning. She was obstinate, and it wasn't that she wasn't charming, but she exuded an unapproachable standoffishness, truly like a different life-form. Plus, she was a stalker.

Suddenly, Ringo looked up around the car, and I casually followed her gaze. One of the walls displayed an advertisement for an upcoming performance by the "East Ikebukuro Sunshiny Opera Company," abbreviated to "E.I.S.C." The title of the performance was "The Tragedy of M." The actress playing Marie, the titular "M," was listed as Tokikago Yuri, and there was a large picture of the actress, along with an otokoyaku actress embracing her from behind.

"Do you like the theater?" The actress, Tokikago Yuri, looked familiar. I'd probably seen her on television or something. But I also felt that I had recently seen her somewhere, far closer up.

"Not really," Ringo spat coldly, her gaze returning straight ahead, falling silent.

Though we had not even reached our destination yet, still stuck on this train with its rhythmic swaying, I already wanted to go home. I wanted to go home and pass my day off in monotonous bliss, like a little old grandpa.

Just as I wished for, Wadazuka Park possessed a peaceful tranquility. It was already ten in the morning by the time we arrived. I followed along with her to the fountain plaza, offering to carry the bento to her meeting place since they were heavy. However, I was not going to find an opportunity to search her bag in so short an amount of time.

Oginome-san sat down on a bench in a gazebo and took out a small mirror, arranging her hair with her index finger, and slathering on lip balm. It was as if I wasn't even present.

"Hey, sorry to keep you!"

I turned my head to look at the owner of the dull voice, which perfectly suited the laidback park. Oginome-san stood straight up, turning around.

It was, of course, Tabuki standing there. He wore a carefree smile and had a number of wild bird pins fixed to the lapels of his strange shirt, and a pair of binoculars hanging from his neck. Even someone like me, who paid little attention to appearances, knew this was a fatally uncool look.

"Hm? Are you with a friend today?" Tabuki smiled, noticing me.

"F-friend? He is definitely not my friend! That man is just a passing acquaintance, but when I started talking about today he started saying that he *had* to come! I'm so sorry, this is such a bother!" said Oginome-san, bowing her head.

While I was surprised at how sweet her voice sounded, even

knowing that she already disliked me, it still hurt a little to hear her say that. Realizing that he would soon figure it out anyway, I reluctantly stood to greet Tabuki.

"Nonsense," said Tabuki with a smile, "A fellow birdwatcher is always welcome." His eyes turned to me, beyond her. "Oh? If it isn't Takakura!"

"Morning, Sensei." Given how frequently I skipped lately, the greeting came out strangely flat.

"Takakura is a student in my class. Wow! I didn't realize you two knew each other. What a coincidence."

As I smiled along numbly with Tabuki's goofy smile, Oginome-san shot a sharp glare at me. I wondered how long she could keep such a strained face before it froze that way.

She stepped closer to me, asking in a low, sharp voice, "How long are you going to stay here?"

"Umm, j-just a little longer. I've got some business around here, too." I had to say. This was painful.

"Oh my! Looks like you get to be with the fabulous couple again today," came a lilting, gorgeous voice.

"Oh, this is perfect, I can introduce you both to my old friend, too," said Tabuki, face relaxing more, stepping to the side. "This is Tokikago Yuri."

"Pleased to meet you!" I said. Tokikago Yuri was shaded from the sun by a wide-brimmed hat, wearing a refined white dress cinched by a belt of the same color, and carried a large basket. Her soft-looking hair waved in the wind, and every blink of her long eyelashes seemed to make a sound.

"The curry woman," Oginome-san murmured. I saw that her cutesy false smile had crumbled.

"Oh!" I muttered without thinking. The curry woman. This woman was Tabuki's girlfriend, who had been at his apartment the night Oginome-san had brought her homemade curry there.

"Isn't she gorgeous? To be honest, she's actually an actress. She's a leading lady with the Sunshiny Opera Company," Tabuki introduced her proudly, his cheeks deepening.

I felt grateful to this woman, who, beyond being a joy to be around, had drawn Oginome-san's nervous attention to something other than me. It should have made it easier for me to look inside her bag, but Oginome-san herself made such a dark expression one would think it was the end of the world. I felt a fresh wave of unease.

Across from us, the "fabulous couple" with their dreadful expressions, Tokikago Yuri and Tabuki were casually chatting. "Wasn't it nice to have such good weather?" and "Thank you for inviting me," and "What are the names of the birds on your pins? Wasn't learning all of them difficult?" The two were lost crafting a world of their very own, white lilies abloom.

Having walked to the entryway with the penguins to see Shoma and Ringo off, Himari swiftly grew quite listless, and dragged her feet back to the living room.

"They're gone," she said, as though this were not some terrible, dreadful event, just mere fact.

"Let's eat the rest of those lunches. Bet you're hungry, huh, Himari?" said Kanba, unaffected, sitting cross-legged by the table.

"Yeah. I'll go make some tea then," Himari said dimly, once more putting the kettle on the stove.

Kanba stood calmly beside Himari as she stared blankly at the kettle, renewing the contents of the little teapot. How could she always take things in stride like this? he wondered. She'd seemed to be having such fun up until now, but she would go flat again in an instant. But there was no mistaking the smile that would jump right back to her face the next time something fun came around.

As his gaze happened to fall upon the flowers decorating her silky, blow-dried hair, Himari muttered to herself, "A date, huh?"

"Are dates fun?" she asked Kanba with a grin.

"Huh? For me? I mean, there's a lot of different kinds."

If Yamashita, his classmate, were to ask him the same question, Kanba would have grinned and cracked back, "Well of course they're *fun*," but talking to Himari was another matter.

"Hmm. I wonder if I'll ever go on a date someday," said Himari, staring at the kettle, her cheeks puffing out meaninglessly.

"A date? You?" That might be true. She would probably end up dating someone one of these days. Someone just like him. However, he would not say that. He was afraid of speaking such a thing into existence. "Well..."

As he searched for the right words, Himari cut in to say, "But I think I'm fine with just you and Sho-chan for a while. I'm still scrawny, after all. I can't even go to school yet."

She did not seem especially distraught about this, but that was precisely why Kanba later regretted not saying something like, "You'll probably be able to go on plenty of dates pretty soon."

"You can do it," he said. "You can go to school, and I bet you'll be killer at racking up friends. You're my sister, after all."

"I can't wait." Himari grinned widely.

This was fine, thought Kanba, silently comforting his own aching heart.

"Water's boiled."

"That's not too heavy, is it?" he asked, watching her slender arms as she lifted the kettle.

"I can handle this much." She poured the water proudly into the teapot. "Let's eat already, Kan-chan." She gave a quiet smile. Flat again.

The pair lined up their chopsticks and dishes, prepared the hot hojicha, and sat around the table with their salmon and pickled plum and okaka onigiri and tamagoyaki, and their asparagus and smashed hard-boiled eggs dressed in mayonnaise. Before they partook in their sausage and cherry tomatoes, or their dessert of apples cut in the shape of rabbits, they each said grace.

"Um, so I think this one is salmon and this one is pickled plum, and these ones are probably okaka," Himari directed, before biting into a plum onigiri. She made sure to give each of the penguins an onigiri as well.

"Mm, this is good. You made these ones, right?" Kanba stuffed his face with onigiri, uneasy at Himari's too-quiet mood.

"Yeah, how'd you know?" Himari's eyes went round.

"Because they're smaller than the others. They're the size of your hands," Kanba answered proudly.

"Oh, I see! You're amazing, Kan-chan!" Himari grinned wide.

Her graceful fingers, holding the onigiri. Her tiny mouth, biting into it. Her innocent eyes, casting glances at Kanba. Her long eyelashes. Every part of her looked pale, small, and fragile. Kanba stopped trying to figure why it was that, despite most women looking small and pale, Himari was the only one who stood out to him. He knew there was no reason for this feeling. But that didn't mean that it didn't hurt him, constantly.

"Was it really okay for Sho-chan to go along on Ringo-chan's date? She seemed angry," Himari said nervously. "I wonder if she'll still want to come over again."

"It'll be fine. Shoma actually went with her to help out. He's her personal cupid," Kanba said with a smile.

"Really? It's not a bother for her? She'll come back again?" Himari stared him in the eye suspiciously.

"She'll be back. It's fine." Kanba wanted to reach out and pat Himari on the head, but she had hair clips in, so he refrained. "It seemed like you two really get along."

"Yeah. I haven't had a normal girl friend in a long time, so it's really fun." She gave a subtle smile, her long eyelashes lowered.

Himari had been enrolled in the hospital's tutoring program while she was hospitalized. However, some of the other children had been released from the hospital and lost touch, and others had even passed away. Kanba couldn't even begin to imagine how Himari must have felt when that happened. But in front of her brothers, Himari always smiled.

"You're going out now too, aren't you, Kan-chan?" Himari asked, in that same hazy tone.

"Ah, yeah. It's nothing huge though." In fact, he wouldn't know for certain if what he planned for the day would be huge or not until he got there, but he still fully intended to get back home as quickly as he could.

"I know you don't have school today, but if you're gonna be late, be sure and call me." She intended to sound calm, but when she spoke it sounded lonesome, and she grew embarrassed, suddenly feeling as though she was a small child all over again.

"Yeah, I know. I'll make sure to get in touch."

After that, the pair silently ate their meals, finished their apples, and once more drank some hojicha.

When Kanba set out with Penguin No. 1 in tow, Himari once again went to the front door to see them off.

"See you soon! Good luck out there!" She waved innocently.

Kanba waved back, wondering just what she wished him luck with.

As she picked up Penguin No. 3 and returned inside the house, Himari noticed the family photo had been turned face down on the cupboard, and stood it back up. Then, she felt a bit tired, and wished to sleep. The best thing to do, when one felt lonely, was to sleep.

I know what you're searching for. See details below.

Kanba looked once more over the text he received.

There was no doubt that it was referring to the Penguindrum. But how could anyone other than he and Shoma possibly know about it? Maybe they were not the only ones who were after it.

The family restaurant where he had agreed to meet the message's sender was somewhere that he had made use of many times before. In the nonsmoking section by the window, Kanba sat quietly, running through simulations of a number of scenarios in his head. After some time, he heard a voice.

"Good afternoon."

He looked up to see Kuho Asami standing there. She wore large, brand name sunglasses, and had her hair in a short cut with lightly teased ends. She wore a casual, pale blue top with ribbons, and lace peeked out like a curtain from the hem of her showy white floral miniskirt. His eyes were especially drawn to her bright red high-heeled shoes.

"Flashy as ever," he said.

Unflapped by Kanba's quiet words, Asami removed her sunglasses and smiled brilliantly.

"Been a long time, Kanba-kun." Her eyes were edged with a thin black line.

Kanba was speechless to see the next two people that arrived after Asami, who sat across from him. Chizuru and Yui sat down beside her cheerfully.

Kuho Asami was one thing, but Chizuru and Yui as well could all be counted among the number of Kanba's former girlfriends, so to speak.

"Damn it, this is a setup." He realized now that he had been overthinking this. How could he possibly have thought that Asami would have had any information about the Penguindrum?

"What a rare sight. Are you flustered, Kanba-kun?"

She grinned, her lips shining with a sparkling, iridescent pink gloss. The pale color of Himari's lips, so smooth from the looks of them, flashed through the back of Kanba's mind.

"What are you all here for?" Kanba asked, ignoring her question.

"We've formed a 'Takakura Kanba Romantic Casualties Club,'" said Chizuru, as if it were the most obvious thing.

"What?" Just from the assembled party, Kanba suspected nothing good would come from this, but that surpassed anything he anticipated.

"Yep, the 'Takakura Kanba Romantic Casualties Club.' Kuho-san was the one who named it." Yui gleefully explained.

"Asami did?" He glanced at Asami, but she coldly averted her eyes.

Asami had not wanted to break up with Kanba, and Kanba was well aware that she probably still had feelings for him. But Kanba had given the relationship a go, and he knew that women like Asami were no good for him. Particularly, the kind of women who would form a "Victims' Club" out of some lingering attachment for a man she had broken up with.

"We decided to gather up all the poor girls you've deceived and start a protest movement. Isn't this fun?" Chizuru made a show of smiling with her mouth alone.

"Today, we are going to set the record straight. You're going to take responsibility for playing with pure maidens' hearts!" Yui smacked the table loudly.

"It's divine punishment."

Kanba suddenly grew worried, thinking of Shoma's warning that morning.

"This will be a while. Why don't we order something?" said Asami, perusing the menu. "It's nice to have some sweets now and then. It's nice that they have the calorie counts written here," she continued, without the least bit of apparent interest, her eyes instead trained on Kanba. This former lover, so long apart from her, had left his mark deeper in her heart than any other man who had ever stood before her, and she could not escape him.

Asami was unsure that what they'd shared had really been love, but it didn't matter. She merely wished to have him before her again. That was what mattered most. Chizuru and Yui and this Romantic Casualties Club were nothing more than a charade she concocted for that purpose. She was only following *that* person's advice.

"What would you like, Kanba-kun? Since you came all this way here. Today's my treat," said Asami, so placidly that one might wonder if she might become an actress one day.

"Coffee," Kanba said dismissively. "I've got a headache, so just black coffee." He swiftly crossed his legs.

The three women sitting across from Kanba felt their hearts skip, just a beat.

When Himari finished diligently washing the dishes and cleaning out the bath, she took up embroidering the edges of the curtains. She was going to increase the area of the flower patterning.

"I hear dates are fun," muttered Himari. She could have as easily been talking to herself as to Penguin No. 3. "What do people do on dates?"

First, people would meet up, Himari imagined. On a day off, they would put on their favorite clothes and wait for a lover, maybe in front of a train station. When their lover finally arrived, they would walk, arms linked or hand in hand, making frivolous conversation.

"I wonder where they go. Maybe to see a movie? Ringo said she was going to the park for some birdwatching. I wonder if Kan-chan goes to the cinema or something." She stopped her embroidery as her hands tired, suddenly growing quite bored.

"People kiss on dates, too." Finally, Himari smiled, and kissed No. 3 on the head. No. 3's eyes popped open, and its cheeks flushed.

Though she had grown healthier, the idea that she was sick still lingered, and it was impossible for her to imagine a future where she herself might fall in love with someone, and have them fall in love with her, and go on dates, and get married. The very idea of it was so surreal its seeming impossibility did not even make her sad.

When her first period had arrived, Himari was in the hospital. One evening, when she awoke and shifted in bed, she felt something strange. She scowled, peeling back the covers to see blood staining the sheets. She'd had a general understanding of menstruation, but she'd had no idea there would be this much blood.

It was embarrassing, but there was nothing she could do about it, so she called a nurse. She did not tell her mother or friends about it. They were all gone, after all.

Her stomach had hurt, and she felt helpless. When she wondered if she was just unlucky, she became even more forlorn, even sadder. Even sick, even lonesome as she felt, time would continue to pass, and her body would continue to grow, eventually transforming into something approaching adulthood. All on its own, without consulting her. Thinking this left her dumbfounded for some time, but eventually she changed her clothes, put a pad on, and got a change of sheets.

Having a body that might one day birth a child seemed utterly detached from her reality.

That day, her brothers received an explanation from the nurse. She hardly ever spoke to them about her period. Though naturally, they had to purchase menstrual products for her plenty of times, so she did have to speak to them about it directly at those points, at least.

Himari clutched No. 3 to her, overtaken with a formless anxiety.

She wished everyone didn't have to go out all at once. At the very least, they could have left Penguins 1 and 2 with her.

Everyone really did always disappear.

"San-chan, do you like picture books?"

The penguin cradled in her arms opened its eyes wide.

"I'll read you a picture book. Let's go." She headed back to her room, urging No. 3 along. In there, Himari could feel at ease, immersed in a place of her own design.

She considered going out to buy some kind of seeds to plant alongside the house, but she decided to wait until she could consult Shoma first. Perhaps she would make dinner tonight. It was getting brisk out, and she wanted to eat Shoma's hot udon. She loved tsukimi udon. The name alone, conjuring images of watching the full moon, gave her a warm feeling.

Himari and No. 3 sat side by side on the bed as she opened the picture book.

"Now listen carefully, okay?" Himari said with a smile. No. 3's eyes sparkled, and it gave a firm nod.

Though Himari was young, she knew instinctively that loneliness meant not being able to share things with others. Still, she began reading with "Once upon a time," and praying that her brothers would come home early tonight.

Himari's high, sweet voice echoed strangely throughout the empty Takakura home, and the house itself passed along just like the events within the storybook.

When she came to again, Himari found herself and No. 3 wrapped up in the blanket, having fallen asleep. She heard an, "I'm home!" from the front door. She quickly sat up; the room had already grown completely dim.

Himari flew out of bed and ran to the entryway.

"Welcome home! Sho-chan, what happened?" asked Himari, looking her brother over again as she rubbed the sleep from her eyes. "Did it rain?"

Shoma was soaked from head to toe, gripping a towel she had never seen before.

"Nothing major. I just accidentally fell into the pond at the park." No sooner had he said this than Shoma let out a big sneeze.

"You're gonna catch a cold! I cleaned out the bath. I'll go heat the tub!"

She retrieved a large towel from the washroom by the entryway, and handed it to Shoma, who still stood on the landing. "Here, Sho-chan."

He accepted the towel, thanking her.

"Did you really just fall into the pond? That seems kind of weird." Beside Shoma, No. 2's face went red. "Did something happen with Ringo-chan?"

"Nothing! Why would something happen? Though, Oginome-san was pulling a lot of weird faces and seemed like she had a lot to work through. Tabuki brought—you'll never believe this—that actress, Tokikago Yuri, with him! She was seriously pretty. There were all these fans wanting to shake her hand, and Tabuki was being all gushy over her." Forcing out the string of words, Shoma flew into the washroom and shut the door. "Anyway, I'm just gonna take a shower. I'll go ahead and heat the bath while I'm at it. I'm fine though—nothing happened, really."

"Well, I'll make you something warm to drink," said Himari, fixing her hair as she headed to the kitchen with Nos. 2 and 3 in tow, and pulled out the tin of cocoa powder.

From Sho-chan's face and the way he talked, something had definitely happened, but he must not have been able to say what. She would ask Ringo covertly about it later, Himari thought.

"You know what happened, right?" she asked, crouching before Penguin No. 2 with a smile.

No. 2 rolled on the floor, its face growing redder and redder, steam rising from its flanks.

"Man. Everyone has so much fun," Himari muttered, sniffing at the sweet smell of the cocoa powder.

On the grounds of Akasaka Mitsuki Station, Kuho Asami was having a few regrets. She wanted to see Takakura Kanba, and succeeded in getting some pointless girls involved in order to draw his attention and calling him here, but she was still nothing more than the poor little girl that he had rejected, and Chizuru and Yui were so irritating, with all their loud prattling about trivial things.

On the other side of the phone, Asami's advisor listened to her report and laughed casually.

"But is this really alright? It seems like now he thinks I'm just some troublesome ex-girlfriend." Still, she had gotten to be with him. She had gotten to see his face up close once more.

"Goodness, we need to hurry up and crush him," her advisor laughed enthusiastically.

"Huh?" Asami asked back. Crush him. That was definitely what her advisor had said.

"It's fine. That's part of the plan, too. After today, I understand the shape of your love. Don't you worry, the next step is already underway." And with that, the advisor hung up the phone.

Just what did it mean for her and Chizuru and Yui's love to be understood? She hadn't been there with them. Thinking this, Asami looked back, shivering. She felt something grip her heart, but she couldn't quite puzzle out what this feeling meant.

There was no way her advisor could have had a view of that entire place; that was impossible. Asami invited Kanba, just as she advised, but she couldn't have known where Kanba met them, nor what seats they would have sat in, so how could she have observed them?

"No, I'm overthinking this," Asami said, climbing onto the escalator. She let out a sigh and muttered, "Still, what was that 'next step' about?"

As if to drown out her whisper, someone's hand shoved her from behind.

"Huh?!" In an instant, Asami's body tumbled down the escalator.

Asami loved the way that Kanba's eyes glinted like a wild animal's sometimes. When he looked at her with those eyes, her heart raced violently, a thrilling pain; in those moments, she wouldn't have cared if he gripped her throat and strangled her to death. When he seized her arms with his angular hands and drew her to him, she felt as if nothing else in the world mattered.

It was all horribly childish, but perhaps a true, childish love that had been there. And now, all she wanted was for Takakura Kanba to look her way again.

A red shoe went flying, and the same shade of red soon began to spread across the brown tiled floor.

This incident occurred at precisely 9 P.M.

PENGUINDRUM

CHAPTER 05

NINE YEARS PRIOR, as the massive Typhoon No. 13 moved north along the east coast of Honshu, passing through the Kanto skies, little Himari was wrapped in a futon, an ice pack upon her forehead, hot breath rolling from her mouth as she suffered a high fever.

Kanba and Shoma sat by her side the whole time. The strange, restless excitement that they usually felt during typhoons disappeared, and their hearts clenched as they watched uneasily over their little sister. The violent rattling of the iron walls, the windows, doors, and cupboards within the house stirred up fear in their hearts.

"All of the ambulances are already on call? But we have a five-year-old girl with a fever that won't come down!" Chiemi's voice unconsciously grew frantic. Kenzan came over and put a hand on her shoulder, pressing down the hook of the telephone.

"Honey..." Chiemi looked at her husband uneasily.

"That's enough." Kenzan looked at Himari, wrapped in the futon, her breath ragged, then looked back to Chiemi. "I'll take her to the hospital."

"But…" Chiemi wanted to stop him, but they had no other options here. Still, the wind was roaring outside, and their whole house swayed. The news was filled with stories about the storm, and a typhoon warning had been issued for their area.

"Don't worry." That single phrase was threaded through with Kenzan's resolve.

Watching as their mother carefully dressed Himari in thermals to protect her from the cold, Kanba and Shoma's fears grew.

Kenzan donned his rain gear and boots, let Chiemi squeeze his hands once more, and then too Himari, so dazed she was practically sleeping, upon his back. Once more, he told Chiemi, "Don't worry," and set out into the downpour.

The brothers swiftly threw on their ponchos in tandem, following behind him.

"I'm coming too!"

"Me too!"

"Stop, it's dangerous out there!" Chiemi gripped the arms and shoulders of her other two children, who seemed to be possessed of an unusual strength, trying to stop them somehow. "Come back here!"

Kanba was the one who managed to escape their mother's hands. Out in the darkness, there was nothing but the harsh, pelting raindrops, and the sound of the wind.

"Daaad!" he screamed at the top of his lungs, but even the

light of the streetlamps was dimmed, and he could not see his father's back. "Dad!" he screamed, again and again. More and more rain spilled into his boots, and soon his socks and feet were soaked.

"Dad!"

When Kenzan noticed the voice and turned around, he saw Kanba, already muddy from having fallen, running full pelt toward him.

"Stupid kid..." he muttered to himself, waiting for Kanba to catch up.

"I'm coming too!"

It was just as Kanba shouted these words, trying to run closer to his father that a signboard blown by the wind suddenly filled little Kanba's field of view. As he reflexively folded his arms in from of him, shutting his eyes, there was a loud, sharp sound. Timidly, he opened his eyes to see Kenzan shielding him, blood running from his arms. In the darkness, the blood dripping from his arms onto the drenched pavement looked black.

"Dad!" Kanba's eyes opened wide in fear.

The metallic scent of blood mixed with the smell of the rain.

Kenzan's breathing was ragged, his face twisted, but he soon stood right back up.

"Let's go," he said quietly, and once more began walking through the deluge toward the hospital.

To Kanba's eyes, his father's face as he protected his family was terrifyingly powerful, and beautiful.

"Make sure you watch your step, it's slippery."

"Okay," Kanba replied obediently, trying desperately to stick by his father as he walked, staring down at his own little feet. No matter what else happened on the way to the hospital, they would get Himari there. Kanba was assured of this within his little heart.

From now until forever, he would protect Himari, as well as his whole family.

Leaving Himari and No. 3 waiting outside of the examination room, I sat down across from Dr. Washizuka. On top of the usual scheduled outpatient examination, today we would learn the results of the recent tests.

Penguin No. 2 stood by my feet, a serious look on its face. By now, I was more or less accustomed to the surreal scene.

"The test results are reassuring, and her condition seems good, so we'll just keep observing her like this for a little while longer," Dr. Washizuka said quietly.

"I see. Thank you very much," I said, breathing a sigh of relief.

Himari seemed healthier every day. But if this was because of, or rather, thanks to the penguin hat, my brother and I wondered if something strange might show up on a test or examination. It seemed absurd, but we'd worried that one of her internal organs might have suddenly gone penguin-shaped, or a penguin-shaped birthmark had popped up somewhere on her body, or something.

"I'm not sure how to put this, but this truly is a mystery. In my profession, you sometimes come across cases that could be called nothing short of miraculous, but your sister's case is doubly so." The doctor smiled gently.

"To tell you the truth," I said, with some hesitation, "There's something I'd like to ask you."

"Sure, what is it?"

Timidly, I pulled the penguin hat out of the bag on my lap and held it out to him.

"Could I ask you to examine this? We think it might be the source of Himari's miracle."

I could tell that Dr. Washizuka was taken aback by my serious manner.

"It's just a theory, but I believe there's a possibility that this hat is actually some kind of alien or supernatural being, and it cured Himari's sickness with some kind of mysterious power."

Right now, this strange hat that I held in my left hand was the key to unraveling all of these mysteries.

The examination room was enveloped by a bizarre silence. Clearly, things had just become awkward.

"You might be onto something!" Dr. Washizuka said suddenly.

"Really?" The doctor patted me on my hunched shoulders.

"You're a pretty funny kid. Super funny. That's wonderful, for your sister that is."

"Huh?" I was deadly serious.

"Laughter! Laughter helps boost your immune system. We're currently seeing a lot of results supporting humor as a medical treatment. This hat's an alien, huh? Yes. It's good to make your sister laugh every day, just like that." His mouth twisted as he tried to say something else, and Dr. Washizuka burst out laughing. "Seriously though, I had no idea you were such a funny kid. My apologies."

Seeing the doctor unable to contain his laughter, I silently put the hat back in the bag.

Himari waited on a bench in the hall, and she looked up from her knitting as I said my farewells and stepped outside. "Was the doctor laughing at something?" she asked me curiously.

"Yeah, he was saying that it's a miracle the results of your exam looked so good. So, he got a little..." I smiled weakly, resigned.

"I see. That's good. Let's do some shopping and head back, then." Himari tucked her knitting away into her bag and hopped right up.

"Yeah." I walked down the hallway, matching her pace. The sky outside was thick with clouds, and somehow dim, as if it was about to rain.

Kuho Asami's private hospital room was in the middle of the floor above the room that Himari always visited for her outpatient exams. Asami stared dazedly at the clouded sky outside.

There was a bandage wrapped extravagantly around her head. The large bouquet that decorated her bedside perfumed the air. On the little table was a heap of get-well cards and presents from her fans. Still, he had not come.

Thankfully, the wound on her head was not especially large, but her condition left it unclear if she would be able to return to work anytime soon. Asami boasted a top spot in the popularity listings of *Sixteen* magazine, but she knew that this was only a fleeting thing. Girls always turned their interests to new things, be it clothing, makeup, male idols, or models.

"Goodness, we had better crush him soon." The voice belonged to Natsume Masako, Asami's advisor, the one who directed her to form the Takakura Kanba Romantic Casualties Club.

"Huh?" Asami turned around to see Masako's almond-shaped eyes looking back at her.

"Aren't you worried? You've been thinking about your career, haven't you?" Masako smiled languidly, but the smile did not extend to her eyes.

Asami looked down at her own hands, at her long nails, gaudy with nail art and at odds with her current appearance.

"This is all my fault. I pushed you to do this, after all." Masako suddenly lowered her eyes in sadness. The shadows of her long eyelashes fell across her cheeks.

"No, that's not true! This isn't your fault, Natsume-san! This happened because *I* wanted to see him!" Asami said, suddenly embarrassed.

Masako stared at her, then sat down on the edge of the bed, gently touching Asami's cheek with her long, slender fingers.

"You poor dear. This incident is unforgivable. To think someone could hurt an adorable little thing like you. Are you certain you remember nothing other than that someone pushed you from behind?"

Unconsciously, Asami found herself captivated by Masako's mature, porcelain skin, and her sharp, glistening eyes.

"Well, actually..." Asami started hesitantly.

Masako's thin, well-shaped lips twisted faintly.

"I don't really remember anything about that moment. But..."

Masako continued stroking her cheek.

"Just before the accident, I think I saw a silhouette." Asami thought deeply for a moment.

"A silhouette?" Masako's fingers stopped moving, her nails curling imperceptibly toward Asami's cheek.

"I remember! I definitely saw them. It was…"

Before Asami could speak any further, Masako cut in, sharply asking, "You saw that?" her expression swiftly turning dark. She drew close to Asami, her face so close their noses nearly touched.

"I, y-yes, but…"

"That's enough already," said Masako, drawing smoothly away.

Asami was bewildered. She could never tell what Masako was thinking. And how did she know so much about Kanba? And why couldn't Asami disobey her?

Right before Asami's eyes, Masako held up an orb the size of a golf ball.

"Natsume-san?"

Masako did not reply. Instead, she used the orb. She had already disqualified Kuho Asami. She was a simple, foolish, boring girl.

"Farewell," she said. "You've been fascinating."

Kuho Asami's affections, or her love or whatever, were nothing Masako could comprehend, nor did she care to try. Not that it mattered. When she left Asami's room two minutes later and stepped outside, she knew it wouldn't be long before they disappeared completely from this world.

Kanba was already in a sour mood by the time their uncle dropped by.

Since the Takakuras had lost their parents, Ikebe was one of the very few adults who bothered to look out for the children. He was a kind man, but there were different kinds of "looking out," and though their uncle always worried for them and always tried to cheer them up, he was still essentially a stranger.

"Come in," he said.

As Ikebe entered the parlor, the entertainment news on the daytime talk show seeped into Kanba's ears.

"Up next, there have been new reports concerning popular model Kuho Asami, who recently suffered an accident at the Akasaka Mitsuki subway station. Shortly after the accident, Kuho-san initially testified that someone pushed her from behind. But according to new information, Kuho-san now says she can't remember anything from the time of the incident. The police intend to continue their investigation, including searching for any witnesses to the scene."

Kanba quietly picked up the remote and turned off the TV. So, she had gotten into an accident. Not only had Asami been injured the night after he met up with her, but now her testimony had changed. Still, Kanba's currently most pressing issue was the man sitting before him.

They faced each other, the table between them. On the table was the usual "Ikebe-ya" package of sweets.

"I was hoping to do this when Shoma was here too," Ikebe said softly, as if unable to bear the silence.

161

Quiet returned to the living room.

"I'm really sorry to put this on you all so suddenly. I mean, when I talked about selling this house, I didn't mean immediately. This isn't the sort of place that sells quickly nowadays. It's just... with this recession going on, no matter how established our shop is, things are getting rough for us." He stopped and started unwrapping the bundle of sweets he had brought as a gift from his shop.

Kanba and the others were already thoroughly sick of eating those sweets, but they were still pretty tasty.

"Of course, I'm going to do right by you all, and take responsibility for your well-being. It might be too much to take all three of you together, but I'll find someone who can take custody of you. It's only two or three years until you and Shoma are adults, right?"

"I'll go make some tea," said Kanba, standing up as if to cut Ikebe off, and heading to the kitchen.

"Plus, you of all people should know, Kanba," Ikebe continued, speaking to Kanba's back. "I don't want to have to say it, but your parents... Chiemi and my little brother, they're never coming back here."

Kanba continued to the kitchen, pulling out two suitable glasses, and pulled some cold barley tea from the fridge, pouring it into both. Then, he returned silently to the living room, the two glasses in hand, and placed them on the table.

"And what about Himari? What is Himari supposed to do? She's sick. You know that." He could never leave Himari on her own. And he could never let her feel lonesome. More than anything, he could not bear to be apart from her.

"I know that. No need to worry. We can look after Himari at our place. If anything happens with her, we'll let you know right away."

If anything happened to her it would be too late. Even now, he had no idea what might happen without the penguin hat. If they didn't find the Penguindrum, she might die again. They were already down to the wire.

Kanba was unable to contain his anger and had to look away from his uncle's face. His eyes fell on the family photo, now standing up again. Out of the corner of his eye, he saw the marks scratched into the beam where he and his brother would compare their heights. Above each mark, their respective names were written in katakana.

If not here, then where could they come home to? Where were they supposed to "make a family"?

"How much?" His voice was low, practically a groan.

"What's that, Kanba?"

Kanba shot a glare at Ikebe, and asked him again, firmly, "I'll raise all the necessary funds. How much do I need to get together so that you don't have to sell this house?"

How many times now had he consciously stopped himself from clenching his fists? To hide how his directionless anger grew hazy and sank down quietly into the bottom of his heart? How much longer would this continue?

"Kanba, I wasn't suggesting anything like that. There's no way you could get that kind of money on a high schooler's part-time salary." Distressed, Ikebe tried to calm Kanba down.

"*Listen!*" Kanba shouted, cutting him off. "*How much do you want?!*"

Ikebe furrowed his brow. His face, as he looked at Kanba, was a mix of sadness, concern, and a little bit of anger.

At some point, Kanba's shoulders had begun heaving. They would protect their family themselves. Somehow or other, he would protect Himari and this house. Kanba steadied his breath, his determination renewed. There was no time to waste thinking through options; he needed to act.

Ringo sat daintily on a chair in a restaurant in a department store in Ginza, feeling a little bit bashful.

She still had not talked to her father, who she had not seen in some time, about *him*. If she did, her father would surely be jealous. Right now, she was still her father's precious jewel. She hoped to remain his cute, sweet little Ringo-chan. That was the sort of affection that a daughter owed her father, she believed.

She gave her order to the waiter standing beside the table, flipping through the menu.

"Two of the seafood curry sets, please. Is that alright with you, Father?"

"Yes." Satoshi smiled.

Ringo turned the page, satisfied, and her eyes sparkled.

"Oh! There's a special Antarctic parfait, look!"

The parfait depicted on the dessert page was decorated with shaved ice and whipped cream like an iceberg, and little penguin dolls sitting on top.

"It's so cute."

"Then we'll have one of those, too." Satoshi said tactfully.

"Hey, we should go to that aquarium soon." Ringo thought that this was a wonderful suggestion.

"Which aquarium?"

"The one in Ikebukuro that we used to go to all the time! Don't you remember when that staff lady got mad at you because you were so interested in taking pictures of the penguins marching that you blocked up the walkway?" Ringo laughed, as though it happened yesterday.

"Did that happen?" Satoshi smiled back at her, but all memories of this aquarium seemed to have disappeared; he found it a little suspect, the idea that he could have been so taken with the marching of penguins.

"It did! And then on the way home all three of us bought matching cell phone charms. Look!" said Ringo, pulling out her cellphone, swinging the little charm of a penguin holding an apple, its coloring worn and faded, in front of him. "It was just a coincidence, but you said that it was like it had been made just for me."

Just then, Satoshi's phone rang.

"Oh, just a sec, sorry." He picked up the phone and stood quickly from his chair, walking a short distance away to take the call. "Hello?"

Ringo's slightly joyful mood suddenly flattened. Her father's phone was missing its matching charm.

"Ah, I'm with my daughter right now. It's that visitation day I mentioned. No, I'll have dinner with you tonight. I'll bring home a cake. Give my love to Aoi-chan, too."

Who was her father returning home to? Ringo had a fairly good idea, but she pretended she didn't.

"Say, Father. On the last Curry Day, Tabuki-san ate my curry that I made all by myself," she muttered, watching as Satoshi chatted on the phone with a far more excited expression than he had shown her, feeling farther away than she actually was.

"He said it was delicious."

It was a hollow feeling, one she was not sure that she could name as sadness.

Ringo recalled being inside the pond at Wadazuka Park. It was painfully cold, and her hair swayed in the water, caressing her cheeks, soft as cotton. A faint light pierced down through the water from the distant sky above, to the depths of the pond. Algae, plankton, and her own pallid hands as she sank. The bubbles of air escaping her throat.

"Thank goodness, you're awake!"

She smiled weakly, worried. "Huh, me?"

Underneath the water, Ringo thought only of being with her family. Was this what they meant by your life flashing before your eyes?

"You fell into the pond and were drowning. We weren't sure if you would make it for a moment, but you got mouth-to-mouth."

"Mouth...to mouth?"

Ringo quickly realized: Tabuki rescued her from the pond. And then he had given her mouth-to-mouth resuscitation.

In other words, they kissed.

Ringo was on cloud nine. She shared her awaited first real kiss with the man of her destiny. She was succeeding. Things were proceeding. Everything was just as she imagined. She and Tabuki were bound by fate after all. There was no space for that woman, Tokikago Yuri, to get between them. She would probably be off somewhere stamping her feet in frustration right about now.

Ringo, soaked through, headed home after that, saying she felt a cold coming on. She only realized later that the insolent interloper Takakura Shoma was gone as well. His presence had thrown a wrench into her plans, but things still went perfectly for Ringo in the end.

After all, she had kissed Tabuki.

Walking home alone from her meeting with her wretched father, Ringo dragged her feet through the shopping district at Ogikubo Station. All of the busy shoppers around only served to magnify her loneliness. Still, she could not lose focus. Today's mission was not over yet.

In her left hand, she held a small box from a cake shop. She pulled her diary from her bag with her right hand, confirmed her destiny, and grinned.

On the way home, drop in on Tabuki with a mont blanc. Of all cakes, mont blancs were Tabuki's favorite. And there was no way that he wouldn't go crazy for Ringo herself, having brought him his cake.

Ringo giggled to herself and lifted her head confidently,

walking swiftly. But the scene in front of her sent her plunging once more into the depths of loneliness.

At the cafe before her, Tabuki and Yuri were facing one another, smiling at each other very much like lovers. Yuri's look was casual but refined, while Tabuki wore a t-shirt that read in large letters, "Crazy About Birds."

Tabuki had his mouth open wide, stuffing his face happily with mont blanc.

"Mm, this is good! I would definitely rank this place on the top of my 'Best of the Mont Blancs' chart!" Tabuki wore a dopey look on his face.

"I swear, Tabuki, you are simply *Fabulous Max!* Take your time with that cake," Yuri said without a hint of rebuke, resting on her elbows and gazing lovingly at Tabuki as he ate.

"This flavor. Oh, gosh, you just gotta go crazy for it!"

Ringo stopped walking and stared dumbfounded at the pair. She dropped the cake box on the ground at once.

She started back through the shopping district she had come through with a hurried pace. With her eyes down so that she would not encounter anything else she didn't want to see, all she could see was her own shoes. Her unreliable, childish, tiny shoes.

She felt a drop on the back of her head, and looked up at the sky just as it began to rain. The sky had gone gray and clouded without her noticing, and rain began to pour.

Ringo felt suitably maudlin, being pelted by the rain. It was not like she could feel any more hopeless.

"Ringo-chan?"

She looked back at the sweet, familiar voice, and saw Shoma and Himari standing beneath a shared umbrella. Shoma held a bag from the supermarket in his hand.

"What's wrong? Do you not have an umbrella?" Himari came closer to Ringo, pulling Shoma along. "There's not much room, but come on in." Himari grinned.

"Are you sure?" Ringo glanced at Shoma.

"I-I don't really mind." For some reason, his cheeks were turning pink.

"Are you heading home? You wanna come to our house to wait out the rain? We can have dinner together!" Himari said in a fawning voice, happily pulling Ringo under the umbrella.

Ringo again looked at Shoma, but not only was his face red, he looked away.

"Sounds good, right, Sho-chan?" Himari asked Shoma, carefree.

"That's fine, I guess."

Then it's decided, Himari's smile seemed to say.

"I swear. Everyone always seems to be coming home soaked lately. What a bother," said Himari, giggling as though this was not a bother at all.

"That so?"

Ringo was relieved. She was surrounded by the warmth of other people, in the midst of a lively conversation, and soon would get to eat dinner together with them. When she thought of this, the whole day seemed worth it.

"Yep. Just like the other day, when Ringo-chan went on that date in the park, right?"

"Uh, no, I mean, that was just an unrelated coincidence," Shoma said, faltering. "Let's get home already. It's getting chilly, and Oginome-san's gonna catch a cold."

What a strange person, Ringo thought. But that had nothing to do with her. Things had gone poorly today, but surely, there was a reason for that. Fate was not something that changed. It could not be changed as simply as that.

The train car was sparse with riders. Kanba sat in a row with Penguin No. 3, scarcely taking in his surroundings.

The man boarded around Kasumigaseki, and leisurely made his way over from the next car, standing before Kanba.

Kanba looked up at the man.

The man, who wore all black, held an envelope out to Kanba. Kanba took it, quickly checked the contents, and said, "Looks right," slipping the envelope into his inner jacket pocket.

The sound of the man's footsteps as he departed intermingled with the keening of the train.

Me and Himari and Oginome-san. I certainly had not expected to have this particular line-up crowded around the dining table. Kanba was probably going to be out late with some girl. Still, I was not sure that I was gifted with the ability to weather these circumstances on my own.

"I love this curry-flavored beef and potato stew! Curry is something to eat with the ones you love, right, Ringo-chan?"

Himari was in high spirits, eating more than usual. We set

aside portions for Penguins No. 2 and 3 on their own little plates, which Oginome-san, who could not see them, seemed to think peculiar.

"That's right. Curry is something to share with the ones you love."

Oginome-san, who looked bashfully pleased at having her recipe praised, apparently remembered nothing of what had happened at the park. I fully intended to forget about it as well, so I felt grateful.

On the day of that "date" at Wadazuka Park, I instinctively jumped into the pond to save Oginome-san after she fell in. If I hadn't, she might have died, after all. Tabuki was so wrapped up in doting on that Yuri-san that he hadn't even noticed that Oginome-san was drowning. I had no choice. That mouth-to-mouth was done purely to save her life, it was necessary. In other words, that kiss didn't really count as a "kiss." I was sure of this.

"Sho-chan, your face is all red, what's wrong?" Himari pointed out, sharp as ever.

"It's nothing! This curry stew really is delicious!"

Despite my sureness, I could not simply forget the feeling of Oginome-san's soft lips, chilled and soaked in the grassy pond water. It was difficult to bear the guilt of keeping silent about this to her. It had been my first kiss, and probably hers as well, after all.

I glanced Oginome-san's way. Even now, the sound of her and Himari whispering and laughing together sparkled in the apartment's air.

I caught sight of the same notebook I had seen that day at the park poking out from the tote bag at Oginome-san's side. This was the chance I needed. I could not be shy about this. What was I going to do if I did not say something to her now?

I slowly set down my chopsticks.

"Oginome-san. I have a big favor to ask of you."

"What?" Both she and Himari looked at me, bemused.

"The other day, when we were at Wadazuka Park, did you have a notebook with you?"

Her eyebrows suddenly knit slightly, and she set down her bowl.

"I was wondering if you could let me borrow that, if you don't mind?" I swallowed thickly. She looked back at me, clearly dubious.

Himari seemed puzzled, and looked curiously between me and Oginome-san.

"Just for a few moments. I'll give it right back when I'm done with it. So..."

Before I could finish speaking, Oginome-san snapped her chopsticks down onto the table.

"Don't be stupid. Why should I lend that to you?"

"Well, I..." I stammered, glancing at her. Himari held the penguins close, looking troubled.

"Absolutely not. You can't have it. It's not something that I can lend to other people in the first place," Oginome-san said flatly, in a harsh tone.

"Why not? It's just a normal diary, isn't it?" *Crap*, I thought, but it was too late.

"So you saw it! You're terrible!" Her face went red and twisted, and she stood, closing in on me.

"I-I just happened to catch a glimpse of it! But all it has is your plans, just things that you yourself want to happen, right?!" It was too late to take it back. This was all for Himari, who stood before us. If there was a chance that that diary was the Penguindrum, then I had to get my hands on it no matter what. Even if it made Oginome-san angry.

"That's not true. What's written there is fate." Her voice went soft, her eyes lowered.

"Fate?"

"My future is written in that notebook. It's my Fate Diary." Her voice grew conspicuously louder, as if she was reaffirming this to herself.

"Fate Diary? What the heck is that?"

She glared at me feverishly, her shoulders heaving.

"Listen, I've been honest with you. Now, it's your turn. How do you know about all that? And why do you need it? Explain yourself!"

I don't know how my brother would have handled this, but I knew that if I didn't explain myself, I would never get my hands on that notebook.

"Alright. I'll talk."

I took a breath, stood up, picked up the penguin hat, and showed it to her.

"What is this?" she asked.

"Oh, that's... a souvenir that we got recently from the aquarium," Himari explained, curiously.

Perhaps uneasy at the rising tensions in the room, Himari had drawn the penguins close to her, and both 2 and 3 were flailing in her grip, flapping their beaks in protest.

I silently placed the hat down in the middle of the table. Once more, I gulped.

"Please try not to be too surprised. The truth is, this penguin hat is actually some kind of mysterious life-form. It might be an alien or some other kind of being."

Oginome-san went slack-jawed. Himari waited for me to continue, her expression unchanging.

"This thing ordered us to bring it your notebook, or rather, your Fate Diary." I was fully aware that what I was saying was absurd, but what else could I do? These were the facts that I witnessed with my own eyes. I could not say in front of Himari that her life depended on that notebook.

"Stop playing with me."

The words came so softly that I barely heard them. "Huh?"

"Stop playing with me! I listened to you seriously!" Oginome-san shot to her feet.

"I'm not lying! Besides, *you're* the one who's messing around and being cryptic with this so-called Fate Diary or whatever!" My protests, bursting out at the sight of her dubious expression, were weak and obviously not doing me any favors.

"Oh? Then what's this 'mysterious life-form'? Did you hit your head or something?"

I could not respond. I would probably have said something similar in her position.

"Survival Tactiiiic!"

I turned around in surprise to see Himari, who sat between us, had at some point donned the penguin hat. Now she was clad in her penguin dress, white lace whipping furiously around her. The otherworldly space spread from out of the gaps in the lace. That sweet scent wafted through the air, and the otherworldly rhythm wracked my whole body.

Himari stroked her slender, corset-wrapped body with her tiny hands. The frills beneath her billowing skirt inflated one after the other, like popcorn.

"Shut the hell up and listen, you filthy sow. You think you can just start flappin' your mouth?" Himari's bright red eyes glistened, and a sudden gust sent her long hair fluttering.

"What are you saying, Himari-chan?" Oginome-san looked around her new surroundings, dumbfounded. "Where are we?"

The being who was both Himari and the penguin hat puffed her chest out haughtily, loudly clicking her tongue.

"That's enough. Hand over that stream of messed-up delusions that comes spewing out your butt, that 'Fate Diary' or whatever, to that brat there immediately!" Himari whipped a finger towards Oginome-san. The rhythm modulated in time.

Even my innards seemed to be vibrating. It was difficult to breathe.

Though I tried to describe the situation, I could not explain what I didn't understand. Oginome-san was so shocked she seemed to forget even to breathe.

"W-wait a second, what is all this?!" Oginome-san looked at me, eyes wide with apprehension.

175

I could not reply. It took all I had just to shake my head slightly.

"Himari-chan, is something wrong?" Still sitting down on the tatami, she looked up at Himari, in her penguin dress.

"You're the one who's got something wrong, you perverted stalker!" Himari forcefully stomped her glistening black boots. The sound seemed to reverberate throughout the entire space.

"Himari-chan, why would you say something like that? Is this a joke?"

"How loathsome for you to speak back to us!" Himari lifted her chin coldly, turned her head to the side and spat. "A filth-brained, muck-wallowing pig like you!"

"That's awful! You shouldn't say things like that!" Tears welled in Oginome-san's eyes.

Her distress was understandable, and very relatable. I kept taking a breath to try and say something, but when I opened my mouth the right words never came. The sweet scent seemed to fill my head with a foggy haze.

Himari gave a signal with her eyes, and a square hole popped open beneath Oginome-san's feet.

"Oginome-san! That's not it! This is Himari, but it isn't Himari!" I finally managed to explain to Oginome-san as she fell into the darkness. Somewhere, deep down in my heart, I sympathized, wondering if I always fell down into the darkness the same way.

"You muck-wallowing sow!" Himari huffed angrily, her hands on her hips.

I stared at the little door into the darkness that opened up in the floor. I wondered if Himari's voice sounded distant to Oginome-san right about now, as she hurdled through the dark.

"Oginome-san?!" I said again. Penguin Hat and Penguins No. 2 and 3 turned at the sound of my distraught voice.

More than shocked, I was half-terrified. From that darkness that always swallowed me so swiftly, Oginome-san's white hands reached straight out, grasping firmly at edge of the floor.

She groaned, murmuring, "Who's a muck-wallower?"

A cold sweat began to run down the expressionless faces of Nos. 2 and 3 at this dreadful turn of events.

Now, one hand gripped the edge. With ragged breaths, bit by bit she scraped her powerful, flexing hand along the floor. Finally, her right shoulder came into view, and as her disheveled hair slunk into sight, the penguins paled and clung to me, leaving me unable to move a muscle.

I was too terrified to draw my eyes away.

"Don't you look down on me." Groaning, Oginome-san dragged the upper half of her body up onto the floor, steadying her ragged breath. From the waist down she still hung in the darkness.

"O-Oginome-san, a-are you okay?" I asked, in a voice so small and pitiful it surprised even me.

"Don't you look down on me!" As she hauled herself up in a most unladylike fashion, her face was shadowed by her hair, and I could not read her expression.

The slimmest, slightest bit of worry crossed Himari's face, but she still stood with her legs wide, glaring at Oginome-san.

What happened next took only a matter of seconds. Just as I noticed Oginome-san making a break for Himari—not saying a word, not even bothering to stand up—she reached for Himari's bewildered face and seized the penguin hat. The crumpled hat was sent flying swiftly away.

"This piece of crap!"

The moment the hat came away from Himari's head, we were back in the parlor. Outside, it rained, and steam still rose from the curry stew atop the table. The hat flew away out onto the dark roadside.

Himari was back in her original state, collapsed in a small heap on the tatami, her eyes closed.

"What are you doing?! That's Himari's!" I shook the penguins off and rushed out to the front of the house. Instead of the sweet smell of the storm from earlier, my lungs now filled with the cold scent of vegetation damp with rain.

My socks sucked in the water in an instant, and chills ran up and down my spine.

The rain poured down more violently than earlier in the evening. I scanned the tiny park right next to the house and the black asphalt, but the hat was nowhere to be seen. The rain pelted harshly on the metal of our home.

My vision began to blur, whether from the rain or from my own tears, and my throat stung. Without the hat, Himari would die. Collapsed on the floor just now, she was probably already dead.

Startled by the sudden sound of a truck's engine, I looked up to see the hat, flapping from the corner of the canopy of a freight truck that was just about to depart.

"Gotcha!" I reached out, but it was out of reach. "W-wait a minute!"

The truck started slowly and cruelly through the rain. Without a moment's hesitation, I ran after it.

"Wait! Waaait!"

With the driving rain, no matter how hard I tried, there was no way that I could possibly catch up with that truck. I ran desperately, wiping my eyes with my hand.

"Kanba!" Up ahead, I saw my brother walking along with Penguin No. 1.

"Shoma, what's up?"

"There!" I pointed to the truck's canopy, before a fit of violent coughing overtook me.

"How?!" Kanba swiftly shed his jacket and looked all around, spotting a rusted bicycle, and shoved No. 1 into it, taking off.

"Damn it, what is *with* today?!" he muttered.

The truck rounded the corner, picking up speed, my brother rushing through the rain behind it on the rusted bicycle.

It was dawn, following that fateful evening nine years earlier. Little Himari was in a bed dressed with clean white sheets, breathing softly and fast asleep, her fever lowered. Kanba sat on a stool set beside the bed, his poncho and boots so filthy, the mud looked like it had been painted on. His hair was mussed, his face weary and dazed. His eyes were bleary. A blister that had formed on his left foot stung terribly.

It was dim in the room with its drawn curtains, the round

clock on the wall the only indication that it was already morning. Beside Kanba, Kenzan breathed deeply.

"We can relax now." His arms looked dreadful, wrapped in pristine white bandages, except where they were dotted with blood.

Kenzan smiled back as Kanba looked up at him. There was a mute appeal in the boy's eyes, unable to form words to express his feelings. Kenzan's large, warm hand rustled over Kanba's head, mussing up his hair even further.

"You did good back there, Kanba."

Kanba lowered his head slightly, happy but also embarrassed. He felt the guilty, tearful storm within him slowly dissipating in his warm heart.

Kenzan stood up slowly and stepped by the window, swiftly opening the curtains. The dazzling morning sun pierced in to fill the hospital room. The sky was fully clear. Birds were singing. It was a beautiful morning, more beautiful than Kanba had ever seen before.

For a moment, Kanba narrowed his eyes. He could feel the heat coming back to his body as sun shone warmly on his skin.

"Every storm passes. But while you're waiting for it to pass, you have to protect the ones you love. Never forget that, Kanba." Kenzan looked back at him with a smile and a glint in his eye.

Kanba finally returned a real smile. Things were going to be alright.

Still soaked by the rain, I grabbed Himari's shoulders as she lay on the tatami, shaking her again and again.

"Himari! Himari, snap out of it! Himari!"

I knew. In the dark corners of my mind, I knew that without the penguin hat, it was pointless. Still, there was nothing else for me to do. Nothing else I *could* do.

Himari's little body only wobbled back and forth, her eyes still closed, motionless as a doll.

"Himari, don't die!" I wasn't sure if I felt hot or cold, if the sensation hitting my body were sharp or dull.

"No way. I mean, it's just a hat. Himari-chan was playing around." Oginome-san was at her wit's end, paling, peering at Himari's face, tears again welling in her eyes.

I could not blame her for what she had done, not that I was thinking straight enough to assign blame. It was completely unbelievable, that that hat would have a hold on Himari's life.

As I waited for my brother, who chased down the freight truck on bicycle, I remembered having such grim, furious, sorrowful feelings about my family once long before. Such scenes, floating hazily in my mind, always made it hard to breathe.

"Himari."

How could I be so powerless?

Oginome-san and I sat at Himari's sides, both of us crushed, trying to hold back the tears.

At the sound of the front door opening, I looked up. There were heavy, slamming footsteps, and my brother entered the living room, looking ragged and gripping the hat, Penguin No. 1 on his heels.

"Aniki!"

He was covered in mud, his pants ripped, stained with blood from his knees down. No. 1 was black with dirt as well; with its round, black eyes, it looked like a black blob.

Huffing, Kanba stomped across the tatami, and gripped Himari's hand tight around the dirtied hat.

He left a meandering trail of mud and blood on the tatami behind him.

For a moment, we all watched Himari carefully, holding our breaths, so quiet the silence seemed to ring.

Just then, Himari's fingers moved, ever so slightly, squeezing the hat. Finally, there was the faint sound of her breathing, and she opened her eyes a crack.

"Himari!"

"Himari-chan!"

Oginome-san's voice joined with mine, both shouting for joy. Tears of joy rolled down my face as I looked up at Kanba. He grinned back. Then he collapsed to his knees, fell heavily onto the floor, and lost consciousness.

"Aniki!" Despite his dreadful state, there was a look of joyful fulfillment upon his face.

In this room, filled with the scent of blood and rain, we were all thoroughly exhausted. Even now, I didn't know if things were good or bad. But at any rate, Himari had been saved.

It would be good to clean up the floor before Himari was fully awake, I thought. I ought to take a look at Kanba's legs, as well.

"So, what is going on, here?" Oginome-san asked in a shrinking voice.

"It's just what it looks like," I replied with a wry smile. Was there any other explanation to give? "It's...exactly what it looks like."

Kanba rubbed the bandage-wrapped wounds hidden beneath his pants legs as he listened to Uncle Ikebe's phone ring. Traces of the soaking rain remained on the tatami, which they had futilely scrubbed with a cloth. Atop the table, beside a half-drunk glass of barley tea, was an envelope, streaked with blood and soaked with water.

"Hey, Uncle? I got that money we were talking about. I deposited it into the shop's bank account, so go and double-check it later. Yeah, it's fine, it's not funny money. Anyway, I assume that means that we're fine to stay in the house for now?"

Kanba quietly put his hand on the empty envelope.

"Himari? No changes there."

From the living room, he could see Himari digging in the dirt by the side of the house, Penguins 1 and 3 at her side. The sun shone through her plaited hair. She had her sleeves rolled up, and donned a floral apron. The look suited her.

"Thanks. I'll be in touch later." Kanba hung up the phone, flashing a smile at Himari, who happened to look his way.

"You should help too, Kan-chan! It's fun!" Himari said, grinning back. She held up a red shovel and fertilizer.

"Guess I'd better, then." Kanba downed the last of the tea in the glass, balled up the envelope and threw it in the trash bin, and stood up.

A smile crept onto his face. It was just like Himari to want to grow strawberries in the yard.

"I can't even think of the last time I went digging in the dirt," Kanba said softly.

"Probably elementary school? It's cool, and it feels nice. We need to pull up the weeds and get this fertilizer mixed in properly," Himari replied innocently.

Kanba rolled up his sleeves, slipped on a pair of rubber sandals from the porch, and stepped into the yard.

As he dug, Kanba's thoughts suddenly took a strange, curious direction. How could this childlike girl digging in the dirt mean so much to him? There were plenty of women who were wiser, more stylish, more beautiful than her. He smiled at his own feelings, so mysterious and yet causing him no doubt. No matter how he might struggle, there was nothing he could do about it; these feelings were as certain as the death that would one day come for him.

CHAPTER 06 →

KANBA WAS BEWILDERED. From the moment he set foot in her hospital room, Kuho Asami looked at him with a complete and utter lack of interest.

"Who are you?" was the first thing out of Asami's mouth. A large, square bandage was affixed to her forehead.

"What do you mean, 'Who,' Asami?" asked Kanba, his face twitching. Certainly, he dumped Kuho Asami in a pretty inexcusable way, and acted thoroughly unimpressed with the "Takakura Kanba Romantic Casualties Club" the other day, single-mindedly sipping his coffee and saying little until he could get out of there. But Asami, of all people, should have known that Kanba would not have reacted well to that. He assumed that she must be toying with him again.

"Might you be one of my fans? I'm sorry, you'll have to go through the agency." Asami looked deeply troubled and a little frightened.

"Asami, have you seriously forgotten me?"

Kanba felt unnerved at how dry her gaze was.

The accident that happened that night. The fact that her testimony changed. He thought that the accident was peculiar, so he had come to visit and check in on her. But maybe it had just been a coincidence. He couldn't begin to understand what it meant that Asami's memories of him had been snatched away.

"Please don't speak to me like you know me. I'll call someone!" Frantic, she reached out for the nurse call button. As she did, her arm collided with the bedside table, and a ball that had been hidden behind an ostentatious flower-filled vase dropped to the floor, rolling to Kanba's feet.

He had seen this charred, golf ball-sized thing before. As he looked at it in shock, he felt his phone vibrate in his pocket.

"I know what you're searching for," read the message. The message was identical to the one he received when Asami and the others called him out to that restaurant, and it was from an unknown sender.

He glanced at Asami, who was still looking at him nervously, and left the room before anyone could arrive.

Perhaps Asami's accident had not been completely accidental after all.

Shinjuku Gyoenmae Subway Station. On the way home from school, Penguin No. 2 and I boarded the train car that we had been directed to. Oginome-san was already ready and waiting for us. From a more innocent standpoint, this was the sort of thing that would have made Yamashita jealous, but I was not here on any date.

"Where's your brother?" asked Oginome-san in a harsh tone.

"I couldn't get a hold of him." When Kanba was unavailable, it was usually because of some girl. He was always leaving the house on some minor errand or other, and I never knew where he was or what he was doing. As a result, I once again found myself in the awkward circumstance of meeting up with Oginome-san alone.

"What useless brothers," she said, casting a glare at me and lightly clicking her tongue.

"I mean I'm here, aren't I? What do you mean, 'useless'? You're the one who called us out here all of a sudden." *Never mind the fact that I'm the one who saved your life*, I could not add.

Oginome-san glared out the dark train window, uninterested in what I had to say.

"Listen. If you try to sneak a peek at my diary like you have been, or take it from me forcibly..." Her eyes flicked to mine.

I let out a deep sigh. "I know. You won't lend me the diary. Or are you saying you'll toss it into an incinerator?"

"Even if it's for Himari-chan's sake, that is the one thing I cannot relinquish. I absolutely cannot slip up in my plan." Her gaze returned to the dark window.

"Plan?"

"Project M. My greatest trial," she said, a significant look on her face, scarcely even listening to my words.

Project M. I watched her serious face in profile, wondering if the "M" might not stand for "marriage" or something like that.

I wanted to believe that even a stalker like Oginome-san would not be thinking that far ahead.

"Are you going to help me? Or no?" she asked.

"I'll help. I should help, right?!" I replied in desperation.

I felt like I spent every free day with Oginome-san. The times I spent laughing with Himari, doing the cleaning and the laundry, already felt like a distant memory.

I gloomily imagined my sister sticking little strawberry-shaped signs where she and Kanba planted the strawberries, looking at me with a smile and saying, "We'll eat them when the berries are ready!" Why was I instead stuck taking part in this stalker girl's weird machinations?

Oginome-san's home, in East Kouenji. I had not been able to step inside her room the last time, and it didn't seem like I'd see it today, either. I could not get past all of the piled-up boxes, after all.

"What is all this? Are you moving?" I was dumbfounded.

"Something like that. Now, carry these," she said promptly.

"Huh? All of this?"

"Of course. That's why I told both of you to come, obviously. But there's nothing to be done for it. All you need to do is carry. Carry them!" She pursed her lips.

Through trial and error, I was able to tie most of the boxes to the mattress, and hoist the whole thing onto my back. It wobbled terribly and was naturally quite heavy.

"Can't you carry a little more?" I asked.

She made a pitying face.

It took so much work just to stand that I was incapable of spitting a reply. By comparison, Oginome-san, swinging a single travel bag around in her hand, was relatively carefree.

"Hrrngh!" I took the first stumbling, miraculous step forward, and then steeled myself and took several steps more, when suddenly I stepped on something soft.

"You idiot!" Before I had a chance to look down, Oginome-san sent me flying back. I went rolling on the floor, burden and all.

"Wah! What the heck are you doing?!" I shouted, collapsed onto my side.

"You just stepped right on Ka-chan and Ot-chan!" She glared at me, cradling a pair of stuffed animals in her arms.

"Wha?" I looked closer to see that they were a stuffed kappa and otter. Thus, "Ka-chan and Ot-chan."

"I'm sorry, Ka-chan, Ot-chan. That must've hurt," she said softly to the pair of toys, tying them securely to the handle of her travel bag.

"Are you taking them with you, too?"

"These children are my family! Obviously, I'd always take them with me!"

"Family, huh?" It occurred to me that I knew nothing about the composition of the Oginome family. What kind of people lived in this spacious, lifeless home besides Oginome-san?

"Do I have to spell this out for you?! C'mon, let's go!"

No. 2 was kind enough to look at me, worry in its eyes.

"We're here." Oginome-san stopped as if for a much-needed breather.

"Of course," I said beside her, looking up at the strange little weathervane-adorned gate of the building that housed Tabuki's apartment.

Just as she had the time that we tailed her, Oginome-san went around the back of the building, sneaking towards Tabuki's place from behind. She didn't intend for me to carry these things underground, did she?

And yet, that's exactly where I ended up, crawling underneath the building, luggage strapped to my back and all.

"C'mon, move!" she said, as though I was blocking her way, and I slowly stood.

She unfurled a blue tarp and neatly covered the piled-up luggage.

"Anyway, this is what we'll hide it with."

"Um, isn't this the apartment where my teacher, Tabuki, lives?" I said nervously.

She cast a glare at me.

"U-um, I mean, it's on the faculty roster. It's close to us, so I just happened to remember that."

Her face abruptly went blank.

"If you want me to lend you the diary, you're going to shut up and do as you're told. You said so yourself, didn't you?"

I swallowed the words I'd been about to say.

"Then just keep up the pace! No unnecessary talking. There's still more stuff to carry."

"Huh? There's more?" There was more luggage. My eyes narrowed to points.

"We're moving all of it! Before this evening!"

I hung my head but said nothing. Directly in my line of vision was Penguin No. 2, casually licking an ice cream cone that it must have snatched from somewhere, watching a line of ants marching on the ground.

The department store's rooftop was filled with playground equipment for young children and artificial grass, a number of white garden tables with matching chairs, and a line of carts selling juice and crepes and ice cream and the like. After school, there was knockoff carnival music from the play place, and the joyful screams of children as they ran around. Students ran around making merry, and lovers walked past holding hands.

In front of Kanba, Chizuru and Yui sat at a table, each casually licking a soft serve cone. Kanba held out his phone to them, which displayed the suspicious text.

"Which of you sent this? This constitutes harassment."

"I'm telling you, I have no idea what that is," replied Yui, sounding bored.

"Yep, the sender's number isn't either of ours," Chizuru added.

"How can you all be so casual about..." Kanba realized how unnatural his own words sounded and cut himself off.

When Asami invited him out, he mistakenly read too much into the message she had sent him, assuming it had to be related to the Penguindrum. However, Asami suffered an accident, and all of her memories of Kanba had been, probably intentionally, erased. Given that he happened to receive a text with an identical message at the moment that he learned this, this time he could only conclude that it was from someone who knew that he and Shoma were searching for the Penguindrum. But this did not necessarily imply that it was from either of the women before him.

After all, how would Asami, Chizuru, or Yui have gotten their hands on such crucial information in the first place?

"I see. But there's someone pulling the strings behind the scenes, right? Listen, this person is way more dangerous than you all think. Asami..." he started to say, then cut himself off.

"What about Kuho-san?" asked Chizuru, head tilted.

"Uh, never mind." It was hard to tell just how much these two knew. Given that they did not appear particularly surprised at the mention of Asami, they probably did believe that what happened to her had been some simple accident.

"That reminds me, I heard from Kuho-san that you had a new girlfriend, Kanba-kun?" Yui scowled at him.

"Never mind that right now."

"I heard that too," Chizuru added, glaring. "Tell us, who is she?!"

"Hey, gimme a break already," said Kanba. His eyes went wide as something like the bead of a red laser beam suddenly appeared on Chizuru's forehead.

"Spit it out!" Chizuru said sulkily, not seeming to have noticed this herself.

"Is she some schoolgirl?" Yui, sitting beside her, was not looking at Chizuru, either.

Kanba backed away, trying to determine which direction the beam was coming from. Just then, there was a terrible sound, and a sparking sphere came hurtling past and struck Chizuru in the forehead. Chizuru's head drooped down, and for a time she was motionless. Kanba and Yui stared at her, holding their breath.

"H-huh?" When Chizuru lifted her head, there was a sphere the size of a golf ball, identical to the thing in Asami's room, stuck to her forehead.

"What is that?" asked Yui, tilting her head, looking closely at the ball.

"Oh heck, did a bird crap on me?" Chizuru showed Yui her forehead, as though it were no huge deal.

"That's kinda big though, isn't it?" As Yui turned around to see where it had come from, another laser beam appeared on her head. Without skipping a beat, there was another bang, and a second sphere came flying and struck Yui in the head. She jerked, momentarily losing consciousness, and then lifted her face. Stuck to her forehead was the exact same ball.

Kanba looked in the direction the ball had come from, suddenly shouting, "Who's there?!" He looked at the rooftops of the surrounding buildings, but there was no sign of anyone. It seemed unlikely that it had come from anywhere on this rooftop.

"Kan...ba...kun...you're terrible."

Kanba's gaze jolted back to the pair at Chizuru's strange sounding words. Her voice was flat, her expression hollow. There was an emptiness to the eyes of both women, sitting side by side.

"Tell me I'm the only one you love."

"No way, I'm the real one."

"Hey, you guys..." Not even Kanba's voice appeared to reach them.

"You're so shameless."

"Are you stupid?"

Their hazy argument over Kanba continued, as though they were under a spell.

Kanba watched, speechless, as the ball attached to Chizuru's forehead suddenly began to spin, moving so quickly his eyes could not keep up. As he watched, a black flame began to rise from the ball. Chizuru opened her mouth wide and collapsed onto her back. Watching the rising flame, Yui muttered, "Oh no, what is that?"

As Kanba reached to try to pull the sphere from Yui's forehead, that one began to rapidly rotate, and another black flame rose. She opened her mouth and collapsed as well.

The soft serve cones the girls held fell, splattering to the ground. The charred balls, now detached from their foreheads, rolled away. Sure enough, they were the same as the one that had been in Asami's room.

"Snap out of it! Are you okay?!" Kanba shouted, pulling Chizuru up.

"I'm fine," Yui said breathlessly. Kanba looked over at her. She was already sitting up, but her head hung down. "But I have a question: who are you?"

"Huh?"

"Speaking of..." Chizuru, propped up in Kanba's arms, lifted her head, her eyes open a slit. "I have the same question. Who are you?"

Kanba slowly backed away from the pair, then seamlessly wove himself into the conversation and bustling activity that suffused the rooftop, as though he hadn't seen a thing, and departed the scene.

Penguin No. 2 and I collapsed on the white corner sofa. We were surrounded by a sea of cardboard.

"Ugh, I'm beat!"

"Hang on, who said you could rest?!" Oginome-san said sharply.

"But we've made so many trips already!"

I thought about the tattered little red sofa back at our house, unsuited to the tatami. If we had a living room and a sofa this big, Himari would have a blast lying on it and reading books and knitting. I could watch her from the adjoining open kitchen as I prepared dinner.

"We have to finish moving all of this before evening! If we don't, then my new house won't be complete!"

"New house?" The phrase, which I could not ignore, pulled me back to reality.

"It's none of your business. Look, just hurry and get back! Up!" She cornered me and grabbed my arm as I lay on the sofa, tugging.

"No! This is seriously impossible!"

I put all my strength into clinging to the sofa, resisting her pulling, when her face suddenly and inexplicably went red, her breath growing ragged as she drew nearer.

"Huh? Wait, what?"

Not saying a word, she pushed her face up against mine, with all the weight of her upper body, her lips pushing inevitably against my cheek.

"Th-th-this is our first night together." She muttered something vaguely terrifying.

"Huh? Oginome-san?"

"I have to feel our sleeping breaths together, side by side."

"Hey! C'mon, stop it!" No matter how I pushed against her, she sank forward, breathing hot breaths. "Oginome-san! What's wrong with you?!"

I felt my terror rising, like a zebra being stalked by a lion on the savanna. Though it's pathetic to admit, it's not like I could have just slipped out around her. Nor could I behave like my brother, who would have probably taken advantage of the situation.

"I'm home!"

Hearing this stranger's lazy voice, without thinking, I reflexively shouted, "No!" even though I should have shouted, "Help!" What I meant was, no this wasn't what it looked like, it was not some indecent scene like my brother would find himself in, it was really just an accident, set in motion by some strange design.

"C'mon, get off me! There's some misunderstanding here!" I desperately shoved Oginome-san away, finally realizing there was something wrong when I saw her face. I pressed my right hand to her forehead; it was burning up. "Crap, you've got a fever."

A woman, who I could see over Oginome-san's shoulder, was frozen in the doorway of the living room, staring speechlessly at me.

I helped the woman, who turned out to be Oginome-san's mother, carry her into her room, intending to apologize and flee immediately, but I wasn't off the hook that easily. Her mother placed warm tea and cookies before me as I sat in terror. The white, angular tea set suited this room perfectly.

"My apologies. I completely misread the situation." She wore a white suit. She had strong, willful eyes, just like Oginome-san.

"I swear, that girl. I told her to take the day off. Honestly, collapsing on the way home from school. Still, it's lucky that a fine boy like you happened to be passing by, Takakura-kun. There have been a lot of dangerous happenings recently." Her mother smiled wide.

Helpless, I smiled stupidly. I gulped down the tea, some variety or other that I had drunk somewhere before. The hot liquid danced down my throat, and a peaceful feeling seeped into my insides. I wished I could tell Oginome-san's mother that there was no one more dangerous than her daughter.

"So anyway, what are you to Ringo?" asked her mother, intrigued.

I choked and spat out my tea, quickly drying my mouth on my uniform sleeve.

"My, no need to hide it. Despite how I look, I'm a very open-minded parent."

She grinned at me in an unsettling way. In this regard, she resembled Oginome-san not one bit.

"No, I mean, we're just friends. Or rather, Oginome-san has been helping out my little sister." I was apparently weak against the women of the Oginome household.

"Whaaat? How boring. And here I thought you passed each other on the way to school and fell in love at first sight!" She sighed, shoulders slumping, looking truly disappointed.

My face cramped somewhat. Just which of us had fallen for the other at first sight in this fairytale of hers? The idea of me falling for *her* at a glance was unthinkable. Though of course, the reverse seemed equally impossible.

"Judging by that uniform, Gaiennishi High?"

"Ah, yes."

"Do you know Tabuki Keiju, then? He teaches biology."

"Ah, yes, he's my homeroom teacher." I was surprised to hear that she knew Tabuki as well. Maybe I was about to get some unexpectedly valuable information.

"My, really? Tabuki-kun still stops by our place now and then. Ringo's older sister was his classmate in elementary school." Her eyes narrowed with a nostalgic look.

"Huh? She has an older sister?"

When we searched the place, we had not turned up any hints that two girls lived here. It was likely she was already living on her own, if she was the same age as Tabuki, but Oginome-san herself had never said anything to suggest the existence of a sister.

"Well yes, but…" Oginome-san's mother suddenly looked very sad. "She passed away, a long time ago now."

Her words flowed softly, like sand. The words of someone who already cried out all their tears and keened until their throat cracked, and whose well of grief had now run dry.

So that was how Oginome-san and Tabuki were connected.

Silence returned to the living room. I got the feeling that this spacious, lifeless room somehow resembled Oginome-san and her mother. Both in their strong eyes, and their bluntness. It was a somehow lonely atmosphere.

Finding it difficult to say that I was going to go home, I instead had seconds of my tea.

Clutching her large, beloved kappa and otter plushies, a little girl scurried down the dark hallway to the living room, rubbing her eyes. A comforting orange light flooded from the room.

"Mama," the girl said. "I need to wee-wee."

Just before she pushed the door open and entered, she froze, hearing her parents angrily shouting at each other in the room.

"So, you're saying it's *my* fault?!"

"No! I'm just saying it's about time for us to make a new start."

"*New start?*"

"Yeah, Ringo's old enough now to understand a lot of things, and I feel terrible that her birthday always has to be 'Curry Day!'"

"But tomorrow is Momoka's..."

"I know, it's the anniversary. But it's also Ringo's birthday!"

"So what? It's our duty as parents to cherish Momoka's memory forever!"

The girl gently peeked into the living room. She hushed herself, and squeezed strength into her shoulders. She got the feeling that she was doing something terribly naughty.

"Remembering her isn't the same thing as dragging things out forever! No one is going to be happy this way! You need to open your eyes already!"

As they jabbed at one another beneath the overhead lamp, her parents' faces were cast in shadow, and she could barely see them. The little girl rubbed her eyes again, and then was shocked when she opened them again. Her parents were gone, and where they stood was the spitting image of the kappa and otter she was holding. The huge kappa and otter were glaring at one another, each holding a cucumber and a clam, respectively.

"No! I don't want to forget Momoka!" The kappa snapped the cucumber in half with all its might.

Fearful at the loud voice, the little girl held her breath, huddling up more.

"But we have Ringo now, don't we?!" said the otter in tears, banging the clam on the table over and over again.

"We'll love Ringo in Momoka's stead. That's what we decided five years ago!" The kappa now munched on the cucumber, beginning to cry as well. "But this is pointless. Ringo and Momoka are different people!"

"Even so, aren't you Ringo's mother?!" The otter stood up on the chair wildly, throwing the clam down on to the floor. "It's just fate!"

"Fate?" At that word, the kappa looked down. Finally, it stood straight up on the chair, and said, "That's too cruel!" It ripped the plate from atop its head and cast it onto the floor. The plate broke with a great snapping sound.

Suddenly, a large-headed eel, longer than the little girl was tall, appeared, trying to slip by her feet. Its eyes shone black, and its mouth gaped wide. It spit bubbles as it twisted its long torso, marked with a plethora of blackish spots, swimming through the gap into the living room.

The fearsome eel swam, fins rippling, flapping about at the kappa and the otter with its flank. Water suddenly flooded the living room, and the kappa and otter wept, bobbing up and down, head over heel.

"This is our fate. Until we accept that, we can't move forward," said the otter. It did not even grab for the clam floating nearby.

"Is accepting it our only choice? If that happens, our family will scatter and drift apart!"

The kappa was still hysterical.

Papa and Mama are crying. I'm a bad girl, because I can't be big sis Momoka. I know that. But I know exactly what "fate" is. If I can be just like Momoka, then Papa and Mama won't fight anymore. We'll always, allllways be together.

Our whole family can be together.

The anxious girl held her kappa and otter plushies tight, the wheels in her head turning. She was so gripped by sadness and guilt, she couldn't take another step.

On the floor, the puddle leaking out from her spread, sadly and silently.

The eel and the water flooding the living room vanished without her noticing, and her parents returned to their normal, shadowed human shapes.

It was seven years later, the thirteenth anniversary of Momoka's death. Ringo and Tabuki sat side by side, eating the curry her mother made. By now, Ringo and her mother had started a new life, in a spacious, tidy condo along a slope.

"Don't hold back now. Eat as much as you like!" Her mother took off the apron that she wore over her mourning clothes, folded it up, and sat down at the table.

"I will, thank you very much," Tabuki quietly replied, clothed in a suit he was unaccustomed to wearing.

"Thank you for always being Momoka's friend, Keiju-kun," her mother said wistfully, but with a smile.

"Oh, no, of course." Tabuki's eyes lowered behind his glasses, and his hand holding his spoon stopped moving. "Momoka-san was my entire world when we were young. It was fate."

Hearing that word, Ringo's head snapped up, and she took a firm look at Tabuki's throat and chin and cheeks and the skin of his forehead and eyes and damp-looking eyelashes. This man seemed far more mature than her, she thought.

Walking along the evening road with Ringo at his side, Tabuki watched their shadows stretching across the asphalt with a tranquil feeling.

"You didn't have to walk me all the way to the station." His eyes fell toward Momoka's little sister, still so young. He could not deny that there was something in her aloof profile that resembled Momoka. But obviously, she was a different person. "What's the matter? You've been so quiet."

Ringo, clad in her black dress, asked him somberly, "Tabuki-san, was my sister really that special?"

Stunned at the unexpected question, his eyes widened slightly, and he looked again at little Ringo's serious face.

"Ringo-chan, do you know how to ride a bicycle?"

"Uh-huh." She gave an obedient nod.

"Well then, what would you do if, back before you knew how to ride, someone told you, 'Come ride this bike, right now?'"

"That's impossible. I'd fall. And also..."

And also, what? What was she trying to say? Ringo's pace slowed.

"The moment you learned how to ride, you forgot what it was like not to be able to, right?" As he turned around to face her again, Tabuki's face was lit by the orange glow of the setting sun.

"Uh-huh."

Tabuki's eyes narrowed, and he looked up to the sky.

"In that same way, it's thanks to Momoka that I learned how to ride. The feeling of wind rushing past my ears, pushing forward through the air. The scenery rushing by so quickly it was startling. Momoka changed what should have been a familiar world to me into something special in an instant. She really did change me," he said emphatically. "When I was with Momoka, the sky and the birds and the clouds, even the little pebbles at my feet, seemed like treasures, concealing new possibilities. Riding in tandem, we could ride on forever."

Having said that all in one breath, Tabuki let out a sigh. He inhaled softly, and a lonesome look returned to him.

"But I can't ever go back to that time. I still know how to ride a bike, but I can't remember what those treasures were. Now and then, I suddenly think, 'Why is Momoka no longer in this world?' To me, a world without Momoka feels incomplete."

This was a complicated conversation, Ringo thought. But it was not as if she didn't understand. It was just that Tabuki was incredibly sad, and the fact that his sadness would never end sunk into Ringo's heart like the setting sun.

"Tabuki-san, are you not happy?"

When he finished speaking about Momoka, more than being simply mature, his face in profile looked like that of an old man, one who had long since been left behind.

"I loved Momoka. So, I still have a lot of sadness and anger that I don't know what to do with. But, if this was all part of fate's plan, then surely there is some reason for all of it. At least, that's what I'd like to think." Finally, the youthful look returned to his face, and he smiled.

It was then that Ringo knew for certain what it was that she had to do, in accordance with fate.

When she returned home, Ringo headed straight for the desk in her room. In the bottom of the lowest drawer in the desk she inherited from Momoka, her diary was hidden. She picked up the diary, which had the name "Momoka" written on the back cover in little letters, considering "Fate's Plan." If finding the diary now, at this stage, was also fate, then everything was unfolding as it should.

She opened the cover reverently and drew in a breath.

"Here, I write the fate of the world," Ringo read aloud, her voice steady. "When the future that is written here becomes reality, the things that I cherish should become eternal." The sentences scrawled here in round, childish letters were engraved deeply into Ringo's heart.

Ringo needed to become Momoka. That was Ringo's destiny, and both her father and Tabuki were surely waiting for it to come to pass.

Now, delirious with fever, Ringo clutched the diary to her chest.

If Ringo could become one with Momoka, then everything she cherished would return to her. And she would be happy forever.

"Survival Tactiiiiic!!!"

A wind of white lace blew. The fluttering cloth brushed my cheeks, and that sweet, sweet, mind-melting smell filled my nostrils. Between the gaps of the flood of lace, red-eyed Himari appeared. With the penguin hat atop her head, the heels of her boots clacking, in an instant, she changed the room into that alternate space.

"You worthless nothings were given your orders! You must obtain the Penguindrum!" She stretched her hand out, placing her foot forcefully atop Penguin No. 3's head. The sleeves of her dress swayed.

"No, c'mon, this is impossible! Today, she collapsed with a fever, saying something about her first night, and how it was fate and some stuff, and, uh? Aniki's not here. Is it just me today?" A familiar hopelessness seized me.

Paying me no mind, Himari pointed at my nose, and said, "It is the duty of you cretins to actualize that 'fate' immediately, and snatch the Penguindrum from her! Listen. Whether it's a first night or a deflowering or what have you, you are to make that pervert girl's desires happen!"

"Stop saying filthy things through Himari's mouth!" I said, raising a somewhat irrelevant objection. The penguin hat's speech contained a malice that was utterly incomparable to the normal Himari.

"Silence, heretic!" Himari clicked her tongue.

"You're the one who's a heretic! Taking people's little sisters hostage!" I suppressed the urge to cover my ears.

"A first-class heretic in the Promised Land! I will end you!" she spat.

"What the hell are you, some kind of thug?! That's so out-dated!" I already had a premonition of what was to come.

Penguin No. 2 was already scrambling away from me. "W-wait! No. 2, stop! Hey!"

The button was pressed, and I was flung into the darkness. What the heck was I supposed to do here? All I wanted was to save Himari.

"Shall we initiate the Survival Tactic?!"

Though she realized it was a very old-fashioned strategy, Ringo arranged her bed's pillows to look like a sleeping body, and then slipped out of the house in her nightgown. All she had to do was board the train from East Koenji to Ogikubo, and then the train would carry her straight to his side.

"Our first night together. There's no changing fate," Ringo said vaguely to herself, taking a seat in the corner of the empty train.

It was already dark as she slipped into the familiar grounds of Tabuki's building, pulling back the tarp.

Tonight was her first night with Tabuki. She needed to hear his sleeping breath nearby. Clutching only the luggage that she could carry, she squeezed herself beneath Tabuki's apartment. Rolling on the ground, breathing raggedly, she picked up the sounds from his room.

There was Tabuki whistling, and the sound of a frying pan moving skillfully.

Ringo shut her eyes tight, listening to those sounds for a while, then pulled out a camping stove and began her slapdash cooking, still lying on her stomach.

"The first thing we did as a couple was make dinner together.

It got a little burnt, but Tabuki-kun told me it was delicious, like he always does," Ringo recited from the diary.

Guessing when Tabuki would be sitting down at his table, Ringo began eating her own, purposely burnt, vegetable stirfry.

"And thus, our carefree life together began. Tonight, however, both he and I were to finally truly touch one another."

Tabuki finished up his meal while watching a documentary on wild birds, and then slipped into the bath. Ringo pulled out a small washbasin and toothbrush as well. She filled it with mineral water from a bottle and went through her evening routine.

"We even bought new toothbrushes for tonight. Tabuki-kun's is blue, and mine is pink."

Tabuki stepped out of the bath, brushed his teeth, laid out his futon, and turned out the lights in his room. Ringo listened as he took off his glasses and snuggled into the futon. Judging by the sounds alone, Ringo crept around the subfloor space, trying to get close to him in her simplistic reproduction of the room.

She spread out the mattress from her room on the ground and made a partition with a blue cloth. Within was Ka-chan and Ot-chan, and the special picture of all three of her family together. She had a pillow shaped like a jellyfish, and her favorite tea set. The peach-shaped alarm clock was there, too. Decorating the inside of the little space with a beaded curtain and the ornaments that had hung from her chandelier, this space was now unmistakably Ringo's new home.

On the humanoid outline drawn on the ceiling, directly in her line of sight as she lay down, she'd affixed a photo of Tabuki's face. Ringo began speaking fervently within her mind.

Tabuki, do you remember? That day, when you told me that everything happens for a reason. I believe in that. Fate is like a hopelessly enormous ring, a wheel that's constantly spinning, drinking up everyone's joy and sadness.

Ringo lay down, just beside the space where Tabuki would likely be sleeping. She might have been underground, but for Ringo, this was no different from sleeping beside him.

Ringo knew. She had been born into the orbit of Momoka's fate. Tabuki loved Momoka. And so, Ringo would become Momoka.

Despite the floor between them, Ringo embraced Tabuki, both body and soul. So that the future written in her diary could become reality. So that the things she cherished could become eternal.

Natsume Masako looked up at the night sky through a tall window, drinking milk tea, as was her routine before bed. She unconsciously rubbed together the pointer finger and thumb of her left hand.

Masako was vaguely amused by the girls who flocked to people like her and Kuho Asami. Their movements were entertainingly predictable, but this was nothing more than the prologue to the project she was soon to begin.

The soft melody of a piano tune echoed through the apartment, the second movement of Symphony No. 9 by Antonín Leopold

Dvořák: "Going Home." The fire burning in the fireplace threw off warmth and flickering shadows into the room. Steam rose from her gaudy porcelain teacup.

"Yes, yes indeed. Everything is proceeding according to plan." Masako smiled faintly, stroking the head of the penguin that sat atop her lap, eyes glinting.

"Yes, it has been confirmed. The orbit of fate is within our grasp. Soon, Project M will be underway," said the voice on the other end of the receiver.

Masako chuckled. Her beautiful curls swayed gently as she laughed.

CHAPTER 07

OGINOME-SAN, predictably, was lying on the mattress in her new home beneath the floor, her diary open. Through the beaded curtain that served as the entrance to her room, one could see her listening to the sounds of Tabuki's daily life, through headphones attached to the receiver by her pillow. She smacked her cheek, crushing a mosquito that landed on her face, and grinned.

I slowly approached her, my eyebrows already knit in concern.

"Are you, are you plotting something again?" I asked, plopping a hand down on her shoulder.

"Eeek!" She clutched the diary to her chest in shock. The headphones fell from her head.

"When will you get it through your thick skull not to invade other people's privacy?!" she coughed, trying to ward off the smoke, after shooting me a glare. "What is this? You trying to smoke me out?"

"Just use this for now. The tiger mosquitoes must be terrible down here, right?" I once more offered her the lit mosquito coil.

"There are other ways to get rid of bugs these days!"

Not knowing what else to say, I silently placed the mosquito coil in the corner of Oginome-san's so-called "new home," then picked up two teacups off of the nearby tray. I peeked inside to make sure there was no dirt, lightly brushed them off and looked around for some tea to pour into them.

"So, um, how long do you plan on keeping this up?" I poured some green tea into each of the cups from a plastic bottle set among the sweet bread and chocolates.

"Until my plan is finished. I told you about this, didn't I? Project M!" She peered in the mirror, making sure that the recently dispatched mosquito had not bitten her.

"That M in Project M doesn't stand for 'marriage' or something, does it?" I politely offered Oginome-san a teacup, kneeling and curving my back for some reason. The phrase 'house husband' floated unpleasantly through my mind.

"That's not it at all."

"I-I see." I was relieved at her emotionless reply.

She turned back toward me, straightening up her back as far as she could, and added, "Project M is a large-scale creative project, the likes of which you could not even imagine."

"Creative?" I repeated, even now worried my head might collide with the ceiling.

"Oh, I wonder what Tabuki-san is doing right now," she suddenly muttered, distracted and ignoring me.

"Well, he lives alone, so he probably watches dirty videos on the internet at night, wouldn't he?" I muttered.

"Tabuki-san does not watch such things," she said resolutely, sipping her tea as if this were perfectly obvious.

"I wonder." Just because she didn't see it didn't mean it didn't happen.

"If you're finished here, shouldn't you be heading home?" she said, declaring me a nuisance, a crinkle forming on her nose.

"I am not here because I enjoy it!" I was here because I needed to borrow that diary, the Penguindrum, from her. That's why I was here, looking out for her like this.

She sneakily pulled out her phone, looking at the screen as if to hide it from me.

"I'm not gonna peek at your phone."

"You see! He *wasn't* watching dirty videos," she said, then thrust the phone out in front of my eyes. "He was writing a love letter to me!" She smiled, satisfied.

"If you don't mind, would you like to go see a play with me next Sunday? I was given two tickets to a popular show. I think you'll enjoy it, and it would be a nice break from studying," I mumbled, reading the text aloud. It was no love letter, but at the very least it could be interpreted as an invitation to a date.

"What a liar, that Tabuki-san, saying someone *gave* him the tickets. Alright, let's do this, Ringo! Forward, onto our destiny!" She pumped her fist, which collided with the low ceiling. "Ow!"

"Won't he get suspicious if you keep making all this noise under the floor?"

It seemed unlikely that he would lie about receiving the tickets. I doubted that a simple man like Tabuki had that kind of imagination. Plus, didn't he already have that beautiful lady?

There was the graceful and refined Tokikago Yuri-san, kind, with an indomitable smile and good at cooking to boot, who somehow had eyes only for Tabuki. Would someone with a girlfriend like that really be swayed by Oginome-san, even mistakenly?

"Wonder what I should wear?"

I could think of nothing to say to Oginome-san, who clutched her jellyfish pillow in ecstasy, but I hoped she wouldn't get her hopes up too much.

I flashed a look to Penguin No. 2, who stealthily hunted for sweets. He misread my look and rushed over, handing me a chocolate.

East Ikebukuro Sunshiny Playhouse was a far larger and more impressive place than she imagined.

Sitting in her assigned seat, Ringo's eyes fell to the playbill in her hands, with an expression like she had just swallowed a fly. *The East Ikebukuro Sunshiny Opera Company presents, "Death and Paris—The Tragedy of M."* A photo of Tokikago Yuri, dressed as a queen and with an otokoyaku actress embracing her, was boldly splashed across the front. An extravagant, sparkling chandelier, smattered with crystals, hung from the high ceiling like a joke. Tabuki, sitting beside Ringo, looked incredibly pleased and a little excited.

When Tabuki said that he "was given some tickets," it had not been a lie.

Ringo had worn a cobalt blue dress, her favorite one. Unlike usual, she paired it with a rather sophisticated-looking handbag. Normally, she wore only lip gloss, but today she perked her eyelashes just slightly with a curler and applied a light coat of mascara. Not that Tabuki noticed in the slightest.

"This is the first time I'm getting to watch this play properly. I'm excited." Tabuki, clad in an unassuming jacket, smiled, a slight blush forming on his cheeks.

How could his voice be so lacking in malice? Ringo wondered. And why did no one ever consider what a terrible thing it could be to be so kind?

"I see," Ringo replied with a wry smile.

Finally, the starting announcements came, and the house lights slowly grew dark. The way that they were sucked further and further into darkness resembled the state of Ringo's heart. It was difficult to breathe.

"It's starting!" Tabuki said softly, fixing his glasses.

The deep crimson curtain rose along with the music. A spotlight flashed down on the pitch-black stage, to show Tokikago Yuri standing there. This alone brought cheers, sighs, and applause from the audience.

"Oh, there's Yuri! Heeey!" Tabuki waved his hands innocently.

Ringo subtly pursed her lips, puffing out her cheeks.

The play depicted a striking romantic tragedy. Dazzling dresses and gorgeous voices soaring in song. Ringo kept looking at Tabuki, but his eyes were glued to the stage, to Yuri, leaving Ringo feeling very alone.

Yuri, portraying a heroine toyed with by fate, was dazzling and beautiful. When Ringo first encountered her at Tabuki's apartment, and when she came to Wadazuka Park, she was always gorgeous, flawless. That alone irritated Ringo and made her feel wretched.

Why would Tabuki invite her to watch this play? As she watched him take out his bird-patterned handkerchief and dab his tears, Ringo's loneliness grew deeper.

Yuri received a wave of applause from the audience as her voice rang out high. The curtain call ended, the curtains fell, and finally the lights came back up over the seats.

Ringo was exhausted.

"Ah, that was amazing! I've still got butterflies," Tabuki said to Ringo, his eyes and nose reddened, presumably from tears.

"Yeah, me too," she replied, then bit her lip.

The entrance of the green room was backed up with throngs of female fans holding bouquets and presents. Tabuki pulled Ringo along behind him, purposefully giving the fans a wide berth. If he reached his hand out to her so that they would not be separated, so that she would not get lost, Ringo would have gladly taken it. She would have even been able to forgive the group of shrieking women, she thought, hazily watching Tabuki's back.

"Gosh, that was so moving. Real live actresses really are amazing. That last line of hers was so good," said Tabuki, his eyes sparkling, as though he had not yet fully returned from the world of the play.

Suddenly, the fans were abuzz. Yuri appeared, escorted by a male-clothed actress. She wore a slim dress that accentuated the lines of her body, and she smiled gently.

The fans descended on her like an avalanche, pushing Tabuki and Ringo aside.

"Wah, we'll never get close this way! I wanted to take her to out to eat or something, as a thank you," Tabuki said with a wry smile. "That's too bad. Should we go somewhere with just us two?"

Ringo lifted her face with unintentional force. Just the two of them. Tabuki definitely said that just now. Go somewhere, just the two of them. Anywhere was fine. Maybe even somewhere where he could notice that she was slightly more made up than usual. Somewhere where he could plainly see how hard Ringo was trying, wearing her favorite dress.

"Y-yes! I'd love to!" It was a strong reply, leagues more impressive than the calls of staff at a local izakaya. "Let's go somewhere, just the two of us."

"Oh sorry, just a sec." Just then, Tabuki apparently received a message on his phone. "Oh, it's from Yuri. Says she wants to avoid starting rumors or something. Oh wow, she's so sensible. She's already made reservations for a restaurant." Tabuki looked back, excited.

Ringo glared at Yuri, surrounded by her fans. When Yuri noticed her gaze, she returned a placid smile, waving just her fingertips at her.

"This is perfect, Ringo-chan! It's an invitation from a star, I'm sure it'll be her treat!" Tabuki laughed foolishly.

Once again, Tabuki had not the slightest idea how the sweetness in his voice made something crumple in Ringo's heart.

The restaurant that Yuri booked them for dinner was gorgeous and showy even from its brick façade. When they arrived, still wrapped up in the atmosphere of the theater, it was like delving into an even more profound, sophisticated world.

Tabuki nervously gave the staff the name on the reservation, and with a polite greeting and a quiet smile, an impeccable hostess led them to their seats. The thick carpet covering the floor silenced their footsteps.

There were white tablecloths, and little lamps decorating each of the tables, and red roses. They quietly took their seats in the chairs pulled out by the staff. The other diners nearby were calmly and gracefully enjoying their meals.

The hostess gave a perfunctory "Please enjoy," and was gone.

The interior furnishings, mostly colored in a wine red, were highlighted here and there with deep gold accents. A dim light passed through the murals etched in the glass on the ceiling, reaching to their hands.

"This place is sort of intimidating," said Tabuki with a faint smile on his face, looking around nervously.

Frankly, Ringo was a little moved. A world of even greater luxury than the playhouse or the theater itself unfolded before her eyes. Beyond the faint light, Tabuki was nervous, but he was still an "adult," still far closer to this world than Ringo. He was moving further and further into this world, drawn along by Tokikago Yuri. This was meant to be a message to Ringo, wasn't it?

A waiter finally appeared, suggesting they might order some aperitifs while waiting for Yuri, but Tabuki refrained.

"So sorry to keep you waiting," said Yuri as she finally arrived, without a hint of hurry, guided along with a clutch in one hand.

Her freshly applied makeup was understated, but more than enough to make an impression on Yuki's face, gorgeous in its own right. Her well-made, elegant dress and delicate accessories were nothing compared to her own beauty, and her smile shone like an endless firework, distorting everything one could see.

A sea of gazes followed Yuri as she languidly took her seat at the table with Ringo and Tabuki.

"Look, it's that actress, Tokikago Yuri!"

"Goodness, she's even prettier than on TV."

Ringo could hear every one of the insolent voices, but the actress in question merely took the menu that was brought to her, not caring a whit.

"The two of you must be famished. I was thinking of ordering a prix fixe, but would that be alright? Is there anything you can't eat?"

"As long as there are no carrots, I'm fine," said Tabuki, his cheeks reddening, completely taken with Yuri.

"That's right," she tittered. "Ringo-chan, what about you?"

"I'm fine with anyything," she answered in a tiny voice, glancing at Yuri.

As she smoothly gave their order to the waiter, Yuri was so lovely that even the women in the room could not take their eyes off of her. Even the waiter's cheeks began to redden.

Once she finished ordering, Yuri took a breath, and then a single swallow from her glass of water. Her throat moved silently. In the soft, orange light, her skin looked pale and delicate, and her glossy smile turned slowly toward Ringo.

"Thank you, truly, for coming to watch me today." Gently, she took Ringo's hand.

"Of course." Seeing Yuri's face so close, Ringo found herself enchanted, flustered.

"Tabuki-kun begged me, he insisted that you absolutely had to see me up on the stage. I hope it wasn't too much of a bother." Her eyelids shone with a meticulous liner. Her long, lustrous eyelashes framed jewel-like eyes, which could be clearly seen even from the distant audience. Her hand in Ringo's was soft.

Without waiting for Ringo to reply, Tabuki said, "Seriously, I loved it. Ringo was totally lost in the story the whole time, too. Right?"

His guileless voice grated at Ringo's little heart.

"Yes. It was...quite wonderful," she replied, forcing a smile. She pulled her hand swiftly away from Yuri's and unconsciously shifted slightly away.

Why did she have to start blushing when Yuri of all people gazed at her? Especially since this could be some sinister plot on Yuri's part, using her status as an actress to get Ringo to give up on Tabuki.

Tokikago Yuri *was* an actress. She could probably muster a kind smile in front of anyone. There was no doubt behind that beautiful glass mask, she concealed the true soul of a killer whale, a predator that slunk through the raging seas of the entertainment world. She had cosumed countless prey before now, and was always on the prowl, watching for the right moment to gobble up her target.

Tabuki had been thoroughly deceived, smiling within her trap, and that was no good. This wolfish woman had surely risen to her position through some nefarious means, and if you scratched the surface, you'd find a darkness in her body and soul. Tabuki, weak and innocent, would surely be swallowed whole.

"How about next Sunday?" Tabuki suddenly asked.

Ringo jerked back to her senses with a "Huh?"

"Are you free?" he asked.

"I've been planning a little party," said Yuri, smiling gently. "You'll come, won't you Ringo-chan? You can even bring that cute boyfriend of yours from the other day, Takakura-kun, was it?"

"That was not my boyfriend!" Ringo protested, louder than intended. That Yuri would bring this up in front of Tabuki was just more evidence of the dark nature churning within her.

"Oh dear, really? That's too bad. I thought you made a lovely couple." She cast her gaze at Tabuki, looking for assurance.

"Well, that's alright. You can invite Takakura anyway. He's a fellow birdwatcher, after all. He definitely has an interest in wild birds," said Tabuki, positively elated.

That was not how she wanted him to smile at her. That first night. Of course, it had only been in her imagination, but his kindness had been incomparable. In her mind, he gazed at Ringo with warm, glistening eyes and stroked her hair. He complimented her, told her that the slight fierceness of her gaze was adorable, and he held Ringo tight, so that they would not grow cold.

He could not be here in this flashy world of adults, clinking glasses with this black-hearted whale woman and happily discussing parties. It seemed fake, like a movie.

"Then it's decided," said Yuri, once more lifting her wine glass.

Tabuki lifted his glass in turn. "Cheers," he said, smiling wide.

Ringo slammed her tepidly raised glass of iced tea down on the table.

"Are you alright?" asked Yuri. "I know the play was long, perhaps you're a bit worn out." Suddenly, her long, white fingers brushed Ringo's cheek.

Ringo looked at her in shock. She felt her cheeks unwittingly growing hot.

"That dress you're wearing today is terribly cute, but make sure you dress up for the party as well," Yuri added.

For a moment, Ringo was unsure if she was saying this seriously, or out of malice.

The dress that she had so carefully chosen had been called cute but once today, and of all people, it was by that loathsome, black-hearted whale woman.

In the spacious courtyard, surrounded by a moonlit white mansion, the sounds of a live string ensemble resounded. The electric lights woven through the trees shone like scattered jewels. This was by no means just a "little" party.

People in formal wear passed between the round tables and numerous catering carts, champagne glasses in hand. In the middle of this stood Oginome-san, wearing a red floral print dress, with a similarly red headband upon her head, and myself, wearing my best jacket, with a folded-up shopping bag in my pocket out of habit, each of us holding a glass of orange juice. At my feet was Penguin No. 2, chomping devotedly on some food it requisitioned from somewhere.

"This place is kind of amazing," I said. It was like Christmas, out of season, or a theme park at night. At any rate, I had never seen such a sight. It was a beautiful, otherworldly, balmy evening.

There was a stirring amongst the guests, and I looked up in time to see Tokikago Yuri enter the terrace from the house. Her swept-up hair was decorated with a white lily, and she wore a long, pearly pink gown that showed her shoulders, frills flowing abundantly from the chest. A string of diamonds swayed from each of her ear lobes, glittering and refracting the light.

"Oh, it's Yuri-san." Shoma straightened up. "Wow, she's even more sparkly today."

"Hmph! Everyone's just fooled by that woman's appearance!" Oginome-san crossed her arms, seeming particularly displeased, and chugged her glass of juice in a single gulp.

"This again? Look, why don't you just give it up already? There's no way you can win with a rival like that." Unfortunately, this was my sincere opinion. Even leaving aside the fact that she was an accomplished actress, Tokikago Yuri was exceedingly beautiful, kind, and sincere. She was also calm, or at the very least, she would not glare at anyone like Oginome-san glared at me, laying her emotions bare.

"Don't be stupid! Everyone's just fussing over her because she's an actress. I know far more about Tabuki-san, anyway!"

Oginome-san snapped her hand open, and started counting on her fingers, babbling insecurely. "I know what time he wakes up, and that he loves his toast with lots of marmalade, and what toothpaste brand he prefers. I know he's good at making vegetable stir-fry, and a little bad at discarding the water from a yakisoba cup. I know what tunes he's been whistling lately, and what kind of things he says in his sleep. I'm the only one who knows all of this!"

I could not listen to anymore of this nonsense. I overcame my embarrassment at being just a terribly average high school boy and called softly to a nearby waiter. I had only reluctantly agreed to come along because I'd been told there would be lots of good food. My house husbandly heart filled with sadness of wanting to let Himari and Kanba eat some of this food as well.

"Excuse me, this red dish and this yellow thing here, how many could I have packed up to take home with me?" I pointed to the dishes heaped up on one of the round tables, the names of which I did not know.

"Hang on, what are you doing?! That's so embarrassing!" Oginome-san shouted, walking briskly over.

"I'm taking some home to Himari! Also, do you think I could get an autograph from Yuri-san? I brought an autograph board."

She grabbed my ear and tugged hard.

"Owww!"

"Were you listening to a word I was just saying?!" she grumbled in my ear.

"I was listening!"

"Then you understand, don't you?" The tone of her voice suddenly dropped. "Just what exactly did you assume I brought you here for?"

"What for...?" As I considered her question, I continued my appeal to the waiter. "Oh, also, could I ask for one of those cake-y things?" I gave him a stupid smile. The waiter grimaced in reply.

Hearing this, Oginome-san yanked on my ear even harder.

"Owwwwwwww!"

"You're here to watch and make sure that black widow doesn't get any closer to Tabuki-san!" she said in a loud whisper.

"But that's ridiculous." I looked at Yuri-san, who was making rounds amongst her guests, offering them polite greetings. But convincing you to go along with her ridiculous plans was just a terrifying superpower that Oginome-san wielded.

"The diary. You want to borrow it, don't you?" It helped that she already had solid leverage against me.

"I do." I hung my head, finally released. Just how far would I have to go before she was satisfied?

Though I had told her to give up, given that her rival was someone as amazing at Tokikago Yuri, it wouldn't be that simple if she really loved Tabuki. Still, judging by her progress so far, the issue here wasn't what she'd learned about through her stalking. Even she should know that, deep down.

Suddenly everyone's attention was drawn to the sound of interference from the microphone.

On a little stage that had been erected in front of the house stood a striking, short-haired woman, wearing a tuxedo. She was more than likely an otokoyaku actress from the East Ikebukuro Sunshiny Opera Company. She stood quietly before the microphone, looking sharper and more masculine than I certainly did.

"Ahem, we know that the night is currently in full swing, and everyone here is busy enjoying themselves, but now, Tokikago Yuri has a very important announcement to make."

Even her voice had a manly ring, and I had to wonder if it was intentional.

"Come, my love!"

As I stood there, moved by the woman and her quip that would have been unthinkable for any man, and the power of the Sunshiny Opera Company, the music swelled. Yuri-san ascended the stage, the ends of her dress fluttering marvelously. She bowed deeply, and applause rose as she lifted her head.

"Everyone, thank you sincerely for taking the time out of your busy day to join me here."

The applause gradually silenced.

"Now then, I know this is sudden, but I have gathered you all here today to announce that after finishing the tour currently underway, I will be retiring from the East Ikebukuro Sunshiny Opera Company."

The crowd stirred in surprise.

I was shocked as well, and looked at Oginome-san, to see that her eyes were open wide. She had just condemned the woman for being fussed over for being an actress, and now it looked like she was quitting being an actress, after all.

"And, there is one more thing." Yuri-san looked to the side of the stage. There, approaching timidly, was Tabuki, dressed in thoroughly unsuited formalwear. "I would like to introduce you all to someone. This is Tabuki Keiju-san, and I am honored to announce that just the other day, we became engaged!"

There was an instant of silence before the applause erupted, along with the cries of "Congratulations" and "Best wishes!" Yuri-san held back tears, her face reddening, and Tabuki grinned bashfully.

"Thank you so much. I will be retiring from the stage in order to start a new life with the man I love, but the irreplaceable treasures I acquired there will always live on in my heart, both as a person, and as a woman."

Yuri-san bowed her head deeply, her throat tightening with a rush of tears.

Tabuki smiled at her, similarly moved, and placed a hand on her back.

My jaw dropped. This was not the commotion one would expect of a "little party." This story would definitely be all over the entertainment news tomorrow morning.

"Stop! Stooop! Banish this gloom from such a joyous occasion!" said the woman in the tuxedo. Her beautiful voice echoed across the entire grounds, as she held Yuri-san tight. "Let blessings rain down upon my most beloved partner and this dreadful man who is stealing her away from me!" She spread her arms cheerfully, pretending to strike Tabuki on the shoulder.

The grounds erupted in laughter.

Oginome-san had frozen, her hand still gripping my ear. I tentatively turned to look at her. Her hand swayed from my ear like a pendulum.

Just as I wondered whether or not I should say something to her, she fell backward as though struck, inadvertently sending Penguin No. 2, who devoured the hors d'oeuvres piled on the table behind us, scrambling to get out of her way.

The string ensemble changed into a lively dance number, but we were unable to dance.

It was quiet on the train, with only the steady vibration and noise moving us. We were speechless for a while. Oginome-san sat in a seat separate from us, as if cornered, clutching to the handrail as though for dear life.

I had never comforted a broken-hearted girl. I never even had my heart broken myself. Honestly, I felt the urge to rub salt into her wound. However, for Himari's sake I would have to go along with this.

"Um so, about the diary," I finally started, speaking my mind. "Given the recent developments, you don't really need it anymore, do you?"

The silence was more awkward than I predicted, and fell heavy on my shoulders. I would have far preferred the usual irrational words she threw my way to this.

"I mean, look, Tabuki's gone, engaged to Yuri-san. There's no room for you to get between them anymore." My grip on the paper bag I received from the waiter tightened slightly.

"No," she said softly, to no one. "This sort of thing is no setback to Project M. Victory is still within my grasp, and I am the one who will live with Tabuki-san under one roof." Her voice was hoarse and weak.

"Under one roof?" So that was her end goal after all, the dream she trying to force into reality. The fact that she coerced me to help stung, but she certainly was not living with him or anything like that.

"Plus, there's still more to the diary. That is proof. The fate that binds he and I. Yes, this is nothing more than a test of our love." Her face, as she lifted it, was no longer pale or clouded.

I had begun to empathize with her the slightest bit, but now I was stunned beyond words. This went beyond mere optimism. She really *was* a stalker, after all. This was the hollow shell of a self-centered, one-sided love, where she could only interpret everything that was happening as being in her favor.

"By the way." She stared at me, a devilish look in her eye. "How old are you?" I had seen that particular grin plenty of times before, but now it sent a shiver down my spine. I got the sense that nothing good was coming my way.

As the bizarre comedy of Shoma and Ringo unfolded, on a train several lines over, Kanba checked the contents of an envelope.

"Looks right. Now we can stay in our house for a while longer." He stuffed the envelope into his pocket and continued, "And then..."

From the opposite pocket, he drew out that burnt black ball.

"There are only so many people who use these. I don't suppose this particular sequence of events is *your* doing?" he asked. He carefully watched the person he was addressing, paying more attention to their reaction than their answer itself. However, even his sharp gaze missed the sight of Natsume Masako, who observed him from the next car over.

Standing by the wall, Masako was enrapt in Kanba's voice.

"Goodness, we'd better crush him soon," she whispered, gently rubbing her index finger and thumb together. She spun around, looking at Kanba's back out of the corner of her eye.

In her bag, her phone vibrated, right on time. She pulled it out and put it to her ear.

"Yes, I'm making the delivery now. Understood. I'll continue things on this end. Project M must be achieved."

There was no beauty at all in such simple, businesslike exchanges, Masako thought, but her conversation partner had absolutely no use for exchanging beautiful words. She breathed a little sigh and slipped the phone back into her bag.

Despite how stylish the building seemed during the day, the school at night had a dreadful atmosphere. All I wanted was to get home before the doggy bag the waiter packed for me got damaged.

Oginome-san, always needlessly prepared, took a small flashlight from her handbag, shining it at our feet as she led me along. I would never have imagined that I would be setting foot in Oukagyoen Girls' High School in such circumstances.

We cut through the wide, expansive courtyard and entered the building, hurrying down the utterly silent hallway.

"Hey, is this really okay?" Penguin No. 2, at my feet, clung to my legs in fear. It was difficult to walk like that, so I had begrudgingly bent down to pick it up.

"It's fine. I looked at the guard rotation. Even if we get caught, I can just say I forgot something and came back to get it, and we should be fine."

Oginome-san must have intended on dragging me into the school at night from the beginning. I doubted she just happened to have packed a flashlight and looked up the guards' rotation just because she was a stalker.

"In your case, maybe! A high school boy sneaking into a girls' school at night is totally..." I trailed off when I saw a doorplate reading, "Special Girls' Changing Room." What was so special about it? Not that it mattered, since going in was completely out of the question. Perverted. A special kind of perverted.

I nervously followed her for a while, when suddenly she came to a halt.

"We're here. Though I'd hoped to end things without doing this."

I looked up to see we were at the science lab. My face twitched as I imagined dangerous chemicals and experiments. It was harrowing to know that I was the only one in a position who might be able to stop to Oginome-san's reckless behavior.

As quietly as possible, we entered the pitch-dark lab. Oginome-san opened the curtains one after the other. As she did, the once dark classroom flooded with the light of the full moon, illuminating what looked like a magic circle made of fluorescent paint on a large lab table.

"Wh-what is this?" I stumbled back, my lower back colliding with the table just behind me.

Ignoring my question, she lit a candle and pulled off the cloth covering something square on another table, like a magician. Beneath it was a terrarium, with a large, bizarrely colored toad.

"Whoa, a toad?"

No. 2's eyes flashed at the toad from my arms. It leaned forward and tumbled onto the floor.

Oginome-san took out a laptop and booted it up, loading a page that read "Dulcamara's School of Magic Potions." When she clicked through, it had a photo of a toad, just like the one in the terrarium, along with an explanation.

"Read this," she said, handing me the laptop before double-checking the markings in her magic circle.

"The Tamahomare Toad is a miraculous toad, emerging from underground once every sixteen years. On the night of the full moon, have this toad lay its eggs on the back of a sixteen-year-old male. The powder made from drying and crushing those eggs can be made into a love potion, and when two people drink it, they will be bound eternally in love," I read earnestly, in a soft voice.

"This thing reeks. Where did you even find this toad? Don't tell me you painted this thing yourself?" I grimaced reflexively.

The toad's head was a brilliant green, its belly yellow, and the rest of its body was covered in black spots. Its eyes were huge and jet black, and bizarre markings trailed across its back. It definitely did not look like something that would appear in Japan in autumn.

"Obviously not. Now, strip," she said, as though this were perfectly obvious.

"Huh? Strip?"

"Did you not read it? The Tamahomare Toad is going to lay its eggs on your back!" Her eyes glinted as she donned a pair of rubber gloves.

"Huh?!" The sixteen-year-old male in question was me?!

"You want the diary, don't you? For Himari's sake."

"I... do. But—"

"Then strip."

Despite an expression suggesting that she hated this as much as me, Oginome-san reached into the terrarium and timidly picked up the toad.

Feeling as though I was about to cry, I quietly removed my jacket.

In the center of the magic circle, I lay on my belly, bare from the waist up, with candles standing in each direction. The desk was chilly, the huge, slimy toad sat atop my back, and Oginome-san hurled abuse at me every time I moved a muscle. It was cold and absolutely miserable. I felt like I was being tortured, or else laid out like some kind of sacrifice.

"That's weird. It's already been two hours, but it hasn't laid a single egg!"

Oginome-san slammed the desk in frustration, narrowing her eyes and looking at me like a mad scientist, twisting her neck back toward the laptop and reading over the instructions again.

"It's for Himari, it's for Himari, it's for Himari," I muttered. If I kept chanting at that rate, I just might have attained spiritual enlightenment.

"It looks like the ideal birthing temperature is one hundred and seven degrees." She turned around, asking me sincerely, "Can you do that?"

"I cannot," I denied.

After that, using every available lab apparatus, somehow the surrounding air temperature was raised to over a hundred degrees. Buckets of sweat poured off me, and I felt nauseous. Oginome-san held a hair dryer in both hands, blowing hot air directly onto the toad, which croaked strangely and fidgeted on my back.

"That's it, just a little more! *Hee-hee-hoo! Hee-hee-hoo!*"

"*It's...for Himari!*"

Just as I was ready to give up entirely, casting my eyes to the brilliant full moon outside as if throwing myself upon its mercy, the toad made a strange sound from my back, and laid a mass of lukewarm, viscous eggs.

"Eeek! There they are! That's so gross!" Oginome-san screamed, shutting her eyes.

Well, obviously, I thought, twisting my neck to check just what miserable state my back had been left in.

"Ah!"

I noticed No. 2's acute interest in the toad, but...did penguins normally eat toads? With a fire blazing in its eyes, No. 2 waddled over, and before I had time to stop it, it cleaned off my back in a single slurp.

"You little..." I looked at its face, dumbfounded, just in time to see the last trace of the toad's leg disappear into its beak.

"Huh? What? Where are the eggs? Where's the toad?" Finally opening her eyes, Oginome-san raised her voice in confusion.

No. 2 panicked and swallowed.

"Hey, what happened? Where is my Tamahomare Toad...?"

There was no way I could possibly explain.

"Wh-who knows? It probably magically set off to somewhere far away?" I stretched out languidly on the desk in exhaustion. "Where *did* it go, I wonder?" I said, glancing at No. 2. If No. 2 had been visible to Oginome-san, she probably would have burned it at the stake.

"But why? I wonder if I didn't draw the circle well enough. I checked it so many times..." she sighed, all the determination drained out of her.

No. 2 rubbed its belly in satisfaction.

"Let's go home already," I squeaked. "You've done all you can, right? Please, just let me go home."

"Survival Tactiiiic!!!"

The gust of white frills swept the takeaway boxes, me—finally feeling clean after washing the toad's sticky remains from my back—and my brother, sour-faced as ever, away to that alternate space.

"Surely, you worthless nothings have been told! You must obtain the Penguindrum!"

No matter how many times I saw it, I never got used to the sight of Himari in that black penguin dress. Her red eyes gazed sharply at us.

"Look, this is impossible! Tabuki got engaged to Yuri-san, so there's no way Oginome-san and Tabuki will get together! Plus, I faced terrible horrors tonight! I thought I was gonna die!" I gestured wildly, trying to convey to her how awful it had been.

Penguin Hat walked forward, her boots clacking slowly across the not-quite-there floor.

"Hmph. It is your duty, my servants, to do something about that."

"Enough already! I can't be around that occultist psycho anymore!" I pouted. It was completely unfair that my brother had somehow managed to avoid dealing with Oginome-san's madness.

"Come to think of it, didn't that M plan or whatever refer to marriage?"

"Mm-hm." I nodded, puffing out my cheeks.

"There's still a possibility." Kanba put his hand to his chin.

Penguin Hat looked to Kanba.

"The essential point here is that Oginome Ringo wants to have *some* kind of relationship with Tabuki, right?"

"This again?" My face cramped.

"In that case, there might still be something we can do. Guys can get cold feet, after all. Tabuki is a man, so if we hit that weak point just right, there might be a chance for one night's indiscretion," Kanba said with a grin.

Relations, indiscretion...it was impressive how easily those words just flowed from his mouth.

"Aniki, you are making a suuuper creepy face right now."

"Then do it! Servant Two!" Penguin Hat pointed at me, as though completely on board.

"Huh? Me?" I looked at Kanba, wondering if he wasn't better equipped to handle these kinds of things, but he averted his gaze.

"Hang on, Aniki!"

"You do it. There's other stuff I need to do," he said, evading my complaints with a bizarre seriousness.

"Obviously, you useless fool! You don't get to choose the means. You and Oginome Ringo fight, and entice Tabuki! One strike! Two! Three!"

"Stop making Himari say—" I was already anticipating it, but I still forced out the words. The floor opened with a snapping sound, and the hole into which I was to fall opened. "—such filthy thiiiings!!!"

"Shall we initiate the Survival Tactic?!"

I could not bear to see the Penguin Hat in my sister's form, saying such things and gesturing that way. Our little sister was pure.

How could someone as pure as me, with a pure little sister like her, facilitate some kind of 'one-night indiscretion' between Oginome-san and Tabuki?

Late that night, Tabuki Keiju brushed his teeth, wearing his white pajamas with a swan pattern. The sound of this reached Oginome Ringo, who had taken up residence beneath the floorboards.

Ringo, who wore only a soft, gauzy nightgown over her bare skin, went through her own bedtime routine, and opened her diary with those sounds of daily life as her background music.

She relied too much on dubious methods. It was a mistake to put her faith in those magic circles and toads and whatnot. She sucked with those kinds of things anyway, and dealing with a toad that big creeped her out.

"Today marks one whole month of living with Tabuki-kun. We haven't once had a quarrel. He really is my soulmate," she read aloud, taking a breath. Thus far, everything written in the diary had come true. And yet, if that was so, then why had Tabuki and Tokikago Yuri gotten engaged?

Ringo looked quietly up at the ceiling and touched the photo of Tabuki's smiling face. Her fingers traced from his cheeks to his lips. Tabuki was right above her. In this way, he and Ringo were together. She could not grow weak now. Fate was absolutely on her, Tabuki, and Momoka's side.

Ringo cuddled her jellyfish pillow and buried her face in it, calmed by the sounds Tabuki made, and rested her body until it was time to execute her midnight project.

She tracked the passing time on her peach-colored alarm clock. As the night grew deeper, a thundering rain began to fall, and Ringo wrapped herself in her sheets, shivering from the cold. Winter was steadily approaching. Again and again, she reapplied her lip balm, and gazed at the pale peach polish painted on her nails. Everything was in order, her preparations complete.

She picked up the diary from beside her pillow and flipped it open. She looked firmly down at the page, where the words, "Project M = Maternity: Huge Success!" in Momoka's childish handwriting. Ringo steeled her determination and took a deep breath.

"I'm going to bear Tabuki-san's child. That's right! This will be true, supreme proof of our undying love!"

Thunder rumbled violently. On nights like these, a woman wanted to sleep in the protective embrace of her beloved. There was no mistaking that fate deemed this night appropriate.

Ringo knew that there was a single floorboard in Tabuki's apartment that could be opened. She pushed firmly from underneath with her full strength, noisily prying up the board. She carefully slid the floorboard away and crawled up onto the floor. There was a sliding door between the dark, silent kitchen and the bedroom. Beyond it would be Tabuki, asleep. Ringo held her breath, clutching the breast of her nightgown, and slowly approached the screen.

As might be expected, Ringo was nervous. In the back of her mind, a loop of unverifiable information played, gleaned from magazines and comics and friends of friends, about what someone's "first time" would be like. But the reality wouldn't matter; as long as there was love, nothing else mattered. Even if it was scary, she would see it through.

"When the future becomes reality, everything dear to me will become eternal," she said in a tiny voice.

Slowly, she opened the screen, and once more there was a great peal of thunder. Lightning illuminated Ringo's face and the room for just a moment. Ringo slowly stood, walking to the futon. The room smelled of sleep.

She smoothly undid the decorative ribbon at her chest, undoing the little buttons one by one, letting the gown slide from her slender shoulders. The cloth falling to the floor made a soft noise.

Though shrinking back at the thunder, she forcefully pulled back the blankets where Tabuki would be sleeping, only to find it deserted. "*No*," she whispered in a strangled voice, staring speechless at the slightly crumpled blankets. There by the pillow were a small plush bird, and a cute plush egg, sitting in a row.

CHAPTER 08 •••→

I STARED AT THE ROUND CLOCK above Tabuki's head as he spoke in front of the blackboard. Soon enough, the day's lessons—my only relatively tranquil time these days—would be over.

"Now then, we're soon going to start studying genetics. It's a slightly complicated subject, so everyone be sure to read through your textbooks ahead of time," said Tabuki, drawing things to a close and slamming his textbook shut.

While waiting for the closing signals of "Stand up! Bow!" to end, Tabuki let out a big yawn. My classmates scattered and left the classroom.

It was hard to believe that this disheveled, bespectacled, bird-crazy schoolteacher had gotten engaged to a popular actress, and moreover was the object of affection of a high school girl like Oginome-san, who really wasn't so bad herself, at least as far as appearances went. There are so many mysteries in this world.

While Tabuki rubbed the dirty blackboard eraser atop the cleaner, he rubbed his eyes sleepily. Then, he let out another giant yawn, this time without trying to hide it.

"You look pretty tired, Sensei."

I worried about what Oginome-san's next move would be. That night, after having failed at making her weird potion from those toad eggs, she'd told me that she was going to try a more direct method.

A direct method, such as confessing to Tabuki out of the blue, or chasing after him, ripping her clothes off, or something like that. Maybe if he rejected her outright, she would actually give up. In that case, maybe she would lend us the diary. On the one hand, the penguin-hatted queen and my brother foisted the plan of giving Tabuki cold feet off onto me. I was disinclined to do anything unreasonable, if at all possible. The only move I could make now was to press Tabuki for information.

"Oh, Takakura. Looks like you caught me looking foolish." He laughed softly, stopping the cleaner.

"Guess you're really busy preparing for the wedding, huh?" I noticed faint dark circles under his eyes, but he did not appear to be ill.

"No, it's something else. Last night was kind of a big ordeal." He scratched his head.

"A big ordeal? Don't tell me something huge crawled out from under your floorboards or something? Like, some black, human-sized shadow that came for you?" I asked, slightly frantic.

"Floorboards? What are you talking about? Have you been watching too many horror movies?" He placed the now clean eraser on top of the lectern.

By some measures, if Oginome-san had come out from under the floor, it *would* have been a horror movie. But I was relieved to hear that she apparently had not yet enacted her next scheme.

"Well, you said something big happened last night." What could have been that big a deal, then? I could not ask so bluntly, but just then, my brother passed by.

"So it was a more adult kind of evening?" Kanba asked with a grin, leaning on the lectern.

"Wh-what are you saying, Aniki?!"

"No, that would've been nice, though," said Tabuki a bit awkwardly, scratching his head profusely. His already disheveled hair became even more unruly.

"H-huh? Then last night, you and Yuri-san didn't...*Fabulous Max* it?" I lowered my voice.

"Hey now, this is a school, Takakura!" Tabuki said, so jovial and friendly that I could practically see the sparkling emoji at the end of his words. Did that mean that if we *weren't* at school, he would have happily discussed the details of that "fabulous max" with us?

"Sensei, please instruct dear little Shoma here about the 'biology' of men and women," said Kanba with a stern expression and a solemn air, but flashing a grin as he looked at me.

"Okay, okay, very well."

"Well, Shoma, listen closely," said Kanba, waving a hand as he left the classroom.

Honestly, the moment he stepped out of the house, Kanba said everything that he would never say in front of Himari. I don't think he did it intentionally, though he also wasn't the type to avoid offending other people.

My nose wrinkled as I glared at Kanba, who urged me on secretly from outside of the classroom.

"So, Sensei, last night?" I said.

"What? You're really persistent. I mean, there was just some flooding in the house. Yuri called me suddenly, and we both ran around like crazy. But it's a new place, so thankfully it didn't end up being that big of an issue."

"New place?" I looked back at him. "Sensei, are you moving?"

While straightening up his handouts and the class roll, he pulled out a postcard and handed it to me.

"Here you go. When things calm down, you and Ringo should come and hang out."

On the postcard was a moving notice. It featured a large photo of Tabuki and Yuri-san wearing matching, intensely garish bird t-shirts, snuggled together and smiling.

Once I thought about it, Tabuki's apartment was probably too cramped for two people to live in, and more importantly, the person moving in with him was Tokikago Yuri. Moving seemed like a natural step. That said, the fact that she would wear a t-shirt like that just for him also meant that she was a wonderful, big-hearted, and unpretentious person.

"On that note, I'm moving today, actually, so that invitation might come sooner than you think." Tabuki grinned, his cheeks steadily reddening. He certainly didn't look like someone likely to get cold feet. "I wonder how the contractors are coming along right now."

"Congratulations," I said dazedly.

Tabuki was moving out of his apartment. I was sure that this would be vital information for Oginome-san to hear.

After school the next day, I accompanied Oginome-san to Tabuki's apartment. Already cleared of belongings, the place was empty and surprisingly spacious. Nobody would be able to listen to the dull sounds of his life here from underneath the floorboards.

Oginome-san went to the curtainless window and stopped dead, speechless. Then, she weakly muttered, "No way," and collapsed delicately on the spot.

"I think it's time for you to give up, now," I said to her, stretching out next to Penguin No. 2, in what probably used to be the kitchen. "Starting today, Tabuki and Yuri-san are living together in a new condo. So, it's time to—"

Oginome-san persisted, cutting me off.

"No way. That can't be possible." She was still on the floor, not moving.

"Enough is enough, it's time to face reality! Tabuki is never coming back here. I don't know about this fate diary or whatever, but no matter what schemes you've cooked up in your wild imagination, it's never going to happen!"

My voice suddenly went wild in irritation, and I sat down beside her, peering at her face. Her eyes were staring somewhere far beyond the window. At the edges of her eyelids, her long eye-lashes were trembling faintly.

"Are you listening?"

The only thing you could see from the first floor of the apartment building was the plain view of a residential district—it was overwhelmingly boring. There were cinderblock walls and telephone poles and waste disposal spots, and someone's broken-down old bike.

"No. That can't be. This diary. This diary is my and Momoka's..." She twisted her body and pulled the diary out from her school-bag. "That's impossible."

I wondered if she was going to start crying. I wondered what I ought to do if she did, but she did not. She just slowly closed her eyelids, and went quiet for several seconds, as though she were about to go to sleep. Then, she let the diary thunk onto the floor.

"Let's go home. I'll help you move your things from under the floor again." I picked up the diary. "And also, um, I'm not sure how to say this, but I hope you can find a more honest romance next time. Your mother's going to worry if you keep doing such dangerous things."

Oginome-san sat up, slowly opening her eyes, and stared at me as though I said something distasteful.

"Don't touch that without permission," she said, snatching the diary from my hands and shoving it back into her bag. Then she stood straight up, smoothed her uniform, adjusted the pleats of her skirt, and quickly fixed her hair with her hands.

"Oginome-san?" I looked up at her, still sitting. That fierce light returned to her eyes.

"This diary is special. It's impossible for things to stray from the fate predicted here." She put her shoes on in the entryway ahead of me, turned back, and said, "Hurry up."

"What's with you? You were just on the floor!" My complaints fell on deaf ears as she opened the front door and left without me.

I let out a sigh, and looked at Penguin No. 2, who was trying to tilt its nonexistent neck up to look at me.

"A broken heart is a terrible thing."

As I slowly stood, I took another look around the empty room. The bleached wallpaper and tatami. The smell of wood and insect repellent.

I felt bad for Oginome-san, but there was nothing to be done. With such joy on their faces, it was clear that Tabuki and Yuri-san were ready to start building a family together, hand in hand. They would eat meals together, and sleep together, and live with one another, seeing each other's vexing parts and wonderful parts and beautiful parts and not-so-beautiful parts, until they finally grew old together. That was a wonderful thing, and no matter how cursed anyone might think their relationship was, they were sure to be happy.

Just as Kanba and I felt about Himari, there was no doubting that Tabuki knew deep in his heart that as long as he took Yuri-san's pale hand in his, and never let it go, then they would be happy.

"Now then."

It was time to move the luggage under the floor. I followed Oginome-san, leaving Tabuki's empty apartment behind. If we didn't hurry, the sun would set before we knew it.

Himari embroidered the curtains while watching the evening news. On the red curtains, she made letters and flowers and fish, and the patterns spread by the day.

"Tokikago Yuri, who recently announced her engagement to an unknown gentleman, will take the stage tomorrow for her final run in her countrywide tour. Apparently, the theater has been bombarded with inquiries from fans devastated by the star's retirement. According to Tokikago-san herself, her new fiancé is a kind person who loves animals. He must be a wonderful fellow," said the female newscaster, cheerfully wrapping up the segment.

"So Tokikago-san really is retiring! I was such a fan. That's too bad, isn't it, San-chan?" Himari muttered, in a voice that suggested she wasn't sure if that was too bad or not. She stroked Penguin No. 3, peering into its face for confirmation. Atop No. 3's head was an artificial flower crown.

On the table sat three steaming teacups. Himari stood in front of it, stretching and contracting her arms and legs and spinning them around. Now and then, she spun herself, too. Maybe it was a strange dance, or some new game with No. 3, or perhaps some form of exercise.

It was pleasant to watch, and a grin grew naturally on my face.

I stood beside Kanba in the kitchen, listening to Himari's joyful sounds through the open sliding door, breathing in the steam rising from the pot. It would be finished soon.

"So you're sayin' that cold feet plan was a bust?" Kanba asked quietly.

"You saw for yourself how he talks about her! Should he even be talking that way to students?"

Tonight was a little bit chilly, so we were making special soup, stewing up the rest of the vegetables in the fridge, partly to clean it out.

"No choice then. In that case, it's time for some drastic measures," he said, wiping his hands on his apron.

"Drastic measures?" I repeated, briefly wondering what those could be.

"I've been thinking about this for a while, but your methods are too slow, Shoma. You can't go along with every one of that stalker girl's wild delusions. You need to hurry up and just take that thing." His tone was as detached as ever.

It was true, my methods were different from his. I resolved to save my sister, but playing with other people's lives was, I felt, somehow too much. But I understand how my brother, who could not accept this, felt. We would never get the Penguindrum in our hands if we played by the rules.

"Saying 'if you play with fire, you'll get burned,' is just a figure of speech. People see how weak you are and just walk all over you," Kanba spat.

"But I don't want to just *take* something from her," I eked out.

"What? You feelin' sorry for that pervert girl or something?" His tone was cold.

"Huh? Obviously not! And why would you put it that way?!"

"Are you even serious about saving Himari?"

"*You're* the one who's always pushing Oginome-san off on me! Where have you been running off to? And why?" How many of her crazy plans had I been subject to while Kanba was away?

"Sounds like a fight's a-brewin'!" Himari said from behind us.

"Wah! Himari, how long have you been standing there?" I raised my voice, looking at her.

"Anything I can help with?" she asked, sliding between us and looking at each of our faces with a grin. That innocence of hers calmed my heart.

"No way. We're taking care of dinner today. You gotta wait until it's finished!" said Kanba with a smile, slamming a lid onto the pot.

"Really? I see..." Himari's lips pursed, but she obediently re-treated several steps, then added softly, "You two have been gone all the time lately, and now you're fighting. I might just collapse again from loneliness."

Kanba whirled back toward Himari with shocking force.

"I-I'm sorry, Himari! We weren't fighting or anything, right?" He looked me in the eyes, not dropping his strained smile.

"O-of course not. We were just having a disagreement about preferences for seasonings, right?" I got the feeling I was not as good at deception as my brother. Even if I got better at lying,

I always chickened out in the end. I wasn't sure if that was a virtue or a flaw.

"Really? Well, that's good, but..." Himari gave a teasing grin. "No fighting."

"C'mon, I told you we weren't fighting!" Kanba forcefully wrapped his arm around my shoulders.

"Alright, now, you wait out there until it's done, Princess!" I pushed Himari hurriedly back into the parlor.

"Whaaat? Boo, that's boring," she sulked, returning to in front of the TV. "Wanna play something, San-chan?"

"Anyway," whispered Kanba, "The next time you mess up, I'm gettin' in there and taking it by force. Got it? For Himari!"

"Understood. For Himari!" I repeated, as if assuring myself.

Our goal was to be happy. To live as one big family, happy and healthy and getting along. When we were little, that seemed like such a simpler thing to achieve, accomplished by simple means. But now we knew. Everyone worked very hard to achieve a normal life. Laughing, crying, eating, and sleeping normally required an immense effort. And we were stuck halfway down that difficult path.

"Huh? That smell, you sure this isn't burning?" I looked in the pot, and quickly added more water.

"It's still edible," Kanba said calmly, stirring it with a ladle.

We knew each other well. We were doing well.

A little girl ran around the aquarium, along with her beloved father. Every tank was full of beautiful fish and kelp. Of them all, the penguins, tottering around happily, were some of the cutest.

When they arrived at the gift shop, the girl spotted it, as though she had been drawn in.

"Uwah! Papa! Hurry, hurry! Look, look! This penguin has an apple!"

"You're right! It's probably just a coincidence, but it's like this charm was made for you."

"Hey, Papa…"

"Well, I guess I've got no choice. Let's get a set, then, for Papa and Mama and Ringo!"

"Yaaay!"

The little girl did not yet have a cellphone, but she decided deep down that she would cherish this. Her beloved penguin charm, bought by her father at her beloved aquarium.

Even now, she still cherished it. This charm seemed like it had been put there just for her.

Presently, Ringo stood in a corner of the souvenir shop, her phone in one hand, searching for a phone charm with the same design as the one she already had, a penguin holding an apple, but of course it seemed that the shop no longer carried it. Her expression did not change noticeably, nor did she sigh. A quiet simply fell to her heart.

It made sense; it had been years since then, after all. The one Ringo had was already tattered and faded.

Sunshiny National Aquarium in the evening was filled with families and couples. Each time Ringo looked at them, she sighed just a little in jealousy. Who was she to be coming to a place like this all alone? She should have at least reached out to Yukina or Mari. She couldn't talk to them about the Project, but it would have been more fun than coming to a lively place like this alone. After visiting the aquarium, they could have done a bit of window shopping, sat for a bit and drunk some tea. Something like that would have been better.

Faced with the fact that Tabuki had moved, Ringo felt a bit helpless. Everything was destined to follow the course of fate, but it was just as true that from now on, Yuri would be part of Tabuki's life. When Ringo thought of this, she somehow felt lost.

"Uncle, hurry, hurry!"

Ringo turned around reflexively at the sound of a young girl's voice, hiding behind a nearby shelf in surprise.

"Come on, Aoi, no running!" said the girl's mother, walking in with a smile.

"Let her have a little fun," said a man, walking beside the girl's mother, smiling. It was unmistakeably Ringo's father, Satoshi.

"Goodness, you're too soft on her, Satoshi-san."

The three of them together were a picture-perfect family. The girl named Aoi's excited voice sounded just like Ringo's once had.

"Hey, Uncle. I've got a class observation day coming up. Everyone said that their Papas are coming." She tugged on Satoshi's shirt sleeve in practiced fashion. "So, um, I want you to come too. You can be my Papa."

Ringo felt light-headed. Satoshi was Ringo's father. He was Ringo and Momoka's father.

"Hmm, I see. That's something you have to ask your Mama about," said Satoshi. He looked at the girl's mother, beaming. His expression was awkward, but his eyes serious; it was a look Ringo had never seen on his face.

"Oginome-san, that's, well..." The mother looked away demurely.

Satoshi stepped closer to her.

"I know this is a strange place for it, but this is for you."

He abruptly pulled a small box from his jacket pocket. Even from a distance, it was obvious what was inside that box.

"Satoshi-san, you..." Her eyes went wide in a joyful surprise, and she clasped her hands to her mouth.

"Could I ask you to consider making the three of us a real family?" He looked at her searchingly.

It was the face of a person in love, which Ringo had seen in the mirror now and then. Ringo began to feel a bit ill. She wasn't a little girl anymore and was fully aware of the sort of relationships that blossomed between a man and a woman, but...

"Yes, if you're alright with us, then happily." Aoi's mother nodded, tears forming in the corners of her eyes.

"Yaaay! Yaaay! Aoi's got a papa!" Aoi clung to Satoshi's legs happily. Satoshi smiled, lightly picking Aoi up.

A family. Such a ridiculous scene could not be unfolding before her eyes. Satoshi could not possibly have any family besides Ringo's mother, and Ringo, and Momoka. So why was Ringo hiding, watching Satoshi in fear?

Ringo's heart, which had quieted before, and mind seemed to slowly submerge into darkness, as though she was diving into the deep sea. All these ridiculous things. These impossible, ridiculous things.

Even walking dazedly through the crowds of Ikebukuro at night proved difficult. After proposing, Satoshi and the others would certainly be eating dinner together as a "family." Aoi would order a kid's meal, and the adults would watch over her, smiling. A little flag would stand on the rice heaped up on the kid's plate, and it might even come with a little toy. Aoi would be thrilled by this. Just as Ringo once was.

Everything was coming to an end. Hard as she tried, everyone was leaving her behind. Things were scattered and confused.

Tears suddenly welling up, Ringo tripped over the asphalt in the middle of the crowds and took a painful spill.

"Ow!" She smacked her forehead in embarrassment, and then lifted her head angrily.

Suddenly, a cold wind blew before Ringo's tear-filled eyes, and her bangs swayed. Her face twisted in frustration, but she swallowed back her tears, refusing to cry.

She took her diary from her bag and drew herself up off the ground.

It wasn't over yet. She couldn't quit. No matter what underhanded means his fiancé employed, there was no reason Ringo should lose Tabuki. She still had an ace up her sleeve to ensure victory.

Ringo clutched the diary to her chest. Ringo had something that that woman did not. She had a destiny. As long as she had that, there was no changing the future. Ringo was bound to Tabuki, and Ringo would make a family with him. Project M would inevitably come to fruition.

"*Destiny!*" Ringo held the diary up high in the middle of the darkened street.

The crowd's eyes focused on her. A car approaching from in front of her honked its horn.

She would never hand Tabuki over to Tokikago Yuri. Ringo had to let her know, once and for all, that there was no defying fate.

The sounds of Dvořák's "Going Home" on piano flowed through the room at low volume. On the round table in the middle of the long, narrow, high-ceilinged room sat a tea set and an antique telephone made of black and subtle gold. Sitting lightly in a chair beside it, gazing at the checkerboard floor as if stroking it with her eyes, Masako let out a quiet sigh.

She lifted the receiver, rubbing the fingers of her other hand together in irritation, and glanced at the penguin sitting in the chair beside her. She dialed the number as if resigned. The person on the other end did not let the phone ring even once. This was no surprise; it was just as they arranged.

"Yes, it's finally happening. Project M. There is no room for failure," she said shortly, then hung up the receiver with an exaggerated clack.

Masako walked over to her tall window, reaching out to stroke the edges of the thick curtains. The penguin followed quietly, standing beside her.

"Goodness, we better crush him soon." She lowered her eyelashes in the sun, biting her lip lightly.

The penguin, who dexterously held a teacup with an aloof expression, flashed its eyes in reply.

It was my first time in a girl's room that wasn't Himari's, but I felt no butterflies. Instead I shut the door, my head hung.

"Ugh, I'm beat. It really is tough moving stuff the second time." I sunk down onto the cool floor, sighing deeply. Having strategized based on what happened last time, I was able to move Oginome's belongings back from beneath Tabuki's apartment much more efficiently. I could feel my house husband proficiency rising.

"Did you put Ka-chan and Ot-chan right back where I told you to?" Oginome-san asked, not looking at me.

"Yes, yes. They're separate from the other luggage, lined right up by the pillows." I looked to the heavens, cracking my neck.

"Then that's good." Oginome-san stood in the kitchen, a serious look upon her face. However, it did not appear that she was about to offer me a cup of tea, or anything like that.

"So, um..."

"What?"

"I'm guessing I still don't get to borrow that diary from you yet."

Until things were settled with Tabuki, I assumed I would not get an affirmative out of her, but I still had to ask, just in case. I held up frayed fingernails, dirty with earth and cardboard.

"It's fine. You can have it."

"I figured—wait, what? Really? Are you sure?"

I stood up, leaning over the kitchen counter, and stared at her. I pleaded silently for her to say yes before she changed her mind, and to put the diary into my hands.

"That is, once the upcoming task has been safely completed."

"Task?" I cursed myself for being a soft-hearted, feckless fool, to have believed for a second that Oginome-san would hand the diary over to me unconditionally.

"Alright, it's done." I looked at her hands, to see her just closing the lid of a little white box.

"What's that?" I asked, briefly meeting eyes with Penguin No. 2, who stood beside Oginome-san, staring at the box.

"Wait here, I need to get ready to go out."

She entered her room and slammed the door shut, ignoring my question. Before ten minutes had passed, she reemerged carrying a sports bag.

"Let's go," she said, picking up the white box.

I gave a response that was somewhere between, "Yeah," and, "Huh," and followed her out.

"Thanks for carrying all those. See you." She gave me a nod of parting and began walking off alone.

"Wait." I had to ask her. "Where are you going with those?"

"Where? I'm heading to Tabuki-san and Tokikago Yuri's condo," she said coolly, taking out the postcard with Tabuki and Yuri-san's moving notice.

"That postcard! I got one of those just yesterday. I thought it was here in my bag..." I stuck it in the outside pocket of my commuter bag, but it was nowhere to be found amongst the shopping lists and receipts.

"Is that box a housewarming gift?" I asked.

Oginome-san looked at me silently, with a quiet expression.

"So it is! Girls really do bounce back quickly, huh? Now that I think about, the girls that my brother rejected have been surprisingly the same way. There's always rumors of them getting new boyfriends after not too long. Oh, in that case, this is a special occasion, so I'll go with you to congratulate them!"

"You..." she said, more quietly than I had heard from her before, glaring at me, "What nonsense are you speaking?"

I froze, my genuine smile still on my face.

"That woman is in Osaka today, on a nationwide tour. Tabuki-san will be alone at their place tonight. This is my last chance. Now, goodbye." She turned her back on me, her stance rather gallant.

"What? Wait a second!" I could not go home and leave her like this.

Apparently, she had not yet given up on Project M. Inside that white box was something that would help her grasp this so-called 'last chance.'

"I'm not waiting," she said crisply, back straight, with a strange coldness. Her limbs swung purposefully.

"What are you gonna do *now*?! What's in there?!" Penguin No. 2 and I matched her steadily increasing pace. "Stop already!"

"I told you that I would lend you the diary if this goes well, so don't interfere."

That was true. Whatever plan she had in mind, whatever was in that box, so long as Oginome-san achieved her goal, I would get the diary. Whether or not she could attain this twisted love of hers, and whether or not anyone was hurt by her actions, it had nothing to do with me and Kanba, or Himari's life.

It had no connection to my, to our goals.

"I can't just do nothing." I just wasn't capable of thinking the way my brother did. "Plus, if it does go well, I want to take the diary home with me right away. I absolutely need it."

In lieu of a reply, the corners of Oginome-san's mouth turned down, and she glared at me.

I followed the blank-faced Oginome-san, boarding the train along with No. 2. Oginome-san sat in the empty seat she found in the crowded car, staring down meekly at the white box. I sat a short distance away, careful not to lose sight of her, and pondered this Project M.

So, the "M" of Project M did not stand for "marriage." What else could it possibly stand for, then? It would have made sense if it was in either of Oginome Ringo or Tabuki Keiju's initials.

"M... M...Mix, miracle. Magical. Marvelous," I muttered silently, thinking of various words. None of them seemed to hit the mark, and there were only so many words I was aware of with my limited English vocabulary.

"M. Ma…Mad, madness." Madness. Oginome-san might be afflicted with madness, but that was merely my perception of her.

"M. M? Murder?" The word popped into my mind, and I shivered.

Indeed, "murder" began with M. What would I do if, in the depths of her obsession, she was after a lovers' suicide with Tabuki? Considering her actions up to now, it did not seem at all impossible that that box contained a homemade explosive or something.

I hated to get wrapped up in this, but I could not let it alone. I had to get her to abandon this project of madness. If she was gone, Himari would be sad, and if the diary was ruined, things could not be undone.

I followed frantically after Oginome-san, who swiftly disembarked at Akasaka Mitsuki station, and prepared myself for the worst.

I looked up at the high-rise building towering beneath the thinly clouded sky, and my jaw dropped. We greeted Tabuki at the large entrance, and the door unlocked. We passed through the wide lobby, decorated with sofas, headed for the flat where Tabuki and Yuri-san lived.

"This place is amazing." As we walked down the wide, carpeted hall, I was shocked at how quiet and clean it was, only realizing now how drastically Tabuki was proverbially "marrying up."

Oginome-san proceeded down the noiseless hallway without hesitation.

"Calm down, would you? It's unseemly," she said.

"But this is like a completely different world."

We pushed the button on the intercom beside the large white door, and Tabuki soon opened the door with a "Hey," and a smile. Today he wore a bright, blue-striped shirt and beige slacks. They were probably to Yuri-san's tastes.

The entryway was surprisingly large, and to the side was a shoe shelf for Yuri-san. There was a separate walk-in closet for clothing as well. There were two bathrooms before we even reached the living room, and there was even a bar just before the living room. The idea of Tabuki and Yuri-san living here was hard to imagine. It didn't seem real.

"Sorry for barging in on you so suddenly, Tabuki-san, especially when you've just moved in." Oginome-san sat modestly on the living room sofa and smiled gently, greeting him as a pure and humble maiden would. "But I just couldn't wait to congratulate you."

"No, I'm glad you came. We've sorted out our things surprisingly fast." Tabuki loaded a classy-looking teapot and teacups onto a tray in an unfamiliar manner and carried them over. He set them on the table, looking up at the weather report showing on the large TV screen. "It's just that Tokyo's supposed to get a lot of rain tonight as an effect of the typhoon, and I'm worried about you getting back home."

"That's just fine. After we have a little bit of a celebration, we'll be out of your hair," Oginome-san said cheerfully, sliding down from the sofa and kneeling on the wooden floor. "I'll do it," she said, diligently picking up the tin of tea leaves and the tea spoon.

"Ah, sorry about that. I have at least drunk tea on my own before," said Tabuki scratching his head. "Though normally I'd just grab a mug and a tea bag and be done with it."

"Whoa, these ceilings are so tall!" I wandered around the spacious living room, shamelessly unable to calm down, seriously moved. "The floors are so smooth, and the kitchen is huge. I wonder what Himari would say if she saw this."

This house was beyond imagination. Tabuki's former living space couldn't even hope to compare. It almost seemed a little *too* big. But considering that it was the home of a popular actress, it somehow made sense that the living room would be furnished with a chandelier with a design that looked exceedingly difficult to clean, and that there would be a sofa the size of Himari's bed. A spacious balcony surrounded the corner room, on which one's laundry would surely dry briskly on days with nice weather. Currently, the whole sky was covered with flame-colored clouds.

"You too, Takakura, thank you for coming. Have a seat."

"Thanks. I just sort of ended up tagging along." Oginome-san glanced at me out of the corner of her eye as I contemplated the scenery outside. I looked back to see that Penguin No. 2 had made itself completely at home beside her, and busily popped sugar cubes into its mouth.

"I don't mind! I did tell you that you should come and hang out, too."

"Anyway, Tabuki-san!" Oginome-san said suddenly, placing the white box she cradled on her lap onto the table. "I put my heart into making this for you two."

My ears pricked up, and I slowly turned around.

"You should enjoy it with Yuri-san, if you like."

"Huh? What is it? I'm excited," Tabuki said, carefree, staring at the white box.

"I'll open it up then." With a grin, Oginome-san put her hand on the lid.

I hurriedly shoved No. 2 out of the way beside her and said, "Wait!"

"What?" Oginome-san glared at me as I reached out for the box, a cold sweat running down me.

"Don't be hasty. If I have to, I'll throw it out the window!"

"What are you talking about?" She opened the box at once.

"Oh, that looks amazing!" Tabuki's eyes glittered.

"I hope that it suits both of your tastes." She slid the box slowly toward him, shrugging her shoulders bashfully.

The contents were, as far as I could tell, a large mont blanc.

"Man, I'd love to enjoy this with Yuri, but she just left for her Kansai tour. She'll be in Osaka a while," said Tabuki, in a husband-like *Sorry about my wife* sort of way.

"That's too bad. It came out so well, I was hoping she could see it too."

Though speechless at the conspicuous way Oginome-san tilted her head, eyebrows drawing to a peak, I breathed a sigh of relief.

"It's okay, you went to all the trouble, let's eat it together," Tabuki said happily, heading to the kitchen for some dishes.

"What? Isn't this just a normal cake?" I said, in a cowardly voice.

"It's not *normal*. Look closely. It's a special curry-type mont blanc, with my heart and soul in it."

Wondering what she meant by curry-type, I looked the cake over again. Rather than curry, the squeezed out chestnut paste on top looked like pasta. To have a curry-type mont blanc was weird. Mont blancs, by nature, were supposed to resemble Mont Blanc, in the Alps, so for it to be a curry-type mont blanc was essentially calling it a "curry mountain cake." Of course, I wouldn't know for sure without biting into it, so I just looked at her, not voicing my concern.

"So, what are you making a fuss for?" she asked.

"Ah, well, I was just surprised that you genuinely wanted to congratulate him."

She pouted, then gave a faint smile.

"If you don't mind, please eat up, and let me know what you think of the cake," she said in a soft, but somehow boastful voice.

Having never seen such a sweet and normal Oginome-san at any point in the past, I smiled and said, "Of course!"

This was good. She'd gotten it through her head. She was finally trying to move on from Tabuki. There was no need for me to fret over her doing something reckless. I was sure that on the way home, she would apologize and lend me the diary.

"Now then, I suppose we'd better partake of this mont blanc for our happiness," Tabuki said merrily, returning with plates, a cake knife, and forks that matched the tea set.

We gave our thanks, and Tabuki politely sliced the curry mont blanc for everyone.

Outside the window, rain began to fall, and from the steadily darkening sky came booms of thunder. Rain struck the window fiercely, but the cheerful atmosphere in the living room remained protected by the thick glass.

The cake was incredibly delicious—or would have been, had it not been poisoned. Oginome-san really *wasn't* interested in congratulating Tabuki and Yuri-san.

I forced my heavy eyelids open a crack, moving my sluggish body slightly, and looked at Oginome-san. She was standing over us proudly, looking down on us, collapsed on the floor.

"That took effect faster than I thought," she muttered in a low, hoarse voice, putting her sports bag on her back. She put her arms under Tabuki's, who collapsed on the table, and pulled him up, taking him from the living room with a slow, dragging sound, making the spine-chilling expression of a serial killer.

Tabuki, who loved mont blancs, gobbled down a large helping of the cake without any suspicion, and was now fast asleep. I had not eaten as much, so my breathing only grew more subdued, my body relaxed, dying for sleep.

I thought of ordering Penguin No. 2 to go and do some recon, but out of the corner of my eye I could see No. 2 passed out on the ground, motionless.

I had to do something. Whatever Oginome-san was intending to do, I had to stop her.

I tried to force myself up but slammed back down on the floor. I breathed deeply to try and calm myself, but my ears were ringing with the sound of the rain, falling more and more violently, and the roar of thunder.

"O-Oginome-san." My voice, too soft for her to possibly hear, was drowned out by the peals of thunder and its accompanying bolts of lightning. At the same moment, the lights in the living room went out.

There was no light in the kitchen or hallway, either. This *was* the perfect time for a power outage, huh? Even though the apartment was so big you didn't know what to do with yourself. If I didn't catch up with Oginome-san quick, who knew what she would do?

Just what did the M stand for?

I crawled across the floor out of the living room. I caught a glimpse of Tabuki's white socks, rounding the corner of the hallway.

"Wait." I gripped the wall, standing shakily, and slowly began walking. When I turned the corner, I saw an open door at the end of the hall.

It was a bedroom. I sat down in the hallway, keeping the wall at my back, and peeked inside. Even in the dark, I could see the hazy silhouette of Tabuki, lying on a large bed, and Oginome-san sitting beside him.

"I really didn't want to have to do this. I wanted you to love me for me, Tabuki-san."

Slowly, Oginome-san began to strip. I squeezed my eyes shut.

"But there's no more time. Soon, you'll awaken. You'll be so dazed, you won't be able to tell who is lying next to you."

What was she talking about? I slowly re-opened my eyes. Wearing a fluttering nightgown, she climbed onto the bed, straddling Tabuki.

"Tonight, I will be your bride. But not as myself."

I knew that she was Oginome-san, but her hair swayed in long, beautiful waves, just like Yuri-san's.

"What a beautiful engagement ring." She took Tabuki's hand, taking a long look at his ring finger.

"Hey, what are you doing?" I finally managed to stand, entering the room and leaning on the door.

She turned only her eyes to me, and clutched Tabuki's hand in both of hers, enveloping it.

"Looks like the medicine wasn't strong enough. Fine. You're here, so I'll tell you. This is our fate. This is Project M."

I slid my heavy body along the wall, trying to get closer to her.

"What the hell is the 'M' for?"

"Conception," she said sharply. "The M is for Maternity!"

Illuminated by a flash of lightning as she turned around, her face looked much like Yuri-san's, but it was not a beautiful face at all. A loud peal of thunder shook the whole room.

My chest stung with fear, and I was overtaken by nausea. Finally, I understood exactly what it was that she was trying to do.

I tried to run to the bed, but I lost control of my legs, and tumbled across the floor. What she said wasn't correct. This was the M of the truly deranged, of *Madness* through and through.

I crawled across the floor toward Oginome-san, who arranged the wig with her hands.

"This is weird," I called. "Was this written in your diary too? Just what the hell is this 'Fate Diary'? This whole time. To say that trying to make the things written there come true by force is fate... Isn't this all just your own selfish delusions?"

"You're wrong. It's not a delusion! If I don't do this, then my family will..."

I continued, cutting her off.

"Whatever reason you have, doing it this way is wrong!" I finally reached the edge of the bed, clawing at the white sheets and dragging my upper body up.

"I don't care what anyone says. This is the only choice I have left," she said, her breath ragged. She yanked off Tabuki's horribly white socks, then practically tore open the buttons of his shirt to expose his chest. Then she undid the belt of his pants.

"Stop it!" I shouted weakly at the rustling sound.

"This is my destiny. Just leave me alone!"

She forcefully removed the leather belt and put her hand to the zipper of his fly.

"Like hell I would!" I shouted, flinging myself toward her.

With some difficulty, my hands reached her waist. As I clung to her, the long hair of the wig whipped in my face, and I couldn't see a thing. Still clutching her, I fell dramatically off the side of the bed. My back ached as it struck the wooden floor.

"Oginome-san, are you okay?" I started to say, when the lights in the room came on. Everything went monochrome before my eyes in the blinding glow. The power must have been restored.

"Hold it, what are you doing?!"

"Huh?" My vision cleared, and I realized it was Penguin No. 2 wriggling in my arms, the wig crooked on its head.

"O-Oginome-san, why are you naked?!"

She was crouched atop the bed without a single stitch on her body. I whipped my whole head away, averting my gaze. She had already cast the nightgown away to the side of the bed, and apparently had not been wearing any underwear from the start.

"Hey! Don't look!"

"I'm not looking! Now put something on already!" I wondered if I had already become unsuitable as a groom. Not that I had planned this, of course. "And go home!"

"I'm not going home!"

Just then, a buzz from the intercom made us both leap up in shock. Whoever had just showed up, nobody could mistake this scene as anything other than a crime, perpetrated at the hands of a high school girl.

As we instinctively looked at one another, we heard Yuri-san's gentle voice from the intercom.

"I'm home, Tabuki-kun! My flight got cancelled because of the typhoon. I'm going to take the first bullet train out tomorrow instead. The automatic lock isn't opening though, probably because of that power outage earlier. Could you open it? Hey, Tabuki-kun, can you hear me?"

"Oginome-san, go!" I staggered to my feet. "I'm going to go open the autolock, so get out of here before Yuri-san gets back to this room!"

"But!" Though she hurriedly re-dressed herself in the night-gown, she was persistent.

"Just hurry up already!" I grabbed her clothes that were scattered across the floor and stuffed them into the sports bag, wondering what to do about the state of the living room. Even if we cleaned it up right away and left, I didn't know what Oginome-san used to drug Tabuki, and there was a chance he might remember us stopping by. But there was no way he would think Oginome-san planned on assaulting him. Not letting Yuri-san find out was our top priority right now.

"I'm opening it," I said, activating the autolock before Oginome-san had a chance to argue. Then I gripped her arm and exited Tabuki's room.

There had to be an emergency exit somewhere. It would be best to make it out of the building without running into Yuri-san near the entrance.

"Wait!"

Holding the wig in one hand, Oginome-san tried to yank her other hand out of my grip, but there was no telling what she might do if she got away from me. Plus, she was still in her costume. I wanted to avoid the other residents of the building seeing her, if possible.

What was I even doing here? I was supposed to be trying to save Himari, but just like Kanba said, all I seemed to be doing was looking out for Oginome-san. Was it really love if you were sabotaging other people's happiness in order to make someone yours? The shape of love was different for everyone, and maybe

Oginome-san's way of doing things was just one variation, but this was far too selfish and warped.

Was not disregarding the feelings of the one you love, in order to satisfy your own desires, not fundamentally disrespectful to both you and them?

That was when I realized: I stopped feeling love at a very young age. I looked at women in a sexual and age-appropriate way, but I had never truly liked anyone romantically, let alone *loved* them. I had no idea if my own ability to love was even functional. I thought of Kanba and Himari and our uncle and school and my friends, and Penguin No. 2 and even Oginome-san each in a special way, but I had no idea how to confirm whether that was a type of love or not. Was I even capable of loving someone?

The emergency escape stairs were outside the building, where it was already completely dark and raining hard. With some difficulty, we sat down on the covered stairs, shoulders heaving with breath, listening to the sound of the distant thunder.

"I was almost there!" Oginome-san suddenly stood, throwing the wig she held to the ground. Her hair, normally brushed down smooth, was thoroughly disheveled.

"It's better this way. Doing something like that wouldn't be any good for you, either."

"Are you saying you know what's good for me? Don't lecture me!" Her voice echoed loudly down the stairs. "I'm going to be the one to bear Tabuki-san's child. If I don't, the ring of fate won't be connected. That was my final chance! Tabuki-san's life with that woman will be starting soon. When that happens, everything will seriously be ruined! It has to be me!"

She talked like I was in the wrong here. I stared at her narrow back.

"What?" She made a horrible face as she looked back, her eyes devoid of purpose, of sweetness.

"Listen, do you not care about Tabuki and Yuri-san's feelings?"

She froze for a moment, but it was no good.

"That's not it! The fact that Tabuki-san is with that woman in the first place is a mistake!"

The cold air drained the color from my vision. I rubbed my eyes and looked again at Oginome-san.

"You are the most cruel woman I have ever met!" Even though the words were coming from my mouth, my voice sounded like something I had never heard before. For some reason, I suddenly felt as though I wanted to cry.

Oginome-san's face paled, clearly wounded. The unforgiving rain started to fall sideways, soaking slowly into her hair and nightgown.

"You don't know anything." Her voice was like a mosquito's whine.

"I don't want to know anything."

It felt like, for the first time, I saw Oginome-san's real face. Her pale face, still looking ready to cry. And yet, she did not avert her eyes from me. Her mouth pressed into a straight line, with zero regard for her sopping state.

I was suddenly struck with regret. I had said too much. But it was too late.

"Can you really..." she said, in a warbling voice, "...say that you know everything about your own siblings with a straight face? Aren't you just glossing over your own family, pretending that you don't see it?! Who are you to tell anyone to see reality?!"

"What are you talking about?" I raised my voice ever so slightly, feeling that I had been touched in some empty place lurking in the depths of my heart.

"You should know just by looking at Himari-chan! That girl is always smiling and playing, but..."

I was afraid to hear the rest. I stood up at once, grabbing her by the collar and shoving her against the railing.

"Ow!" she yelped softly. The railing made a rattling sound.

She was afraid, looking down and shutting her eyes tight. I slid and sat down, still gripping at her chest and pulling her down with me.

The feeling of the nightgown, thin and silky and soft in my hand, and Oginome-san's scent. The sound of my own strained breathing, and Oginome-san's gentle sobs.

I came back to my senses, and quickly let go. I was afraid of how I'd lashed out, and thought I should say something, but I couldn't do more than flap my mouth silently, like a fish out of water. My hand trembled faintly.

"That's fine. From now on, I'll just do everything on my own. If I don't keep working to become Momoka, the circle won't be joined. Papa and Mama will drift away. Our family will be torn apart."

"Family?"

"This is all for the sake of my family. My duty, the reason I was born. It has nothing to do with my feelings."

"So then you, and Tabuki..."

"I like him. I *love* him. Because Momoka did, too!" she said firmly, interrupting me.

I rewound through all of Oginome-san's actions in my head. Who said they loved who? Who had done what, and why, because they loved someone? I thought that Oginome-san was merely in love with Tabuki, but perhaps I had made some grave misunderstanding.

In my ears, the sound of the rain had gone past comforting and was now irritating, and I couldn't get my thoughts in order.

"Momoka is your big sister, who died a long time ago, isn't she? What are you saying? What is this about?"

She stood up, not answering my question.

At this point, I could not accept any of this unless I got an explanation I could understand. This wasn't just for me. Oginome-san was completely mixed up.

"Oginome-san."

"I told you this has nothing to do with you!" She shoved me back violently, grabbed up the sports bag, and started down the stairs away from me at once.

"Wait!" I grabbed her by the arm.

"No! Let me go!"

It was then, as she jerked her body, trying to shake my hand off that the diary tumbled out of the open zipper of the sports bag, and then slipped through a gap in the iron railing of the stairs and into the rain.

"Aah!" Oginome-san shouted in terror, leaning over the railing to see where the diary had fallen, and then rushed down the stairs.

What would happen if the diary was ruined? Even without Oginome-san burning it, if we lost the diary in some other way, what would become of the Penguindrum?

I hurriedly followed after.

Her heart was cruel. As she rushed down the stairs, Ringo's head was filled with those words. A heart crueler than any other woman he had ever met.

As she stepped out onto the drenched black road, she swiftly spotted the diary. She rushed over and picked it up, wiping the soaked cover on the sleeve of her nightgown, and clutched it to her chest. Those terrible words had nothing to do with her. The diary gave her directions, and all she had to do was follow its words. She was certain of it. It was fate, after all.

Was her heart really that cruel? She squeezed the diary tighter.

She snapped her head up at the loud sound of an engine, mixed with the driving rain, and was blinded by a bright headlight. She thought that the motorcycle was going to rush right past her.

"Huh?"

A black hand thrust out, grabbing the diary she was gripping so tight to try and snatch it away. She reflexively steeled her hands.

Right before her eyes, her fate, in the form of Momoka's diary, was ripped in half. The bike vanished in the blink of an eye, taking half of the diary with it.

She felt the blood rush from her head, her body light and unsteady. As she stared silently after the bike, which had already faded to a distant speck of light, she felt the cold rain seeping into every cell of her body.

Maybe it was true. Maybe all the things she cherished were being taken away from her one by one because she was so cruel-hearted.

In the middle of the road, all she could sense was the smell of the soaked asphalt.

Who liked who? Loved who? What did I want? What did I need? What's important? And what am I doing here, looking like this?

By the time the sound of a car horn reached her ears, it was already too late. There was no time to even be afraid of the big black car barreling toward her on the dark road, like a monster. She prepared herself, shutting her eyes tight.

"Watch out!" She heard Shoma's voice. Well, obviously she should watch out. There was a car barreling down on her, after all, Ringo thought coldly in her subconscious. But the impact that came next was not what she expected.

Her body struck the pavement as she was flung into the opposing lane of traffic. As she sat up in shock, there was the sharp sound of a collision. With her eyes now adjusted to the dark, she could see Shoma's body, struck by the car, bouncing like a ball.

Shoma, who was not of particularly sturdy build, rolled lightly on the wet pavement.

"Shoma-kun!" She felt a terrible pain in her right elbow and knee as she stood. It stung more as she knelt beside him. Tears clouded her vision, her diaphragm tightening with cold and fear, making it difficult to breathe. "Shoma-kun!"

Shoma lay in a heap, motionless as a rag doll. His body sunk away into the rain in an instant.

This couldn't be happening. Even if Ringo was, in fact, the most cruel-hearted girl in the entire world, there wasn't a single word in the diary about Takakura Shoma suffering an accident. But now, she only had half of her beloved diary, and her dear friend no longer answered her.

CHAPTER 09

THAT DAY, Himari enjoyed a visit to the Sunshiny National Aquarium with her brothers in tow, for the first time in ages. There was the fun fluttering of her flared skirt, and the difficulty of walking through the crowds. In the streets of Ikebukuro, the smells of every person and thing intermingled.

Himari Day was the start of a new kind of tedium for Himari, after having been finally released from her endless tedium of the hospital.

She leaned forward, watching the penguins flocking on the artificial rock face, thinking, *the room stinks*. All around the aquarium was the smell of the ocean, and a strange, almost intoxicating atmosphere lent by the thick glass of the large tanks. In the tanks were glittering deep sea fish, as well as tropical fish. Swaying kelp and coral. Penguins, diving into the water, one after the other as if being pushed from behind.

Were penguins birds or fish? Himari looked for a signboard with an explanation, but only found a funny little sign reading, "A request from your friendly local penguins! Please don't touch the penguins!"

"Whoa. The penguins are such good swimmers!" Beneath the water, the penguins swam so rapidly, so freely, that it was hard to believe they were the same creatures she'd seen on land.

"Yeah. Even though they look a little silly on land," Shoma said beside her, nodding.

"I bet the penguins would be annoyed to hear that coming from you, Shoma," said Kanba, teasing his brother.

"What's that supposed to mean?"

Himari's ears pricked up at her brothers' childish exchange, and she smiled softly. These sorts of things would fill her daily life from now on. She would be immersed in this peaceful, joyful tedium.

She looked across the area, trying to get a good look at all of the penguins, when she noticed there was something weird about one of the penguins that had suddenly entered.

"Hmmm?" She leaned forward immediately, scrutinizing this weirdly spherical penguin. None of the other visitors around seemed to be paying this penguin much mind, but as far as Himari could tell, it looked incredibly distinct from the others. It seemed misshapen, and it moved in a weirdly humanlike way.

The moment its round, black eyes gazed at Himari, she found herself unable to move. This mysterious penguin was clearly looking at her. Their eyes met.

"Hey, Sho-chan," she said, pointing right at the mysterious penguin, looking at Shoma, who was right beside her.

"Ew, I wouldn't want to catch Kanba's filthy playboy germs." Shoma did not appear to be listening at all, busy cracking jokes about Kanba.

"Hey, look, that penguin over there..." She looked back at where she was pointing, only to see that the penguin vanished. "...It's gone."

Just then, a little boy went running by, wearing a souvenir penguin hat.

"Honey, no running, you're going to hurt someone," came the kind and graceful voice of his mother, in the way only a mother could speak. The boy's father followed leisurely behind.

The last time they had come here, Himari and her brothers played this way too, watched over by their beloved parents.

Distracted by the boy's sweet laughter, Himari started to forget about the strange penguin. Surely, she had just seen something wrong, or it was just her overactive imagination. She had spent so many days in a hospital bed that she probably was not yet fully reacquainted with reality.

The gift shop overflowed with treasures every way you looked. There were stuffed animals like the ones in Himari's little room, and little lamps and snow globes and tapestries. Both during her time in the hospital, and in the Takakura home, Himari's room had been obsessively decorated. Himari's room was her universe, her sanctuary, and the bulk of her world, after all.

As Shoma established that it was "Himari Day," he made a show of declaring that he'd buy her anything she liked. Genuinely pleased by her brother's consideration, she looked around at all the treasures in the shop.

The hat with the penguin face that Himari chose was a rather childish item, but she found it oddly pleasing. It was partly because she had seen the little boy from before wearing it, but somehow it seemed very important. Plus, it was moderately priced, so it wouldn't cause trouble for Shoma.

While waiting for Shoma, who was in line at the register, Himari felt a strange sensation behind her, and slowly turned around.

That strange penguin was just exiting the gift shop, waddling away.

"That's the one from before."

As though it noticed Himari's muttering, the penguin glanced back at her, then suddenly picked up the pace.

"Wait!" She had no idea why she followed it, but she knew that she had to. Himari could not resist following such a cute and strange little creature.

Himari ran strenuously all the way to the elevators in pursuit of the penguin she now called "San-chan." Just as she glimpsed sight of its back, the elevator arrived with startling timing, and the doors slid open.

Seeing the penguin board the elevator without hesitation, Himari shouted, "Wait!" and ran into that same elevator. The moment she was on board, the elevator doors closed, as if timed.

There was no one on the elevator besides Himari and the penguin.

It had been a long time since she had run like that, Himari thought while carefully catching her breath, looking at the back of the penguin's black head.

"Hey, Penguin-san," she called out, not sure if she wished to ask it something, or simply if she wanted to make friends. More importantly, where was this elevator headed? Just after she thought this, the whole elevator swayed violently, and Himari let out a small shriek.

The elevator went steadily down, the numbers on the electronic display quickly decreasing. Finally, they arrived at the second basement floor.

"Gosh, that startled me," she said softly, looking at the utterly still penguin. As she did, the penguin straightened up and reached for the elevator buttons. There was one more button, which Himari had not seen before.

The penguin pushed the button with its flipper.

Frightened by the mechanical sound the elevator had begun to make, completely different from the one before, Himari looked up at the display and the ceiling.

The elevator once more began to jerk violently downward. Perhaps unable to keep up with the elevator's speed, the display no longer properly showed any number.

"Where are we going?" Himari asked, but the penguin said nothing and did not look at her. "C'mon, tell me."

Had she really just been at the Sunshiny Aquarium? Himari

wondered. Along with her brothers, she changed her clothes, eaten breakfast, and boarded the subway. That hadn't been a dream, had it? If not, then what was this? Could this moment, where she followed a mysterious penguin and now was headed off to some unknown place, really be reality?

She heard a *ding*, signaling their arrival, and the elevator doors slid open.

"Oh." Before her was a white building surrounded by trees, which Himari had seen before.

The penguin exited the elevator, heading toward the building as though it were the natural thing to do. With no other option, Himari followed quietly behind it.

A gentle, warm sunlight shone through the gaps in the trees, and she could hear the warbling of little birds.

"This is that library we always go to," she suddenly realized. She looked down and saw she was somehow carrying several books under her arm.

The inside of the Central Library appeared perfectly normal. It was spacious, with a high ceiling, numerous patrons, and a fair number of staff moving about. The penguin at her feet notwithstanding, she saw nothing strange about the place.

Himari went to the counter, placing down the books she couldn't remember picking up, and called out to the apron-clad female staff member.

"I'd like to return these." On the counter were *Christine* by Stephen King, and *Sputnik Sweetheart* by Murakami Haruki, as well as *How to Sustainably Increase Your Income Ten-fold* by Katsuma Kazuyo. All of the books felt like ones she had read before, but also completely unfamiliar. Still, there was no mistaking that she had borrowed these here.

"Thank you. A return, then." The employee pulled the books closer, flipped open the back covers and swiftly finished checking them all over.

"Um, where could I find the book 'Frog-kun Saves Tokyo'?"

"Just a moment." The employee turned to her computer screen. "We don't have any record of that title," she quickly replied.

"I know I've seen it here before. It should be here..."

"Maybe you mistook it for a similar title? Are there any other search terms you recall?"

Himari had completely forgotten everything about it besides the title. She did not know the name of the author or the publisher, or even the genre.

"I'll go take a look myself. I'll probably find it if I follow the same path as when I saw it last time." She gave a nod to the employee and dove into the wide sea of bookshelves with the penguin.

"Frog-kun...Saves Tokyo... Frog-kun...Saves Tokyo..." She scanned the spines as she walked through the stacks. "I know it was somewhere around here."

She stopped in a certain spot, looking carefully from top to bottom. As she did, the penguin following at her feet looked around the shelves, too.

"Are you helping me search?" She smiled at it happily.

The penguin steadily advanced, still searching the books.

"Ah, wait!"

The penguin rounded the corner. Himari followed in pursuit. The penguin did not look back.

"Hey, where are you going?" Even as she followed the penguin, Himari had no idea why she had come this far.

The penguin was oddly fast, despite its waddling, and every time Himari thought she had caught up, it was always just a little ahead. She turned corner after corner, following the little black back. Just as she rounded another shelf, finally catching up with it this time, between the towering shelves on both sides, a large, old-looking wooden door came into view. A damp smell wafted from this odd amber-colored door to Himari.

"Huh?"

She silently and slowly approached the door through the space that should have been the library. Why would there be a door in a place like this?

Himari heard a strange cry and looked up at the ceiling. It sounded like a bird, but naturally, she saw no such shape there. She turned her gaze back to the door, just in time to see the penguin, which must have been hiding somewhere, opening it.

The door creaked slowly open, and the penguin slipped through the crack to the other side. Suspicion hung in the corners of Himari's mind, but against her better judgment, she followed after it.

Beyond the heavy door were bookshelves, strung together, endless and distant, into a gentle helix. The ceiling was so far away, she couldn't see it. The bookshelves were connected with long, narrow ladders, and spread throughout the space, drawing an arc. It was like a large-scale three-dimensional puzzle, or a wooden mosaic.

Unlike the bookshelves from before, these shelves were lined with large, sturdy, dense-looking books. The faint smell of old paper and mold that characterized most libraries was slightly more prominent, with a different quality.

Though they were underground, the space was full of light, and Himari narrowed her eyes.

"Penguin-san, where are you?" Himari nervously began walking down the white geometric-patterned floor. "Penguin-san!"

The penguin was nowhere to be seen.

"Isn't it marvelous?"

Startled at the voice from above her head, Himari looked up to see a young man, standing gracefully atop a ladder. With one hand he gripped the ladder, leaning against it, and held a large book open in his other hand. He snapped the book shut, and practically slid off of the ladder, standing quietly before her. The floor seemed to pulse in a soft, gentle rainbow.

"Welcome. What book are you searching for?"

He tilted his head gently, smiling kindly. His eyes sparkled with a light so brilliant it was impossible to tell where he was looking; it was like looking at tiny galaxies. His neatly gathered hair was white, practically transparent, with streaks of pale peach pink and light green mixed in.

He wore a plain white V-neck and a library apron, along with a loose, long beige cardigan, and denim jeans. Despite his nimble movements, he wore a pair of blue, slip-on sandals on his feet.

"Oh, um..." Himari did not feel afraid, but something about the young man stirred her heart strangely.

Once more, he tilted his head, smiling suddenly with just the corners of his mouth.

"Welcome to the Central Library's Sora-no-Ana Annex."

"Sora no Ana...Hole in the *Sky*? But aren't we underground?" She had no idea that there was such a place.

"This is most certainly the Sora no Ana. I am Sanetoshi, the librarian of this place. Come, your wish is my command." He gave a gracious bow, speaking in a polite, relaxed tone that clashed with the vibe of his hair and clothing.

"Um, then, could I ask you to find me a book called 'Frog-kun Saves Tokyo'?"

One of Sanetoshi's eyebrows shot up. "Very well," he said with a smile. "Since you have made it here, I am certain that we can locate the volume that you desire from within this vast sea of consciousness and memory. Just as one might pluck a single pearl from out of the seven seas. I, Sanetoshi, shall lend my aid with all of my being."

Himari was taken aback by his grandiose manner. Just what sort of a facility was this Sora-no-Ana Annex?

"What a strange person," she said softly.

The man with starry eyes looked at Himari with a smile, and began walking, leading her into the maze of bookshelves.

Himari walked through the labyrinth of books with Sanetoshi as her guide, as freely as though she was flying through the sky. At some point, the penguin had begun following behind her.

Now and then, Sanetoshi would stop as if remembering something and take a book down from the shelf, but then would mutter, "Ah, not this one," or, "No, this one's wrong, too," and put it back in its place.

"Um, is this really a part of the Central Library? It kind of feels a little too big for that."

As they walked, Himari's anxiety slowly grew. Where she had come from, how long she'd been here, and her goal had already blurred within her mind. Something about the mysterious colors of Sanetoshi's swaying hair as he walked in front of her was rapidly giving her the chills.

"It is the annex of the library," he said with certainty. "Though, you're our first visitor in some time."

Sanetoshi smiled brightly. Himari tilted her head in confusion.

"This is not a place that just anyone can visit. This is a special library, where only chosen patrons are permitted." He spoke in a low, relaxed, melodic voice as he walked along, fingers grazing the spines.

"So that means I'm special?" Himari trudged along the road of bookshelves, overwhelmed. She hazily wondered if she had really been looking for a book called "Frog-kun Saves Tokyo" or something.

"Yes, you are a special visitor, chosen by fate. Ah, there it is!" He quickly pulled a particular book from the shelf, opening the cover at once and showing it to Himari.

"Here is the one you were searching for: 'Your Story.'"

It was an impressive book, bound in wine-colored cloth and fastened with thread, an unusual binding nowadays. The mysterious letters, written in an unfamiliar alphabet, were gilded in gold, and the title was embellished with a pattern of vines.

As Sanetoshi flipped through the pages, he cleared his throat softly and began reading aloud.

"It happened just three years ago. The girl had two friends. Two dear companions, with whom she shared dreams of the future. The three girls shined on one another, like three stars, drawn together by a gravitational pull."

The empty classroom after school. Himari, Hibari, and Hikari seated themselves at the desks in the corner, grinning at each other as though shining light on one another. A magazine, *Sixteen*, was open between them. Printed in it was a large announcement for a magazine-sponsored idol audition.

On the digital camera Hikari held, there was a photo of two of them holding a recorder and a melodica, and one of them posing cutely in front of an organ.

"I think this will work." Himari nodded confidently, seeing the photo.

"Alright, then this will be the one we submit!" said Hikari, taking the idol audition entry form bearing the logo of *Sixteen* magazine from her backpack. "I filled out most of this yesterday. Now we just need to print out the photo and attach it."

"Oho, always prepared, Hikari-chan!" Himari was impressed.

Whatever they needed, Hikari was always reliable and on top of things, never forgetting anything she needed.

"Is it all good? You didn't forget anything?" asked Hibari, the most clumsy and forgetful of the three.

"You're one to ask! It's fine, it's the same form as last year. But, what do we do about this?" Hikari's eyes fell to the one spot on the entry form that she had left blank. It was the line for the name of their group.

"Hmm..." Himari and Hibari frowned.

"I've got it! The Otters!" Hibari proposed, her hand shooting up, but Himari and Hikari shook their heads.

"That won't work. That sounds like we're comedians, or something. That was our mistake last year," Hikari admonished.

"Huh, really? Well then, what about the Penguins? It sounds sort of like we're French girls, right?" Hibari emphasized the word "French" in a foreign-sounding accent.

"Do French girls like penguins?" Himari asked, with innocent skepticism.

"The Penguins sounds more like a boy's baseball team." Hikari slumped onto her side, exasperated.

"But it's cute! Penguins!" Hibari persisted.

It was true, penguins were cute, Himari thought. But the name Penguins brought to mind the image of the three of them waddling around the stage in penguin suits. It didn't seem very idol-like at all.

"Aitch," she said softly, a little embarrassed.

"Huh? What?" Hibari and Hikari looked at her, intrigued.

"How about Triple H?" The moment Himari said it, she suddenly felt that this was a wonderful idea, and grinned.

"Triple H?" Hibari looked bewildered.

"Yeah, Hibari, Hikari, and Himari all start with H, so that makes the three of us, Triple H!" Himari puffed out her chest.

"Ah! That's so good!" Hibari sprung up.

"Yeah, that's not bad." Hikari nodded fervently, in a very grown-up fashion.

The three nodded at each other, grinning, and proudly wrote *Triple H* on the empty line of the entry form.

"Oh, this is great! It feels like we've really got a chance this year!" The carefree Hibari swung her legs exuberantly.

Hikari watched her with a smile and started packing up to go home. "Now then, we'll film the application video tomorrow. *Don't* forget your matching ribbons! If you do, we won't make it in time for the deadline," she said, signaling to each of them.

"Aye-aye! I've already bought mine!" Hibari said with a goofy salute.

"You too, Himari-chan, don't forget."

"Yeah, of course," Himari replied with a smile, but she had a slight uneasy feeling. Just the faintest bit.

Sanetoshi shut the book with a loud sound.

Himari's face hardened just a little, avoiding his gaze in the silent atmosphere of the annex, where no one else was present but them.

"Right. I guess that did happen." Her voice was very dry.

"Is this book not what you were searching for?" asked Sanetoshi, his voice slipping into a tone that was neither clearly question nor declaration.

Himari had no idea. The Himari of the present day had no need to remember the past, but something came bubbling up hazily in her heart. No. That was wrong, she had plenty to occupy her mind.

Without waiting for a reply, Sanetoshi returned the book to the shelf.

"In that case, let's look for the next book. There are so very many books here in this place, after all." Sanetoshi pointed forward. Ahead of him were rows and rows of bookshelves with no end in sight.

The place where they stood was strangely bright, but the more she looked, the darker the endless room got as they proceeded further in. It was by no means cold in this place, but as she tried to look for any walls, a shiver of cold ran up from her feet. The penguin pattered ahead of her. With no other choice, Himari followed after Sanetoshi.

"Are you afraid?" he asked, as though seeing right through her.

"No, I'm not afraid," she lied. Since being treated to that story of the past, she had begun to wonder a bit more seriously just where this place was. The Sora-no-Ana Annex. Just where did this Hole in the Sky refer to? This young man did not feel very much like a librarian, and why had she followed this penguin in the first place?

293

She stared at the penguin, but it only glanced back, saying nothing. They walked on and on, but beyond every bookshelf was only another bookshelf. Now and then, something in the landscape seemed to wobble, like the space between two facing mirrors.

"Ah!"

Himari took a few steps forward, and the scenery changed, as though heaven and earth reversed themselves, and she stumbled. Perhaps they truly had reversed. There was still nothing but bookshelves everywhere, but judging by the atmosphere, they had somehow come to a different place, or maybe a different section, she thought.

Sanetoshi stopped in front of a particular bookshelf, and once more pulled out a book.

"Now then. Here is our next tale." He coolly turned the page and began reading. "That night, after pestering her mother for awhile, the girl finally obtained her matching ribbon. Or so she believed."

Kanba and Shoma sat side by side, engrossed in some evening cartoon show. The noisy sounds seeped all the way to Himari.

Himari sat in front of an old-fashioned Japanese dresser as her mother, Chiemi, neatly arranged her hair. Each time Chiemi combed through her hair, Himari's head rocked back and forth slightly. She shut her eyes, entrusting her body to that gentle power.

After tying her hair into twin pigtails, secured by ribbons, Chiemi said, "All done!" and patted Himari on the shoulders.

When she opened her eyes, she saw herself in the mirror, her hair tied up with ribbons different from the ones she pictured.

The warm feeling in her heart sunk, and she grew gloomy in an instant.

"My, what a beauty we have here! With this I'm sure that audition should be a..."

Himari cut in, interrupting her mother, "It's wrong. This won't match at all! It's all wrong!" She turned around, glaring at her mother as if interrogating.

"I'm sorry. The color you were asking for was sold out. But look, see? This is a similar color, and I think that slightly paler colors suit you anyway."

The lack of malice in her mother's smile only made Himari angrier, and she ripped the ribbons from her head, tossing them at her mother. The thrown ribbons fluttered powerlessly to the tatami.

"Himari!" Stunned, Chiemi's voice grew loud, scolding.

"I don't want them! If they don't match with Hibari and Hikari's, then there's no point!" She was incredibly sad. Her mother didn't seemed to care at all about her important ribbon, Himari thought.

Kanba and Shoma turned around in surprise at the shout.

"Sorry. I'll go to the next town over tomorrow and buy you the right ones," Chiemi comforted in a gentle voice, understanding Himari's feelings.

"Tomorrow won't work! I won't be ready in time! You promised that you would go out and buy me the right matching ribbon. You're a liar, Mother!"

Tears burst from Himari like a broken dam as she shouted, her shoulders shaking. She thought of the name of their group that they had written together on the entry form, and the exciting, wonderful day they were supposed to have tomorrow. Himari was old enough to know that this wasn't entirely Chiemi's fault, but her sadness and disappointment at all her careful plans being ruined had no other target besides, unfairly, at her mother.

"Himari." Chiemi was distraught.

"Go buy it right now! You promised! Go out and buy it!" Himari howled like a little beast. She already felt like her fun future with Hibari and Hikari had ended before it began.

It was just then, as she lay on the floor crying, pounding her arms on the tatami in frustration, her legs flailing that her foot struck the dresser, and there was a loud noise. She sat up, thinking she might have broken the dresser.

The mirror fell right toward her.

"Look out!"

For Himari, it happened in an instant. Chiemi covered Himari, and there was a loud sound of breaking glass. Shards of the mirror scattered around them. There was her mother's familiar smell.

Her brothers went pale and started panicking.

"Sh-she's bleeding! Mother!"

"Mother!" Himari called to her mother, who was still covering her, moaning softly and not moving.

She could hear her brothers on either side of them. Her mother said nothing, and when she looked at her face, her eyebrows were knit in pain. It was terrifying.

The sun had already fully set by the time she was settled into a hospital bed. Chiemi was lying down, her head and arms wrapped in bandages, a large piece of gauze affixed to one cheek. Himari sat beside her with Shoma and Kanba, with no clue at all what she should do. She could only stare at her mother's pained face. It already felt like a very long time had passed.

"Your injuries were more serious than we thought, and you lost a lot of blood, so please keep taking these painkillers and come by every day so we can check your wounds," said the doctor who had tended to her mother, standing near the doorway.

"Alright. Thank you very much," said their father, Kenzan, in a deep voice.

"Now, it should be faint, but there's a chance it might leave a scar once we remove the stitches on her cheek."

Himari felt a shock as she heard this from behind. Her whole body ached, and reality seemed to fade away. Her hands, folded atop her knees, trembled faintly.

"Mother," she said softly, so softly no one could hear.

"Himari, look at me."

Himari looked up in shock at her mother's firm voice. Her mother's soft hand reached out to Himari's face.

"You aren't hurt, then?" Her plump fingertips gently stroked Himari's face.

With some difficulty, Himari shook her head.

"That's good. I can't even think what I would do if your face had been cut," Chiemi said brightly, relieved from the bottom of her heart. "You're going to be an idol, after all. Oh, goodness, stop making such terrible faces, you three."

Shoma, Kanba, and Himari all looked crushed with worry.

"I'm sorry, Mother! Mother!" Himari clung to her mother from above the sheets, starting to cry. Kanba and Shoma followed, sniffling and rubbing their eyes.

Kenzan breathed a sigh and watched over them.

Himari clutched the ribbon that she had thrown tightly in her hand.

Sanetoshi closed the book, raising one eyebrow with a cruel smile.

"That was quite something. A tale of a mother and daughter's love. It might even bring one to tears."

Himari was speechless. She was so overwhelmed by emotions that her expression did not even change.

"Hmm, this wasn't what you were looking for, either. My, my, quite the challenging visitor we have today." Sanetoshi's eyes, with their indescribable light, glinted harshly in the direction of Himari's chest, right around her heart, as if searching.

"I suppose there's no choice. Further in, then. Let's go even deeper."

He put the book back in its place, his mood now almost seductive, and started walking.

Himari followed silently behind Sanetoshi in a line with the penguin. As they proceeded up and down, further, deeper through the gaps in the spiral of books, the outlines of the shelves and ladders gradually grew vaguer. In the same way, Sanetoshi's hair seemed to shift colors, and his eyes were so brilliant it was impossible to tell where they were looking, the scenery itself was becoming unstable. Only the rows of heavy books remained clear, unending.

As he walked, his footsteps forming geometric patterns that seemed to bear down upon her mind, Himari faintly wondered if he wasn't trying to play some cruel trick on her. But she had no idea why he would do that. She did not even know who he was.

"Watch your step." Sanetoshi looked suddenly at her.

Though the floor that she walked on certainly existed, as her boots were clunking audibly upon it, she seemed to have dangerously lost any sensation of it beneath her feet. The smell of old books that had tied Himari to physical reality also seemed to have grown. In its place was the smell of fresh greenery, growing stronger each time Sanetoshi's hair swayed.

Just as Himari lost the sensation of her blouse and skirt against her skin, her own existence seemed to be growing indistinct, Sanetoshi suddenly stopped. Then he pulled out another book.

"The next day, the girl revealed everything to the other two: that her mother suffered a wound that would never heal, all due to the girl's selfishness. That she had not been able to obtain the promised ribbon. By speaking truthfully, perhaps she wished some punishment would befall her. That the other two might end up hating her. Believing this, her desperate words began to crack."

After school the next day, the three stayed behind in the classroom, just as they had agreed. Hibari and Hikari already had their hair tied with the matching ribbons.

As Himari finished telling them the whole story, her throat felt tight, and she wanted to cry.

"I'm really sorry. That's why I couldn't bring the ribbon today."

Hibari and Hikari listened closely to Himari's story, meek expressions on their faces. Himari felt like a criminal waiting for a judge to hand down their sentence, endlessly repeating her apologies again and again inside her head.

"You two can shoot the video with just the two of you. And the audition, too."

"Huh? Why?" Hibari asked, voice rising in terror.

"Because I don't have the 'Promise Ribbon.'" Himari forced a smile, her face still tearful. Silence fell over the empty classroom.

"I wonder if there's any way your mother can get better faster," said Hibari. Himari was surprised.

"Hibari-chan?"

"Your mother's in the hospital, isn't she? Let's do whatever we can!" Hikari said forcefully.

"Uh, okay. But, what about the video? If you don't shoot it today, you won't make the...deadline..." Himari's voice tapered off at the end and vanished. She had no idea how to respond to her friends' unexpected reaction.

"That doesn't matter. Our best friend's mother got hurt. We're worried!" Hikari grinned, squeezing Himari's hand.

"Hikari-chan." Himari was moved, her cheeks growing red, desperately holding back the tears that seemed ready to fall.

"Hmm, but I wonder what it is we *can* do." Hibari folded her arms, thinking hard.

"What if we had her eat something extra nutritious?" Hikari wrinkled her face as well.

"That's it! I read it in a book I got from the library, 'Barefoot Gon!' If your sick mother just drinks the lifeblood of a carp, she'll get better!" Hibari flung out in proposal.

As the pair immediately began making plans, Himari was happily dumbstruck. She never expected things to go this well. She never imagined that the other two cherished her so much.

"Let's go to the courtyard, Himari-chan!" Hikari hastily put her backpack on her back.

Hibari picked up her bag too, and gently took Himari's hand.

Himari gave a little nod.

The little pond beside the shed in the courtyard was called the "Friendship Pond." Nobody was sure why; the name had already been set by the time Himari and the others had first enrolled in this school.

A single, colorful carp swam placidly around the shallow, narrow pond, making a burbling noise now and then.

The girls hiked up their skirts and rolled up their pants legs like bloomers, shedding their shoes and socks, and each stepped into the pond. The bottom was slimy with dirt and moss and algae. They waded into the water, in pursuit of the large fish.

"There it is! Over there!" Hikari called to the other two softly.

"Huh? Where, where?" Hibari frantically splashed around the pond.

"Hibari-chan, you can't make all that noise! Himari-chan, it went that way!"

"Got it." Himari was flustered but followed the fish through the water with her eyes.

"Hey, get over there! Over there!" Hibari swung her feet, trying to herd the fish.

"Quietly! Don't rush." Hikari moved through the pond slowly, silently following the fish.

The three slowly surrounded the fish. Then, with a soft, "One, two..." and a single, "Three!" they all reached for the fish at once. With the other two's help, Himari pulled the struggling carp up.

"We did it!" Hibari and Hikari looked at each other and shouted.

"But this is super smelly and slippery!"

The three laid the carp down in the grass. It struggled so much it took both Hibari and Hikari to hold it down, while Himari approached with a bat, taking a stance like she was about to split a watermelon.

"Hurry up and do it! Strike it down in one blow! Smack the life out of it!" Hikari pressed the carp's head hard against the ground.

"Okay." The bizarre situation and the state of the fish frightened Himari a little, but she swung the bat upward, just as Hikari said.

"Hey! What are you all doing?!" The three leaped up, frozen at the booming voice. They slowly turned around to see their homeroom teacher, standing there with a fearsome expression.

The three stood in a line in the faculty room that evening, having dried their legs with the towels they were provided, wearing their slippers over bare feet. All of their lips were pressed tight, looking firmly down and away from their teacher's eyes. A red backpack lay at each of their feet.

The three of them had joined forces to try and murder the school's pet carp. Obviously, their homeroom teacher could not overlook this. However, the trio did not speak a word.

"What in the world were you all doing? That fish was a gift from our alumni. To do something like that..." The teacher, sitting in a chair, looked at them, placing a hand on each knee. "You're not going to answer me? In that case, I have no choice but to explain the situation to your families," he said in a stern voice, reaching for the phone atop his desk and picking up the receiver.

"I-I was..." Himari finally opened her mouth. *I was the one who couldn't bring a ribbon, and it was our special promise ribbon, but my mother bought the wrong color, and I threw a tantrum, and then, and then...*

"It was my fault! I got desperate to drink that fish's blood, and I forced them to go along with it!" Hibari forced out an excuse, seeing the state of Himari.

"Th-that's not true! I was the one who brought them into this! I really wanted to live to be a hundred! I wanted a longer life!" Hikari cut in, swiftly interrupting Hibari. "I heard that if you drink a carp's lifeblood, you'll live longer!" she added in a mumble.

Himari looked at the other two, speechless. Her thoughts jumbled when she tried to speak, but now it had gone completely blank.

"That's not true. The truth is, my mother..." she said in a

faltering voice. She couldn't let the other two take the blame. She was afraid, but she had to speak the truth.

"No!" Hibari shouted.

"That's wrong!" Hikari insisted.

"But..." said Himari, her voice pathetic.

"It was me! So, if you have to call anyone's family, please call mine!" Hikari was fully back to her usual, firm self.

"No, no! I was the one who got them into this! So, you have to call my house!" said Hibari, talking over her.

Finally, the tears Himari held back began to drop down her cheeks. As if in sympathy, tears began streaming from Hibari and Hikari as well.

Their teacher, troubled to no end, let out a deep sigh.

"What is going on here?"

At least the fish was not dead. He stopped them in the nick of time. Plus, judging by the state of the three of them, there was some kind of extenuating circumstance at work, so they had not done this out of malice. They still had to be reproached, but there was no point in punishing them. He reminded the three of them never to do anything like this again and sent the girls home.

It was already growing dim in the halls. The three left the elementary school behind, thoroughly exhausted.

"Hibari-chan. Hikari-chan." They hurried home along the dark road, their three red backpacks in a row.

"Hm?"

"What?"

The pair replied nonchalantly.

"Thank you," Himari said quietly, from the depths of her heart.

"What are you saying?! We're friends, aren't we?"

"That's right. We're Triple H! It's all for one, one for all!"

The three grinned at each other. Their eyes were all red from crying.

Sanetoshi forcefully shut the book with a sigh.

"It would seem that this one has not caught your fancy, either."

Expressionless, Himari averted her gaze from Sanetoshi's strange eyes. She hated how she had no idea what he was seeing, that she couldn't tell which way he was looking, even when he was facing her.

"But that's alright. I understand."

The coloring of the whole annex began to shift again. The light grew hazy and dim, and it seemed the space they were floating through grew clouded, the air heavy.

"Understand..." *Understand what?* she tried to say, but her throat tightened, and she could not form words.

As she steeled herself and looked back at Sanetoshi's eyes, his mysterious-colored hair swayed, its light leaving her dazzled.

Sanetoshi laughed softly.

"Indeed. This is the tale that you really wished to read," he said in a terrifying whisper.

Classes ended at the elementary school, and students were noisily packing up to head home. Himari quickly left the building, walking all alone. She shuffled across the firm dirt of the school grounds. She wanted to get out of there as quickly as possible, but her backpack suddenly felt heavier than it ever had before. She stared at her own dragging feet as she walked.

Something smacked against her backpack. She turned around, but no one was nearby. There were only the students in the window of the classroom she had just left, lined up like little bells and staring at her. Another dirty eraser came flying her way, though it missed her.

The students' eyes studied her with hostility. She was some unfathomable creature, incompatible with the collective reality of their own little world. An ungodly thing. As far as her classmates were concerned, things that they could not understand were bad. Himari thought this unreasonable, but she could not bring herself to blame Hibari and Hikari, who had shrunk back, watching Himari from the edge of the group.

When she looked toward the pair, they vanished from the window, so as to avoid her gaze. A flat silence slowly fell on Himari's heart, which was overtaken by a deep sorrow and pain.

That was probably when it started. Plunged into the depths of huge, violent emotions, feeling as though time stopped, Himari began drifting, all alone. Whatever she might learn, however her body might grow, even if she got sick or cried, all of that only slipped by her, never truly reaching her heart.

It was absolutely required for the continued existence of the Takakura Himari, who always smiled like a pale, little flower.

"I remember. That was the last day I went to school. That was the last time I saw those two, as well," Himari said dully.

"And then, two years later, you were reunited with them. In the cruelest possible way, which you never imagined." Sanetoshi chuckled, but Himari was unshaken.

It happened one day when she was browsing all alone at a bookstore. As usual, she picked up a magazine that she often read, *Sixteen*. She turned the page and was greeted with a headline of "Double H ☆ A fresh debut!" Next to it was a photo of Hibari and Hikari, smiling cheek to cheek and dressed in cutesy clothes. It was a large spread. There were subway posters and advertisements and music programs on TV. Double H secured fame for themselves as a kitschy pop duo; they had become idols, admired by girls of their generation. There was the lovably playful Hibari, and the cool, mature Hikari. The pair were perfect idols.

Above a shimmering stage, wearing darling outfits, Double H danced and sang. There were waves of loud cheers, and glowsticks glittering like stardust.

There was a poster with the Double H logo on it, with their catchphrase, "Don't give up on your dreams!" printed in large, colorful letters. Their bright voices flowed from the TV.

The two of them, dancing together, reflected hazily in Himari's large eyes, and each time she blinked, the image was burned into the back of her eyelids, engraved there.

"If a thing like that had never happened, maybe you would have been singing onstage with them. Yes, as Triple H!" Sanetoshi smiled coldly, bereft of compassion.

"Maybe. But that's in the past."

Himari thought of herself now, out of the hospital, standing, breathing. The world was wide before her, and the man before her was not malicious, merely lining up the facts.

"Oh? Then why were you were searching for this story? To bathe yourself in some piddling self-pity?"

Sanetoshi seemed refreshed. His hair swayed, and a pale blue light spread throughout the annex. The heavy air returned to its original feather-lightness, and the gloomy rows of books now looked like treasure troves of indispensable memories.

"No. I just wanted to be sure that it was really over." The solid, geometric-patterned floor returned beneath Himari's feet.

"Really? The truth is that you resent those two quite a bit."

As Sanetoshi walked, the patterns floated up and vanished in his wake.

"I don't resent them. They were my true friends. Even now, I'm still cheering them on, deep in my heart."

This was how she truly felt. Himari was fully aware that she was far away from any sort of normal, happy life, but she'd never been inclined to get indiscriminately angry or tearful about that fact. She knew that if she did, she would only be pointlessly hurting herself.

"You truly are a wonderful girl," Sanetoshi laughed.

Himari merely stood there firmly, looking back at him.

"And yet, why would such a terrible thing befall such a kind and radiant young woman?" Sanetoshi brought his hand to his chin as if pondering, seeming genuinely curious. One eyebrow was raised, his long eyelashes lowered.

"I don't know."

"You came here to find that answer, didn't you? Because you wanted to know the reason?"

"No. I don't know why I'm here."

Certainly, she wondered many, many times why only she and her siblings seemed to suffer such terrible fates. But no matter how she looked at it, she never came up with the answer. And yet, was it inevitable, or perhaps fated, that she would end up in this place, unconsciously searching for a reason?

Sanetoshi languidly put the book back on the shelf.

"You said that it's all in the past, but has that story truly finished?"

She didn't know when her end would come, but to Himari, that period of her life was a completely different story. And so, she closed that book.

As she fell into a placid silence, Sanetoshi smiled at her gently.

"I told you, didn't I? Somewhere here is a volume that you truly desire to read, deep down in your heart. In other words, your story has not yet ended. For example..." He stopped, slipping his hand between the books, and pulled something out from within. It was the hat with the penguin design. "There are still these sorts of things."

"What is that?"

Looking at it, Himari could not recall seeing this hat. It was different than the one she had seen in the aquarium's gift shop, with a more imposing, elaborate, and mysterious penguin face upon it. Himari stared fixedly at it. It was cute, but there was something deeply unsettling about the lustrous glint of its eyes.

"This is a garland for the bride of fate," Sanetoshi said emphatically, handing her the hat.

"Bride? Me? Whose bride am I supposed to be?" Himari asked, leaning forward and looking at the penguin hat before her.

"That answer probably lies in 'The Place where Fate Resides.'"

"The place where...fate resides? Where is that?"

Distracted by the conversation, Himari didn't notice Sanetoshi's sudden and swift approach, freezing her in place with those universes condensed into his eyes. His hands grasped her slender arms and pulled them near. The two gazed at each other, as if spinning in a dance while the Sora no Ana violently transformed around them. Their long hair whipped in the wind, intermingling.

As Sanetoshi slowly placed the hat atop Himari's head, suddenly, as if bursting open, she transformed into the sharp, red-eyed Penguin Queen. There was a wide ribbon fixed proudly at her chest, a large, voluminous skirt spreading from the frills on the tail of her corset. Tall, black enameled boots. Her long hair billowed out in the white wind. Himari could not draw her eyes away from Sanetoshi and his small universes.

"You don't remember, then? You should know this place. In that case, you'll return to your former world, and I will tell you the answer when I am needed. I will tell you where 'fate' resides, and whose bride you are. Until then..."

Seeing Himari's distress at not knowing the answer, Sanetoshi smiled kindly and moved to press his lips to her smaller ones.

"No." Her fingertips, sticking out from the end of her gloves, halted Sanetoshi's pale, well-formed lips.

Finally, the floating pair stopped spinning, and the Sora-no-Ana Annex itself began to drift away. The bookshelves, the enormous number of books, and the beautiful floor all turned into tiny block and plain lines, or spheres and the lettered lines of many words, and slowly lost their form, scattering away.

"That's a pity." Sanetoshi sneered and pulled away from Himari.

Sanetoshi was the only thing that remained in the space, and Himari fell steadily away. She could see numerous books out of the corner of her eye. Then she spotted that penguin, which was now accompanied by two other identical penguins. All three squeezed themselves down in a row into an insulated box.

Her surroundings grew darker and darker, like she was in the depths of a great big well. Between the fluttering of the sleeves of her dress and her own hair in her eyes, Himari's consciousness began to drift away.

"You mustn't forget this." From far, far above her, Sanetoshi tossed a bright red apple her way. The little fruit, falling slowly down in tandem with Himari, awakened one more memory within her.

A rust-covered electric fan spun with a violent whirring sound. Beside it sat a number of children in stained and shabby clothing, huddled up, arms around their knees.

A little boy, who skillfully caught the apple that came falling down, called out to Himari, who was there as well.

"Let's eat the fruit of fate together."

The little girl's expression did not change, but she was so happy she wanted to cry.

311

"Thank you for choosing me." For Himari, that was unmistakably the fruit of love.

Though it was dim, Himari was stunned by this memory.

That was right. There was someone who was very dear to Himari. He was her fated person. And yet, she could not clearly recall the face of the boy she had seen when she looked up.

Finally, she turned her eyes to a bright light, and there she saw herself, sleeping in the morgue of the hospital. Her breath hitched in surprised, but as all the strength ran from her body, she lost consciousness, as if being swallowed.

Himari awoke on the red sofa in their living room. She was dotted with a strange sweat, ever so slightly. Beside her was the scarf she knitted, and atop her stomach was Penguin No. 3, sleeping soundly. She lifted her heavy head and looked toward the kitchen, where she could see Kanba preparing dinner. There was the delicious smell of dashi. Outside, she could hear a pelting rain.

"Ah, I fell asleep!" Himari slowly sat up, stretching and breathing deeply. "I think I was having some kind of dream. I can't remember it at all, though."

No. 3 woke up abruptly with bleary eyes, rubbing its eyes and looking up at Himari.

"Ngh. My head kind of hurts," Himari said softly.

She stood up suddenly at the shrill sound of the telephone, and called toward the kitchen, "I'll get it, Kan-chan!"

She took a breath and lifted the receiver to her ear, saying in as alert a voice as possible, "Hello, Takakura residence."

Kanba peeked out from the kitchen to see what was going on. "Sho-chan...was in an accident? Ringo-chan, what are you saying?" For a moment, she was suspicious, wondering if this was still part of her dream. But Ringo's sobbing voice on the other line was clearly real. She could not feel her legs, and her voice went hollow. "Ringo-chan?"

PENGUINDRUM

AUTHOR BIOS

Kunihiko Ikuhara

Born December 21. Animation director. Made his directorial debut in 1993 while affiliated with Toei Animated Films (presently, Toei Animation), with *Pretty Guardian Sailor Moon R*. Achieved acclaim in 1997, with the debut of *Revolutionary Girl Utena*, which he independently planned and directed. The original author of manifold novels and manga.

Kei Takahashi

Born October 15, 1980, and raised in Tokyo.